Robbie and Carlo have been involved professionally and personally for twenty years. Lately, though, their architectual practice and their marriage are beginning to falter.

One fall day, Tom Field, a peculiar young man, drifts into their storefront office asking to use the phone. The men get to talking; Tom is curious but enchanting and Robbie ends up playing tennis with him that afternoon, ultimately inviting him home for dinner.

The ensuing evening involves a lot of wine and banter and then increasingly dark coversation, and when the stranger has had too much to drink, the two men insist he sleep in their guest room.

During the night, Tom Field commits an act of violence which shatters the architects' ordered lives so that each man in his own way over the days and months that follow must cope with blossoming doubt and corrosive secrets.

Also by Peter Gadol

Light at Dusk

The Long Rain

Closer to the Sun

The Mystery Roast

Coyote

Silver Lake

A NOVEL BY
Peter Gadol

TYRUS BOOKS

Published by
TYRUS BOOKS
923 Williamson St.
Madison, WI 53703
www.tyrusbooks.com

Printed in the United States of America
12 11 10 09   1 2 3 4 5 6 7 8 9 10

978-0-9825209-1-8 (hardcover)
978-0-9825209-0-1 (paperback)

for my brother Charlie

1

AND THEN IT WAS AUTUMN AGAIN, and Saturdays they would wake early when the first clean light came up over the oak and fir at the top of the ridge and eased its way down across their glass house and overgrown slope, down to the pitched yards and shingled cottages along the street below their street, down across timber and brush and fallen limbs, across the boulevard all the way to the patient lake, where it would linger on the water, an ancient and forgiving light by noon.

These were cold mornings suddenly and so they dressed quickly in fraying clothes. One made coffee, the other swiped jam across toast. They traded sections of the paper. One started in on the crossword, the other scanned the financial pages. Then they headed out to the garage and pulled on work gloves and selected rakes and clippers, and there was little conversation except to agree the movie they had watched the night before was not sitting well with them. A simple story snapped when stretched into an epic. Actually one man fell asleep before the film ended, and the other man had to wake him only to guide him to the bedroom and back to sleep again.

Rain all week had left the air crisp but also made the ground behind their house muddy and not entirely suitable for the chore at hand, yet each man took a flank of hill as if it were his side of the bed and began pulling out the dead sage and trimming back the excess tea bush and clearing out the persistent sumac. There was nothing to be done about the thicket of rosemary, they'd long since given up. There was enough of a drop-off down to the backyard of the property below theirs so that even at the edge of their land, they enjoyed an unobstructed vista of the Silver Lake Reservoir.

"It's so blue today," Robbie said.

"Too blue," Carlo said.

"How can it be too blue?"

"It's like something chemical has been added."

Robbie slid down a patch of mud so he was standing next to Carlo. This was the year they would turn forty. They had been together twenty years, not counting some early semesters of undedicated collegiate messing around. Robbie pulled off his glove and inserted his forefinger through one of Carlo's belt loops, tugging him closer, rubbing his nose against Carlo's neck—Carlo hummed.

It was autumn again and they always looked forward to the season, to the fires they would tend in a stone hearth and the friends at a long table, to what they would roast and what they would decant. They looked forward to the colder nights and the added blanket, the conversations past midnight about new books. The truth was that even before they knew each other (if one could speak of a time before they knew each other), each man was always eager for the decline of summer and the refuge, the rescue of school—and autumn was when they met, and another autumn when they moved to Los Angeles. It was certainly for all these reasons that every fall they felt renewed, but then also because some other heat always abated, because an annual anxiety always burned off and vanished, it seemed, for good. Anxiety related to work and income and debt. Restlessness about lives not lived, the shadow histories that now and then might haunt them, haunt any two people who found each other so early in life. An alien illogical loneliness—it was a kind of ghost grief almost, although to be clear, a grief neither as strange nor ruinous as the one about to wash over them.

"You're a silly man," Robbie said. "A lake can never be too blue. Who's a silly man?"

"I am," Carlo said.

"What are you?"

"A silly man."

Back up by the patio off the kitchen, they collected the figs about to fall from a neighbor's vine that coiled over a high wooden fence.

"Can we remember to pick up some smelly cheese?" Carlo asked.

"Si, signor," Robbie said.

Also in their neighbor's yard, there was a regal Liquidambar with broad long-suffering branches, several of which reached across their terrace, and the men liked the tree because it gave them a graceful canopy and screen, and then they could enjoy the seasonal task (a joyfully nostalgic task since they both grew up back East) of raking leaves. Leaves that this year had turned early, had begun to fall early, and so there was already need to sweep off the table and chairs and the twin cedar chaises. They took turns combing a patch of lawn with their better rake, scraping away the ochre matting to reveal grass that was surprisingly cold to the touch in the morning sun, the ground smelling like sap now, like rich dark potting soil now, like lust itself.

In the house, in their bedroom, they stripped and threw back the blankets and knelt on the bed, facing each other. Carlo fell back against his heels. Robbie held on to Carlo's hips, pale hands against dark skin, until he let go and fell back, too. Then they remained like this a while, facing each other without touching, grinning. It was as if they were waking a second time today. Two men together, two against the world. Astonishing.

SO THAT WAS HOW ONE SATURDAY in September began. Maybe they padded around their glass house barefoot, their feet squeaking against the dark wood, Robbie reshelving some books while Carlo hung a newly framed drawing in the guest room. Maybe they heated up some split pea soup and made grilled cheddar sandwiches for lunch. By noon they would have been riding their matching black mountain bikes, seats set to the same height, out their street to the hill, and down the hill to Silver Lake Boulevard, gliding around the dog park and the basketball court (where the shirtless were routing the shirted), down to the small-town-like commercial strip and their office in a shotgun storefront, their diagonally opposing desks in the back, a set of plywood-and-leather furniture prototypes in the window up front, two lounge chairs and a sofa. It was Carlo's idea to go in that day. He said he wanted to sort through the mail. Robbie didn't see the need but knew if he didn't give Carlo half an hour at his desk, Carlo would fret away the balance of the afternoon.

They had emerged from graduate school with the idea that the best architecture came from the most local engagement, and as much as possible, they had wanted to practice where they lived. At first they were fortunate to be building houses during a boom and in a neighborhood coming into market vogue, but eventually new construction proved too expensive for their clientele, and their primary work became renovations, additions, building out, building up. Then this market slowed down, too, or at least for them it did. Carlo handled their money because Robbie was clueless about money—it was easiest to spare him explication of ledgers with numbers in parentheses—and yet as they locked their bikes in the back and let themselves in, Carlo was thinking a daily thought, that after a slow summer it was time Robbie truly understood how much they owed, how great their monthly needs were. There was some finish work to supervise on a garage-to-guest-house conversion and a maybe a pool house-studio in the works for a screenwriter, but nothing beyond that lined up. Of course Robbie had some idea where they stood, some, and if Carlo once again avoided the conversation, it was because there did remain one prospect that could turn everything around. Carlo tapped the space bar of his computer keyboard and waited as if calling for an elevator.

"He emailed me," he said.

"From Europe?" Robbie asked.

The potential client was a television producer who wanted to build on one of the few remaining undeveloped lots up the street from the office on the sunset side of the Reservoir. The grade of the land, blanketed presently in wild fennel and poppy, was extremely steep, daunting but not impossible to engineer. The man wanted glass and he wanted steel, so he was referred to Stein Voight by a former client, and an initial meeting had gone well, leaving Carlo cautiously optimistic. And were they to build the house from the ground up, the firm would not only be able to post their sign on the property during construction, which inevitably would prompt a raft of inquiries from possible new clients, but also put in play a range of new ideas they'd been unable to try out during their long period of modest renovations. But Carlo didn't want to get too far ahead of himself because before the television producer was willing to commit, he had wanted to be pitched some schemes—understandable but not how Carlo and Robbie operated, although they didn't see that they had much choice and were able to exact a reduced fee for preliminary sketches. In his email now, the producer indicated his enthusiasm for what he'd seen so far. He also indicated he would have some notes, which he would reveal when he returned. When that would be, he didn't say.

"And?" Robbie asked.

"So far, so good."

"I told you."

"We don't have a contract yet."

"We will."

The office was stuffy, so Carlo cracked open the front door to let in some fresh air. He returned to his desk and stared at the stack of mail. It never ceased to amaze him that even when there was no work, the bureaucracy of simply existing required tracts of time. Accounts payable and correspondence with old clients about how to treat various ageing claddings. Invitations to professional association get-togethers, prefab-house competitions they could enter. Half his life was spent filing papers in folders, squaring the piles of folders across his broad plank of a desk into a neat metropolitan grid of smokeless industry.

They didn't have a lot of time to get something going, and Carlo didn't regard this producer well. What was to stop the man from taking the Stein Voight roughs to another architect? And it wasn't simply their anemic finances making Carlo anxious. Ever since his car accident last April (or what he had led Robbie to believe was an accident), Carlo had the sense that he was, that they were, being tested somehow, their way of life in jeopardy. It was silly, he was being silly. Then again, he couldn't deny the pressure— a test before them, a challenge, their future assigned in some part to chance, in greater part to will. Everything was at stake, only Robbie didn't know it, and Carlo didn't want him to know it.

And meanwhile, Robbie had his chair tilted back, his feet propped up, a blank book balanced across his lap, pen poised. His desk was an arctic field of discarded sketches. Robbie was good with pen and ink. Robbie was good at staring out windows. Robbie was good at pacing. He was the quicker sketcher, temperamentally the more instinctive architect (all projects initially were drafted by him), and Carlo watched Robbie now with roughly the same fascination as when he first spotted him sitting alone in an oak-paneled dining hall, hair in his eyes, his shirt cuffs unbuttoned—he remained eighteen twenty-two years later. Carlo knew he himself had grayed some, and if not gained in girth, then widened at the shoulder, whereas Robbie had always lacked weight, lacked gravity—at times he seemed feathery, a little blown about. His fingers danced across the page, Robbie sketching something, blushing the way he did when he drew. With any luck, he was hot with an idea about how to trick the second floor of the new-client project to maximize the view of the Reservoir, possibly cut away some volume for a bedroom balcony, or even go up a floor, although that might challenge codes, and Carlo was the one who pulled the permits, the one cast as the heavy who had to lay down what was and more often was not possible.

He pretended to work while playing computer solitaire. He could hear a stray arpeggio drift out of the music studio down the street and the occasional conversation as customers went in and out of antique stores, but otherwise, the only sound at Stein Voight was that of Robbie Voight's black pen in its journey east and west, north and south across a white page. It was a sound that never failed to deliver Carlo a temporary peace.

EVENTUALLY HE WENT ACROSS THE STREET to buy the cheese they had talked about, to the liquor store for wine, and to chat up a friend at the framers-photo gallery. Robbie watched his lover dodge traffic and disappear, and then he put down his sketch book and rubbed his eyes.

For about five minutes indeed he'd been considering the house up the street, specifically a more integrated way to include a detached rental unit, but the rest of the time he'd been doodling. His idea of a nightmare was Carlo one day breaking a tacit rule and paging through Robbie's stack of old black blank books piled on a credenza behind his desk. For every modern bungalow elevation Robbie allegedly was rendering, for every open-plan floor plan, Carlo would find countless spreads of intersecting planes and graphed vortexes and plump spheres, hard-hatched, soft-shaded—islands and reefs and coves of ink coalescing into a secret atlas of lost ocean continents. Carlo would find evidence of much daydreaming, although miraculously the work always got done, rather last-minute, but done, and anyway, architects needed to daydream, didn't they? The mission of any builder was to look at the world not as it was, but the way he believed it should be.

Robbie needed a shot of caffeine, and he was at the back kitchenette making espresso when someone walked in the front door. It was rare but happened, a passerby trying to figure out what goods were sold at Stein Voight. The man who came in was a young guy, slight, bouncing a bit off his right high-top as he glanced around. He was backlit, hard to see well, so Robbie crossed the length of the office.

"Can I help you?" Robbie asked.

A white baseball cap was jammed in a back pocket of the man's unbelted jeans, which he had to hitch up as he regarded Robbie somewhat sideways. A worn halo of blond highlights had almost grown out. His sweater was torn under one arm and his cheek looked like it had been scratched by a cat. The man was Robbie's height, but scrappier. He vanished from a gallery opening when you looked away, and you never saw him again. You tracked him during a plane trip and then down to the baggage carousel but lost him amid all the arrivals.

The man pointed at Robbie's demitasse and said, "That's exactly what I need. Better make it a double, please."

"Oh, we're not …" Robbie started to say. "This isn't a café."

The man looked around the office, squinting toward the back of the room.

"Do you mind if I use your phone?" he asked. "Car trouble," he explained, although the two metered parking spaces in front of the office were unoccupied.

He also said, "Although maybe I should ditch my car, I hate driving. I hate Los Angeles. The worst thing you can do in Los Angeles is not make a left turn at a light. For the rest of his life, the driver behind you will never forgive you, and it's probably a good thing I don't carry a gun because there have been more than a few occasions when I've seriously wanted to—Sorry, what?"

Robbie was staring. "You'd like to call a mechanic?" he asked.

"If it's not too much trouble," the man said, and again he looked at Robbie sideways, half grinning, probing.

There was something unhusked about him. Robbie guessed his age to be twenty-three or twenty-four. He found the number of a garage and dialed the phone before handing it over to the man. Twenty-five maybe, twenty-six. Robbie returned to the kitchenette to make the man an espresso after all while he waited for the mechanic.

The man sat down in one of the plywood-and-leather arm chairs in the front of the office and slid back, his demitasse nearly slipping off its saucer. Robbie perched at the edge of the adjacent chair. The man looked uncomfortable.

"Y'all sell furniture here?" he asked, concerned.

"No," Robbie said, "no," and chose not to explain that a few years back he and Carlo had entered a design contest but nothing had come of it.

The man crossed his legs, uncrossed them, crossed them again.

"We know," Robbie said. "It looks better than it functions."

"It looks *okay*," the man said.

"We're architects mostly. Or entirely, I should say."

"We."

"My boyfriend is out running errands," Robbie explained.

The man yanked his hat out from his back pocket and pulled it on, his eyes now in shadow. He shifted it to the side, then straightened it.

"I would have used my cell phone," the man said, "but I lost it, of course, because I lose everything. Which is the definition of a loser."

"Not everything," Robbie said.

"No, everything."

"Not your hat."

The man extended his hand and said, "Tom Field."

Robbie introduced himself and for some reason offered Carlo's name, as well.

"I'm glad you didn't say partner," Tom Field said. "In this town, I've noticed, everyone has a partner. A writing partner or a business partner or a boyfriend partner. I have to get out of here."

"And go where?"

Tom squeezed the bill of his cap and said, "Architecture. Nice work if you can get it."

"How long have you been in Los Angeles? Where do you live? What kind of work do *you* do?"

"A year," Tom said, "one eternal infernal year."

It was a mystery to him, he said, how he had ended up living in an efficiency apartment in the Valley with only one friend left in the city (left: implying there had been others whom he no longer knew), this one friend a writer of some repute who traveled frequently (Tom didn't name him), but there it was, that was his life. He took off his baseball cap, scratched his head, put it back on. He was fidgety, maybe coming off of something. He said he thought he merely would arrive and fall into a circle of cool friends, which had worked up and down the Eastern seaboard.

To answer the question about what he did professionally, he said, "I'm not a hooker."

"No, of course not," Robbie said.

"Everyone assumes I'm some kind of escort," Tom said, and he stood briefly and hitched up his pants and then sat again.

He was not currently employed, nor had he worked since moving here, although not for lack of trying. No one would hire him to do what he was best trained to do (which he didn't specify), and eventually he gave up and had been living off savings, which would run out next month. His grandmother who raised him had more or less cut him off and suggested he enlist in the military. What did he do? He slept twelve hours, eighteen hours at a stretch and then drank multiple pots of green tea because he believed by drinking green tea, he would live forever. Then he was awake for twelve hours, eighteen hours. He owned neither a clock nor a watch. What did he do? When he first moved here, he spent his days exploring the city, wandering the southern wharfs and the industrial east and the forested north. He drove along the spine of the hills, he traced the coast. He failed to find a surfer who would teach him to surf. No one wanted to play volleyball on the broad empty beach. He never found anyone in the park for a pick-up game of tennis. He walked the prettier walk-streets and was unable to start up a conversation with women with dogs. He stumbled across a Venice café he liked and loitered there every morning trying to establish himself as a regular, but no one was very interested in talking to him. Or when men were friendly, generally they expected a return on their investment, which was fine, but that kind of transaction had its limits. How did anyone meet anyone? How did a stranger encounter a stranger and get to know him so he was no longer strange?

Tom stared out at the street and said, "I don't think I've ever been more alone than I have in Los Angeles."

Eventually he stopped leaving his apartment very much and somehow passed his caffeinated hours fiddling therein, and the days fell away more rapidly than he would have expected, the weeks, for there was much to learn and there were many things you could teach yourself to do in a musty studio apartment in the San Fernando Valley, and naturally when he needed to go out at night and get in some trouble, he could still do that. He lived as if he were waiting for something in particular to happen, for some inevitable turn, although what he couldn't say, when he certainly could not say.

"Why am I telling you all this?" Tom asked. "You couldn't possibly care, although you are very kind to listen."

The puzzle of it was that Robbie did care. He had no idea why, but he did.

He said, "But you came out into the city today. You're here now."

"In daylight no less. Do you have a map?" Tom asked. "I'm all turned around."

Robbie invited Tom back to his desk and pulled open a deep file drawer that was indeed packed with maps—the top one was the city guide for Los Angeles—but while Robbie was flipping to the worn page for Silver Lake, the page pulling free from the spiral binding, Tom stared at all of the other folded maps and pocket atlases and was smiling again at Robbie in his goofy sidelong way, and it was Robbie now who had to ask, "What?"

Tom took the liberty of reaching deep into the drawer with both hands to take out the pile of maps, which given their variable size, couldn't be sustained as a single heap atop Robbie's desk and fell in a landslide, displacing a few sheaves of discarded sketches. Tom sifted through them, the municipal guides of European capitals intermixed with pleated plats of properties Stein Voight had worked on, all of them soft at the fold. California road maps and tourist maps for archaeological sites. Canal cities, hill cities—a London A-to-Zed—river cities, island cities. There were train schedules for points back East and maps of the Moscow Metro and the Berlin U-bahn/S-bahn. Tom seemed drawn to one pocket guide in particular, the wine-dark brick called *Paris par arrondissement* with its gilt lettering nearly worn off the spine. He flipped to a random page, the particular neighborhood delineated in canary yellow, the streets white, places of note in pink, with the surrounding neighborhoods all a vague mint green, and he flipped the guide around as if he might actually step outside and try to head off for a certain rue or quay.

What Robbie didn't say was that this little guide was his sentimental favorite. With his family, he'd gone to Paris as a child, then back as an exchange student his junior year of high school. It was the one foreign city he had made his own without Carlo.

Tom looked again at the Los Angeles map open on Robbie's desk. He said, "You can study a map of a city you've never been to and think you know the place, but when you finally go there, you're always a little disappointed the actual city isn't quite as neat or logical as the map led you to believe it would be. That's not the case here. That's one good thing I will say about Los Angeles— it looks like its map. The grids are grids and the squiggles are hills."

This was true. "When you get up in the hills at night," Robbie said, "and you look back at the basin, you see the city lights and the traffic and it's like you *are* looking at the map."

Tom glanced around at all the sketches on the desk. He sighed. He said, "I'll tell you something. For a long while, I wanted to become one."

"A what," Robbie asked, "a map?"

"This," Tom said. "An architect."

"And what happened to that?"

"Do you have a cigarette? Keep it quiet that I asked though, because in theory, I quit."

"We don't smoke."

Tom ran his fingertips across the open Los Angeles page as if encountering braille.

"I've been re-reading the Bible," he said. "Or not reading it but listening to it on tape, a little bit at a time before I go to sleep."

"Are you religious?"

This question caused Tom to release a single guffaw: That's a good one.

"You don't know Russian, do you?" he asked.

Robbie did not.

"I bought a Russian phrasebook and made these little cyrillic flashcards for myself, but that's as far as I got. An H is an N, I think. The B is a V. But of course I lost the flashcards."

"Were you planning a trip?" Robbie asked.

"I was reading one of those obese nineteenth-century novels," Tom explained, "and I have to say the translation seemed a little lardy to me."

"You were going to attempt it in the original."

"Did you ever play an instrument?" Tom asked.

"Clarinet," Robbie admitted. "Very briefly. Not briefly enough."

"No way—me, too."

"I have a good ear for other people, but not for myself," Robbie said. "My poor parents."

"That's why I'm sticking with piano," Tom said, "on behalf of my neighbors," and the conversation skidded along like this, Tom chasing various subjects like cats in a meadow, never really grabbing hold: Did Robbie invest at all in astrology? Did he have a good history of twentieth-century physics he could recommend? Did a hammer and a feather truly fall at the same velocity and in what universe did that happen? Did Robbie know of a good place in town to get real gelato? Did Robbie like opera and would he think Tom a heathen if Tom admitted he could never sit through one in its entirety? Robbie answered each question and braced himself for the next, ably tracing the loose threading of Tom's associations.

Tom paused and tapped the map with his forefinger accusatorily. "Do you ever wonder what it was like here back in the day," he asked, "before all of this land was shot through with free-ways? Everyone always says it, but in my case it's a little too true."

"What's a little too true?" Robbie asked.

But Tom didn't answer because at that moment, laden with bags, Carlo returned. Robbie made introductions and explained the situation.

As if waiting for his eyes to adjust, it took a moment for Carlo to say hello. The three men stood by the door an awkward moment.

Far off, a helicopter. Nearby, a chain saw.

"We've met," Tom said to Carlo.

"Have you?" Robbie asked.

Carlo said, "I don't think so. Not that I remember."

"Not that you remember," Tom said.

"Have you?" Robbie asked again, addressing Tom.

Tom didn't speak. He was fixing his stare on Carlo.

But finally Tom said, "My mistake." And then: "If this me-chanic doesn't come in five minutes, I'll walk home. I don't want to inconvenience you."

"You're not," Robbie said, and it was true. He was enjoying talking to this Tom Field, quite a bit.

Tom looked at Carlo again, and Carlo appeared to nod be-fore retreating to his desk. Tom drifted toward the wall of the of-fice decorated with framed photographs and dry-mounted computer-assisted renderings of Stein Voight projects. On an-other wall, rough schematics of the (hopefully) current project were tacked up.

"Tom thought about becoming an architect," Robbie said.

"Did you?" Carlo asked.

Tom was lingering in front of photographs of a project that went up five years ago, another tricky property that required siting the house so it would back out onto the Ivanhoe Reservoir while saving a pair of listing eucalyptus trees, accommodating them with holes through the two stories of decking. The entire house, generous in the eaves, glass-walled, powered by solar panels and built with reclaimed wood, turned into a kind of sophisticated tree house that Robbie and Carlo considered their best work.

However, Tom looked dismayed. He said, "I hope you'll forgive me." He said, "I like windsor chairs and fainting couches. I like shingled siding and bay windows and shutters. Every house should have a big front porch." He said, "Maybe I was born at the wrong time."

A tow truck pulled up outside and he dashed out to point the mechanic toward his car. He was gone a full minute before the two men spoke.

"He just wandered in," Robbie said.

"Did he?" Carlo asked.

"I feel sorry for him. No friends, no money. You don't like him."

"It's not that," Carlo said, and looked as though he wanted to add more but held back.

"You think he's got a grift going," Robbie said.

Carlo shrugged.

"Nobody should be alone," Robbie said.

"You're quoting my father now?" Carlo asked.

"Did you notice the scratch on his face?"

"He's looking for someone to take him to London. New York for a shopping weekend."

"No, see, that's the thing. I don't think he's your typical party boy," Robbie said. "I don't get that sense."

"He just wandered in? He has his price," Carlo said.

"I don't think so," Robbie said. "He's curious—"

"He *is* curious."

"I mean that he's curious about the world."

A short while later Tom returned and said all that was wrong could be fixed with a new fan belt. The mechanic had the part in his truck, and Tom was good to go. Uno problemo. He was short what he owed by twenty-three dollars and change, so he gave the mechanic a credit card, which the mechanic called in to his garage, and the card was declined.

Robbie glanced at Carlo, and Carlo withdrew his money clip. Perhaps this would seem an extravagant gesture to some, but Robbie knew Carlo could read him well enough and knew it would please Robbie to help Tom. Again Tom went outside and said he'd be right back to discuss how he'd go about repaying the loan, and of course it occurred to Robbie that Tom might not return this time. However, he did reappear, dangling something in one hand that resembled a garden snake, the snapped fan belt. Maybe Tom wanted to make sure the men knew he hadn't been conning them.

Tom said, "I'll write down your address here and send you a check. Don't wait too long to cash it though."

The three men stood again by the door. They shook hands and Tom turned to leave.

"So Tom," Robbie said.

Tom was likely a man without a date book, he probably didn't answer his phone, and his sleep cycle would always be too irregular to follow. They would make a plan, Tom wouldn't show up. And yet he was a fellow map enthusiast and deep allegiances had been based in less. What he needed was obvious and not expensive in the scheme of things.

"You mentioned you play tennis," Robbie said.

"Once upon a time," Tom said, "in a galaxy far, far away."

"We should find a fourth and play doubles sometime."

"A fourth?" Tom asked, peering beyond the men into the office as if a doubles partner might be lurking in the shadows.

"Or we could switch off playing singles," Robbie suggested, and he glanced at Carlo.

Cued thus, Carlo said, "That might be fun."

"Tennis," Tom said as if the word were foreign. "Tennis when?"

"Sometime soon," Robbie said.

"Soon," Tom echoed and turned to leave again.

Robbie looked at Carlo, and Carlo hesitated a beat but gave his assent, an almost imperceptible, reluctant arcing of an eyebrow.

"What about this afternoon?" Robbie asked. "We've got a court booked."

Tom looked at Carlo again and said, "You've already been so kind. I wouldn't want to ruin your Saturday."

Robbie was waiting for Carlo, as well, but Carlo didn't respond, and so Robbie said, "You wouldn't be ruining anything. Carlo wasn't even all that eager to play today—Carlo? Would you mind terribly if Tom here and I took the court? You said you had some more gardening—"

"Oh, gosh no," Tom started to say, "I wouldn't want to—"

"That would be fine," Carlo said softly.

"No," Tom said.

"Honestly," Robbie said to Tom, "he would rather putter."

"It's fine, it's true," Carlo said. "I have some things I'd love to do around the house."

Tom flashed his goofy grin at Robbie and said, "I might be terrible."

"Oh don't worry, it doesn't matter," Robbie said, and once again he studied Tom Field and tried to guess his age and settled on twenty-seven. Robbie never actually asked Tom, but later the police would confirm his estimate.

AN HOUR LATER, Robbie met Tom in Griffith Park. Robbie had gone home to change but Tom apparently had not. When Robbie drove into the parking lot, Tom was standing at the open trunk of his banged-up jalopy (its front fender was held on with duct tape), withdrawing clothing from a duffel bag and changing out in the open, without apparent vanity or concern about all the tennis players and hikers coming and going. Robbie was driving a recently washed new car, the foreign wagon that the two men had selected for its safety ratings and reinforced chassis, which educed from Tom an ooh-la-la.

"Nice ride," he said as he pulled a T-shirt over his head.

"Carlo was in a bad accident last spring," Robbie explained, "and we wanted something sturdy."

"An accident," Tom said.

"Fortunately no one was hurt," Robbie said.

The upper four tennis courts in Vermont Canyon were ringed by hills dried gold after an arid summer. Occasionally, preceded by a labrador with a stick in its mouth, a hiker emerged from a trail and headed down the main dirt path. There was no wind, and the dead stillness meant that as the men began to play, their syncopated shots reverberated around the bowl of hills.

It took Tom time to recall his game. Between rallies, he had to tug up his wrinkled cut-offs, and then he would bounce the ball three times before whacking it across the court as if striking a piñata. He had no backhand to speak of and ran around to his forehand, and yet despite his drooping attire and spastic ground strokes, Tom hunted down every ball. He may have been the less fit player—he was panting between points—yet he ceded no corner of the court, and Robbie found it difficult to hit a winner. In this doggedness, there was something appealingly boyish about Tom, at once earnest and playful. Eventually they played points but didn't keep score and whenever the mood suited him, the server opted instead to receive.

On a change-over, they swigged bottled water.

"I'm excited to have a new hitting partner," Robbie said.

Tom rolled his eyes.

"Oops," Robbie said. "Another kind of partner."

They switched sides to share the burden of the angled sun. Then they rallied again without conversation, or the rally was in itself a form of banter. Tom issued involuntary grunts. The longer they played, the more he came into net. Several times he guessed which way Robbie would try to pass him and punched out a professional-looking volley. Quickly his game improved.

At the next change-over, Tom said, "I've been trying to come up with my next career move."

"And what have you decided?" Robbie asked.

"That I want to become a court painter."

"A court painter—like what, a *tennis* court painter?"

"No, silly," Tom said. "You know, a court painter. All you have to do now and then is make a portrait of a princess with some spaniels or a king with his hand on a map, and the rest of the time, you get to work on whatever you want. Ruins, mountains, lakes. Think about it. It's a great gig."

"So all you have to do is find a court."

"Right. How hard should that be?" Tom asked.

And during another change-over: "Do you think there's anything wrong with wanting to make pretty things?" Tom asked.

Robbie shrugged, no, why not?

"I've been going around to all the galleries to check out the scene, and all the art they've got up, blech, it's so ugly. I think you make the world better by adding beauty to it," Tom said, "not more ugliness. But no one seems interested in beauty any more. Are you?"

"Oh, definitely, certainly," Robbie said.

"Well, baby, at least that makes two of us," Tom said.

Little by little, Robbie found out more about Tom. He preferred rhyming poetry to free verse, tart-fruit desserts not chocolate ones, country music more than pop. His grandmother liked to have him read to her at night, the classics, but fell asleep early in the evening, although Tom kept reading aloud while she snored. But what about Tom's actual parents? He didn't mention them. Nor did Robbie discover why (beyond wanderlust) Tom had moved to Los Angeles. Nor what Tom hoped would change in his life once he arrived, or if change was what he sought. He could have been seeking escape or rescue, but escape or rescue from what exactly? What, at base, did Tom want for himself?

Robbie didn't ask too many questions. Mostly Tom talked and Robbie listened, which seemed to please Tom, as if all he wanted was someone with whom he could hold forth. No, not a mere someone—he appeared to like Robbie. He was beginning to confide in Robbie.

After about an hour and a half of tennis, Tom said, "Lately I've been thinking that at any given moment in time, there can only be a maximum of two or three things you find beautiful in the world—out-and-out, breathtakingly, devastatingly beautiful. I mean two or three things you think truly possess grace."

"What makes you say that?" Robbie asked. "Why only two or three?"

"Because any more than that, and you wouldn't be able to function. You'd wander around with your mouth open all the time. You'd go manic."

If Robbie understood what Tom was saying (and he wasn't sure he did), he did not necessarily agree. But he asked, "What's on your current list?"

"Eucalyptus trees," Tom answered. "Bosc pears in a white bowl. A man's back. What about you?"

Robbie didn't know how to respond, so he said, "I like your list. I'll borrow it, if you don't mind."

Tom was looking at him sideways, the way he had back in the office. He was gaunt except when he grinned, and then his face became lunar. He formed a pistol with his first and middle fingers and tapped Robbie twice against his sternum.

"What?" Robbie asked.

Tom tapped him again, bouncing off his sneaker.

He said, "I did know it was an architectural firm I was walking into and not a café or furniture store."

"Did you?" Robbie asked. "Then why—"

With his thumb and forefinger, Tom tweaked Robbie's left nipple once and then again.

Robbie was caught off guard. He pulled back, flustered, wondering what kind of signal if any he'd been sending that Tom would hit on him, a little miffed that his overture of friendship might be misconstrued, annoyed in general at guys always on the prowl, who viewed married men as fair game. Or maybe Tom wasn't making a pass but merely being cocky. That could be all. Robbie returned to the baseline and sent the next several shots sailing wide or long.

A short while later, at the end of one of their longer rallies, Tom framed the ball and knocked it over the fence, over a short retaining wall, and into the adjacent slope. In all likelihood, the ball was lost, but Tom dashed through the gate, hopped up onto and over the retaining wall, and proceeded to rummage through the brush. Robbie joined him outside the court but didn't go over the wall.

"I think it went more that way," he directed Tom.

And sure enough, Tom disappeared and stood up with the lemon tennis ball plus some dried weeds in hand. When he hopped back over the wall, he ended up standing next to Robbie, close, and as he handed him the recovered ball, Tom leaned forward, his mouth barely open but open enough to kiss Robbie. As if to be polite, Robbie kissed him back, briefly, extremely briefly but long enough to get it, to understand the specific way someone like Tom was sexy: Tom the eternal summer kid, barefoot in the backyard. You lay in the hammock with him and he smelled of stolen cigarettes, and then he had his hand down your shorts, but the next day he pretended not to know you, and you would spend the next hundred years searching for Tom Field in every man you met and tried to love.

The police would inquire about a sexual relationship or anything proximate to one, and Robbie would not mention the kiss.

He turned around and headed back onto the court and, once through the gate, pivoted back toward Tom still on the other side of the chain-link, and said, "I shouldn't, Tom. I don't. We don't."

"You don't," Tom said. "Everyone does these days."

"Not us."

"Never?"

"Not in twenty years," Robbie said.

"Get out. Twenty years? No way."

"It's fine for other people, their deals, whatever," Robbie said. "It's not our thing is all."

"Really?" Tom asked—and why did he seem so astonished? "Are you sure?"

"Yes, really," Robbie said. "I'm quite sure."

And then Tom nodded with quick acceptance the way he had back at the office when he was told at first he wouldn't be served espresso (and eventually he was handed an espresso). He ho-hummed, tugged up his shorts, returned to the court, picked up his racket, and headed around to the other side of the net.

Robbie glanced up at the sun. Would he tell Carlo about what had transpired? He might, he might not.

They hit balls back and forth, and a short while later, Tom yelled, "We can do this Saturdays all year long."

Robbie was relieved Tom didn't appear put off by being rebuffed. Maybe Tom's pass was a mere stile to step across. This was Tom: provocative, sexual, testing. But he liked maps, which was to say he knew how borders ran, and now the lines were clear. They could keep walking the way they had been headed.

"That's what you're supposed to like about Los Angeles," Tom shouted, "the weather."

"What's not to like?" Robbie asked.

They played for another half hour, and while Tom wanted to keep going, Robbie had to say, "I should probably get back."

"Just a little longer," Tom pleaded.

"I'm pooped."

"One more game."

"I shouldn't."

"Ah. Okay," Tom said.

They walked down to the parking lot where their cars were the only ones left. It was clear Tom didn't want to give Robbie up to the evening.

Robbie put his things in his car and said, "How about next Saturday? Do you want to play again?"

Tom wagged his head yes.

"I'll book the court," Robbie said, and he should have gotten in his car and driven off, but instead he lingered.

A stranger had appeared that September afternoon and presented an ancient dilemma: How did anyone become a known person in the world—how did a stranger become no longer strange? Maybe it was grand to suggest, but solve this problem, Robbie thought, and it was possible every other wrong among men might be righted.

"At some point," he said, "we'll have to have you over for dinner."

"Dinner?" Tom asked, picking up a bit. "Dinner when?"

"Sometime soon," Robbie said.

"Soon," Tom said, and turned toward his car.

A cirrose armada overhead moved fast across the sky, gunboat clouds outpacing carrier clouds.

"Actually—," Robbie said.

Tom was odd, but Tom had verve, and once again it was not difficult to see that he'd been feeling small in the city. Everyone needed friends. Though he might not readily admit it, Robbie himself had been feeling lonesome lately, for even within the walled estate of a good marriage, loneliness was possible.

So Robbie asked, "Do you have plans this evening?"

And Tom did not.

"Good," Robbie said, grinning, which in turn made Tom grin again, too. "Then why don't you follow me home?"

CARLO MEANWHILE spent the balance of the afternoon at the house, gardening in front. By contrast to the anarchic cascade of flora in back, the street-side landscaping remained well-legislated: There was the flat and shallow lawn, respectfully mown, bisected on the bias by a trim slate path. The two men had eschewed any fencing or border shrubs, and the only plants they'd removed on the property when they moved in were some overly groomed and desiccated arbor vitae. At the northern corner, toward the house, a wise old pepper tree, small in leaf but broad in shade, offered gracious supervision. And to counterbalance the pepper tree, to come under its tutelage, Carlo (the better gardener) planted a modest stand of plum trees at the south, by the street and front path, adjacent to the driveway and garage. These plum saplings, six in all, had grown fast this last year they'd been in the ground, although they remained very uncertain of themselves, at an awkward age, and needed with some regularity to be trimmed up.

He had clipped a few new twigs and untied all the twine binding the trunks to their stakes, and he was kneeling in the dirt, in the process of retying the bands so they were neatly parallel and taut, when he stopped what he was doing for the tenth time in the last hour. Why had he let Tom Field take his place on the tennis court?

In the moment, back in the office, he hadn't known what to do. He couldn't very well tell Robbie not to invite a seemingly fun friendly man with random car trouble to join them—Robbie might have suspected something. But then Carlo should have insisted he still wanted to play and gone to the park, too, if for no other reason than to keep tabs on what Tom might say—and what, he had to wonder now, had Tom said? Why wasn't Robbie home yet?

That Robbie would want to make a fast friend of a stranger like Tom wasn't surprising, because whenever the two men used to travel to Europe, Robbie was always the one who approached scarved widows sitting alone in hotel bars, reliving their honeymoons, or the professors in cafés marking up guidebooks, or the young dark rakes smoking unfiltered cigarettes while writing first novels. Carlo never minded Robbie's transient biergarten friendships—he never was made to suffer any subtraction of loyalty, engagement, or lust. If anything, Carlo fed off Robbie's gregariousness, because while Carlo wasn't shy professionally, outside of their practice, were it not for Robbie they would inhabit a world of two people total, them alone. And then Robbie also had a history of befriending the strangers he would start talking to at openings here at home, or in restaurants, or when infrequently they went out to a bar. It was easy for him, given his innate solicitousness, and at times it seemed like Robbie had too much affection to dispense, more love than could be contained in his life with Carlo, and Carlo didn't like seeing Robbie wounded when inevitably the new friendship lost air. They were younger men mostly—Tom fit the mold—and usually Robbie provided distraction between their romances. They phoned Robbie late and came to rely on his confidence, and (to give them collectively the benefit of the doubt) maybe they thought because Robbie was settled, he wouldn't need anything in return. Fortunately he could never be jammed into a darker mood for very long.

That said, the stakes were different now and Carlo had no idea what Tom's game was—well, blackmail came to mind.

He pulled off his work gloves and dropped them by the ball of twine and clippers. He went inside ostensibly for a glass of lemonade but once in the kitchen, he noticed Robbie's plain canvas sneakers kicked off by the dining table and stared at the way one was caught in the angled afternoon light, its heel fraying, laces fraying, tongue and toe shaped according to his lover's foot—how well he knew this foot, its arch, veins, and freckles; how to hold it so as not to tickle Robbie—

And suddenly a squall: Carlo gripped the counter with both hands to steady himself while he cried. Hours earlier he'd felt good, like a turnaround might finally be in the making—but now? Now he was not so sure. Now he found himself anticipating the expression on Robbie's face when he came home (assuming, as Carlo began to assume, that Tom had in fact revealed something), Robbie looking shocked, enraged, bereft. At first Carlo imagined being relieved, unburdened of his secrets, but then he heard himself spinning an explanation, and he considered getting in the car instead and driving, driving anywhere, giving Robbie space to storm about, and then later on Carlo would return, rueful, the first to speak, apologizing as profoundly as he could.

He took a series of deep breaths. The house was quiet—he tried to quiet his mind, too. Lately he'd been thinking a lot about the man and woman who purchased this home new and lived here for thirty-five years. The husband worked in a studio props department, the wife at the same studio in accounting, and they raised one son, who became a man in the second bedroom, who moved out when he married. His father suffered a fatal heart attack while driving and crashed his car where Silver Lake crossed under Sunset. Thereafter his mother lapsed into a permanent distracted state and died elsewhere. The son sold the house to a single man (according to the title search) who tried to write screenplays and owned a restaurant on Hillhurst that didn't last long (so reported a long-time neighbor down the street), and like many of his friends, he became sick young and died here at home. Other owners briefly held the deed: a decorator who replaced the windows but then faced foreclosure, a sculptor who rented the place to art school kids with dogs. And then Carlo and Robbie arrived eight years ago, this house the first they owned, and given his profession, Carlo had thought he would understand the sentimental grounding that homeownership would entail, but he had not anticipated the daily elation that came with rootedness. Here in Silver Lake, amid the rambling hills that resisted the syntax of any grid, with ambitious trees all around, and of course the placid lake at the heart of the place—in this neighborhood, he could say he belonged.

Was that still the case? Did they, did he still belong here? How did one know when it was time to move on? Where would he, would they go?

Carlo went out front again and finished his chore. He was collecting his tools when he heard Robbie's car pull into the driveway, and his heart skipped—although it wasn't only Robbie arriving home. Robbie pulled in all the way up to the garage, making room for Tom Field's car, which Tom parked in tandem.

"I invited Tom to dinner," Robbie explained as he removed his tennis bag from the backseat.

"Oh," Carlo said. "Did you?"

"I wasn't sure what you were planning on making," Robbie said.

"Nice house," Tom said to Carlo. "Nice street."

"Thank you," Carlo said.

"Or if there's enough," Robbie said. "Do you want me to run out and get something?"

Tom's driver's-side door had been stripped of paint but not reprimed or repainted. He had some difficulty opening his trunk, which was packed with stuff, including a crate of CDs he shoved aside so he could pluck clothing from a duffel bag.

"No need," Carlo said.

"Tom, I'll go and put out a towel for you. You should take the first shower," Robbie said, and then he went inside.

Tom slammed shut his trunk.

"Hi," he said.

"Hi," Carlo said.

"My car really did break down. It's not like I'm stalking you."

"I know that," Carlo said, unconvincingly.

"There you were, crossing the street," Tom said. "I saw your office, I went in. Look, if I'm not welcome—"

"Robbie invited you."

"I meant by you."

"I didn't recognize you at first," Carlo said, "because last spring you were blond. And I think you've lost weight."

Tom brushed his now-brown hair forward with his palm.

"Don't look so worried," he said. "I didn't say anything."

Carlo nodded, wary.

"I don't want anything," Tom said.

Carlo squinted. Why should he trust him?

"Honestly," Tom said, "I don't."

And so Carlo nodded again.

"He doesn't know anything," Tom said.

"Robbie? No," Carlo said.

"You told him it was an accident," Tom said.

Carlo didn't have a chance to respond because Robbie appeared at the front door.

"Tom," he called out, "you're good to go. What? Come inside, for crying out loud, come inside."

WHEN THE TWO MEN BOUGHT THE HOUSE it was because they could not yet afford to build one, and the plan had been to find a place with some clean lines and a clear view, dwell there some months, get to know it, and then renovate. The house

was small, and the assumption was they'd add rooms, yet very
quickly they came to appreciate the choices made by an unknown
peer—the squared-off intimacy of the bedrooms, the simple gesture in main room of a ceiling sloped two feet higher toward the
Reservoir, the built-ins banking the dining area, no cabinets over
the extra-deep counters here in the kitchen, the way the patio off
the kitchen was submerged three steps so as not to obscure the
span of the lake, and so on—and in the end, they decided not to
meddle. They did not add a mantle to the wide stone hearth.
They did not enclose the front entry porch. What they did was
install single-lite doors and floor-to-ceiling birch shelves for their
collection of art books. What they did was paint the rooms green,
forest in the bedrooms, sage everywhere else.

Robbie was doing all the talking while giving Tom a tour
after they had cleaned up, and Carlo couldn't tell whether Tom
cared where the hearth stone purportedly was quarried or what
designer was responsible for the low flat-armed furniture arranged
minimally in the main room. Everyone had quickly emptied their
flutes of prosecco, which Carlo refilled. Their guest nodded politely while Robbie rambled on about the artist-friend who did
the abstract painting over the bed, the mountain browns and the
gash of cadmium red, the lightning cracks of neon green. In the
guest room, however, fingering the fringe of a mohair throw, staring at a color-field triptych, a landscape after a fashion of hori-
zontal bands, Tom was audible when he winced.

"What?" Robbie asked.

"I don't want to irritate you," Tom said.

"No, go ahead."

"Looking at the art you have here—as someone who studied painting, I'd have to say there's not a lot of talent involved. I dated a painter, and he makes what he calls mood portraits—or *something*—and they're abstract but somehow based on guys he meets? I'm sure you'd get it, but it was over my head. We had a fight, I drove off, I haven't spoken to him since. Maybe it's me. Maybe I'm some kind of freak anachronism."

The two men let Tom's aria settle, thinking he'd said his piece, but he was all wound up.

"I don't mean to be rude, or maybe I do a little bit," Tom said, "but, see, it's the face that interests me. If you can draw a man's smile, and draw the way the veins run down his hands, and draw the way he leans back in a chair, if you can do all that, then you will know the man intimately. It's way hotter than sex. You will know him and you will see him—truly you will *see* him—and then when you show your drawing to other people, they'll see him for who he is, too. People ask what is art? *That* is art."

The two men remained quiet.

"I've insulted you," Tom said. "I can leave."

"Don't be ridiculous," Robbie said. "And I don't necessarily disagree with you, at least about portraits. Do you still paint? Carlo used to paint—"

"I want to go back to a time," Tom interrupted, "when men wore gray wool trousers and blue blazers and felt hats and cuff links. Let's the three of us bring back cuff links! But then I have to ask why can't we have all the haberdashery and the civility that comes with it, and also still get all the good new science and the Internet and cancer drugs?

"I sincerely do not get it," Tom said, as if Robbie and Carlo might now proffer and defend a unified theory of modernity.

And yet Tom himself was dressed the way the young men did to go out to the clubs. He wasn't remotely dapper and in fact looked like he'd been wearing the same outfit all week, maybe sleeping in it.

"I own a tux," Tom said, and laughed. "I'm not sure why, it's crazy, but I do. With velvet lapels."

In the far corner of the main room by the window, the men had angled a baby grand with a cushioned bench. The two men no longer played it. Tom tapped a C, then an E, a G—all three keys at once. The piano in all its traditional polish, it was obvious, appealed to him. On the way back across the house toward the kitchen, the steep shelves of books delayed him. He turned his head to the side to scan the spines and withdrew a tome about a Venetian master.

He pulled out another text, a classic of classical architecture, and said, "Okay, you guys aren't total cretins. We can still be friends."

On the back patio, they sat beneath the rustling neighbor-tree and watched the lights come on all around the Reservoir. The lights reflected in the lake looked like unstrung pearls, like loosened fragments of a mosaic.

"We're lucky with our view," Robbie said.

"I don't know," Tom said. "What's the deal with that chain-link fence? I'm not sure I see the point of a lake you can't swim in or take a boat out on."

"I agree with you," Carlos said. "I'm not even sure if it's still being tapped."

It was true that no one could get close to the water, and it was not as though Robbie ever wanted to scull, but it would have been fun now and again to see toy boats out there leaving toy wakes.

He said, "It's pretty to look at though."

"Admit it," Tom said. "Say that just once you'd like to spot a sailboat on that lake."

"Just once I'd like to spot a sailboat on that lake," Robbie said.

They ate the figs the two men had collected earlier, chasing them with wedges of cambozola. They had moved on to red wine and Carlo was feeling quite aerated—Robbie, too. Tom, however, appeared unaffected. He was staring up at the tree swaying overhead, lost briefly in unshared contemplation.

He said, "I don't suppose you two go to church."

"My family is Jewish," Carlo said. "My father is a survivor. I grew up an atheist."

"I'm the resident agnostic," Robbie said.

"All y'all are going to hell," Tom said, and chuckled, sort of.

He said, "I can't find a church I like—a plain, austere, white clapboard, white-spire church. And I miss the liturgy, the old songs. I went to a place near me in the Valley. What was this guy doing with a guitar? No tambourines, please. And I do not want to hear some lame sermon about doing unto others from a minister who the night before, in some sticky back room, was feeding me poppers and licking my ass. I want the old Latin—what happened to the old Latin? *Ad Deum qui laetificat juventutem meam.* Do you know any place like that around here? What?"

Maybe the alcohol had coarsened him. Tom pulled down his sweater sleeves over his palms, gripping the cuffs, hiding his hands.

As dusk settled, the glass house above them became a mirror, framing the immediate hillside. The wind had rolled in finally and scattered their conversation. They were talking about art education, and it was no surprise that Tom had been trained in the Beaux Arts tradition, that he'd stretched and gessoed his own canvases, mixed his own pigments, nor a surprise that he maintained ample disdain for the theoretical approach that had informed how Robbie and Carlo studied what they studied. Tom was in mid-rant when he paused and stared at the two men sitting next to each other.

He said, "Twenty years," and he looked at the men appreciatively, shaking his head, amazed. "Wow."

When they went inside and Carlo began to prepare dinner, Tom said, "You two have been so kind to me. Let me cook for you."

Carlo had planned to roast a chicken, finish it with a splash of balsamic, and also make mushroom risotto. These were recipes from a favorite Italian cookbook that had belonged to his mother.

"I prefer French," Tom said, and fired off a set of questions about ingredients on hand. Satisfied, he announced, "I'm making coq au vin. Try and stop me."

Tom himself now uncorked the bottles of red wine they drank, the same wine that went into the skillet in liberal quantities. Carlo blanched and peeled the onions as directed and chopped celery with rapid percussion. Robbie retrieved ingredients from the pantry or refrigerator: flour, parsley, thyme, bay leaves. Cognac. Mushrooms, butter, bacon. At the same time, Tom prepared rolls to bake—clouds of flour whitened the black counters. Before long there were bits of chopped herb everywhere, the stray coin of carrot, and Carlo's well-kept kitchen was in disarray, although he didn't care, and it was odd, very odd, but he would have to admit he was having fun.

Tom—who ended up with flour-smudged jeans because he kept having to tug them up his hips—Tom clearly was having a good time, as well. Now and then he sang out a chorus line from a song everyone had been playing all summer. He chattered fondly about his grandmother's cook, from whom he'd learned about French country cuisine. He recited his knowledge of the basic sauces. He had a way of bouncing whenever he dropped ingredients in the skillet and stirred them in and knocked the wooden spoon against the cast iron rim. The rolls went in the oven. Carlo insisted on something green and prepared spinach to be sautéed with broccoli rabe. They polished off another bottle of shiraz. Carlo put a symphony on the stereo. He built a fire in the hearth, the first of the season—it was cold enough—and whatever angst he'd been suffering earlier, and whatever uneasiness he had about Tom Field, abated. Carlo decided to take Tom at his word, that he'd shown up by chance, that he wanted nothing. The past was the past and would remain in the past. Life was strange. Life was grand. Maybe it was how much he'd had to drink, but then maybe not: their home was a warm home, a fast fire blazing, the loamy aroma of chicken cooked in wine in the air, an orchestra in full thunder.

While the chicken was braising and the rolls baking, they leaned against the kitchen counters, the two men on one side, arms loosely around each other, Tom opposite, and Tom mentioned that, in case they hadn't figured it out, he had been a bit promiscuous in his life, but he also said that it was never what he wanted or sought, it was simply what happened. He looked like fun, he was fun, but he wanted a proper boyfriend, an old-fashioned boyfriend, and sadly didn't see how this would be in his future.

Tom said, "Used to be a time a couple of years ago I could roll out of bed and look loveable. People invited me away for the weekend, I had places to stay. I read novels on trains. Sunday nights back in the city, I slept beautifully."

"We'll have to think about who we know," Robbie said.

"I have no money," Tom said. "Boys don't want to hear that."

"You're cute, you're intelligent," Robbie said. "Don't give up."

Soon they were dining by the fire, sitting on the floor and leaning back against cushions pulled down from the couches, plates propped up on knees or resting on the coffee table. The coq au vin was earthy and rich. They wiped their plates with the warm rolls. At first it appeared that Tom enjoyed his own cooking, but then Carlo noticed that Tom wasn't eating much food. He did keep drinking, although still to no measurable effect.

While the two men were serving themselves seconds, Tom set down his plate with a loud clink, switched off the stereo and crossed the room to the piano, where he sat down and for a held moment stared at the keys. He stretched his fingers into their fullest span. And then, delicately, tentatively, with a few notable added rests, he played a pared-back rendition of a familiar étude. He would secure a chord with his left hand, then turn his attention to his right, awkwardly slipping his thumb beneath his middle finger, safely repositioning his hand across the keys. He played only the one piece and then mock-bowed and offered an apology about how much he had to learn—he'd been teaching himself— and the men heard none of it, they were entertained.

Back by the fire, Tom was aloft, all of a sudden talky with plans. He had never been to Italy and needed to see Florence, which somehow he would pull off in the next year. He would stay in Los Angeles after all and look again for a job. He would move from his present studio in the Valley over here to Silver Lake and drop by the offices of Stein Voight and keep everyone from getting work done. He would join a gym. He might try to date again. He might sit down in front of an easel again, paint again, because he missed the smell of linseed oil and the feeling of a sable brush against his cheek before it was used the first time. With every statement, the two men were encouraging, although Tom was all keyed up on his own and didn't need winding.

Finally he said, "I will look into going back to school for architecture. It's what I always wanted to do. I will do this finally. Thank you."

Tom's gratitude seemed misplaced to Carlo, given their aesthetic differences, but of course he graciously accepted it, and Robbie, who probably would have offered Tom a job on the spot if he could have, said, "It's a plan."

"Hold me to it," Tom said.

"We will," Robbie said.

And then what happened? This was the moment in the evening to which the two men, days and weeks later, would have to return. There was a lull in the conversation while Robbie stacked dishes in the sink and Carlo made espresso, which Tom declined in favor of emptying a bottle into his glass. Something happened to him during this pause. When they returned to the hearth, Tom looked addled, staring slack-jawed at the fire, mystified, as if fire itself were confounding and troubling. Robbie asked him what was on his mind.

"You don't want to know," Tom said.

"Sure we do," Robbie said.

"Trust me, you don't."

"Go on."

Tom pushed up his sleeves. He waited. He waited a long minute.

"There was a story in the news a few months ago," he said, "about a woman in New York who was home alone on a weekday afternoon with her little boy when a guy broke into her apartment. The guy had a knife."

Tom held out his fist as if gripping the weapon.

"Was he going to rob her? Was he surprised to find her? Who knows? But what we do know is that he made her get down on the kitchen floor and forced her to undress at knifepoint and unzipped his pants and started raping her while holding the knife to her throat. The little boy in the next room naturally was crying …"

Tom's voice trailed off, and Carlo was not surprised that Tom appeared to relish narrating the story, drawing it out.

"And I guess this meant the guy couldn't enjoy his rape," he went on. "So he slid the knife up from the woman's neck to her face and held it there. He pressed the knife against her cheekbone, drawing a drop of blood. The little boy was really bawling."

Tom looked at each man in turn.

"And the rapist said to the woman, 'Your kid or your eyes.'"

Robbie brought his knees to his chest and leaned forward, making himself compact.

"'Your kid or your eyes,'" Tom said again. "An act of additional violence was going to be committed and the man was giving the woman a choice."

Tom paused again.

"She said her eyes," Carlo said.

Tom waited for Robbie, but Robbie refused to guess.

"She said her kid?" Carlo asked.

Tom nodded.

"How does anyone know what she said?" Carlo asked.

"The neighbors heard," Tom said. "They'd called the police."

"And the man killed the boy?" Carlo asked. "Oh no. Did he kill them both?"

Robbie released a muted groan.

"The man pushed himself off of the woman," Tom said, "and started heading for the boy, who backed up into the bedroom. And the woman, we have to assume, must have thought this would give her the chance to grab some kind of weapon, except that she didn't own a weapon. The man turned around and slashed her throat and ran out. The woman bled to death in front of her kid."

The house was still except for the crackle of the fire, although Carlo had not added a new log and the blaze was tapering off.

"What a world," Tom said. And he also said, "Now if the woman had kept a gun in her apartment, who knows what would have happened? Maybe the guy still would have cut her before she got to the gun. But then again, maybe not."

Robbie said, "Then we'd be reading instead about how the little boy found the gun one day and decided to play with it—"

"Great," Tom said in a flat voice. "In fact, if he had been able to play with the gun, he'd have known where it was kept and how to fire it at the man who raped and killed his mother."

"I don't know," Robbie said.

"Now what are you going to say, y'all want gun control? And let me guess, you're also against the death penalty," Tom said. "And you?" he asked Carlo.

Carlo had been silent, his gaze falling elsewhere.

He said, "I agree with Robbie."

"You do?" Tom asked.

"And why are we discussing this?" Robbie asked.

"You asked what I was thinking and lately I think about this all the time," Tom said. "I'm sorry but I do. Somebody comes on my land without my prior invitation, I will fucking kill him cold, and that's my right."

It wasn't Tom's actual sentiment itself that gave the two men pause (although it did) so much as his tone, caustic, bellicose.

"Considering you don't have any land at the moment for anyone to trespass," Carlo said, "we don't need to worry about you taking out any door-to-door salesmen."

"I'm serious," Tom said, fixing his glare on Carlo. "Somebody messes with me, I will get a gun and I will fucking kill him."

"Great," Robbie interrupted. "We get it."

"I doubt it," Tom said. "I bet if someone smashed his way into your lovely glass house here and threatened to shoot you and your monogamous boyfriend for no reason other than you're fags, I bet you'd wish you had a gun in your night table drawer."

Had they offended Tom in some way?

Robbie said, "I'd like to believe I can reason with anyone."

"Reason," Tom snapped. "'Your kid or your eyes'—and you'd try *reason*? That's rich."

"If any two people talk long enough," Robbie insisted, "they will find something they have in common."

"Oh my goodness," Tom said, "you actually believe that, don't you? I don't know what world you think you live in, baby."

"I forgot we have brownies for dessert," Carlo said. To Tom: "There's a new gourmet place across from our office we like—"

"Talk," Tom said. "Talk, talk, talk," he said, pushing himself up and bumping into the bookcase on his way to the kitchen, where he opened another bottle of wine.

"We won't be able to let him drive," Robbie whispered to Carlo.

"You're talking about me," Tom said.

By the fire again, he cradled his wine goblet. He was lying back in such a way that his sweater and T-shirt rode up and revealed a patch of his pale abdomen. The dark clouds had passed again—he seemed calmer. He rested his free hand on his stomach, his thumb inserted into the exposed waistband of his boxers.

Before long, the fire was mostly embers, and Robbie claimed he saw figures moving in these embers, ecstatic dancers, dogs in full stride, cross-country skiers. Carlo pictured static things, numismatic profiles of famous men, the shapes of states, planets in revolution around minor suns. Robbie asked Tom what he saw.

Tom said, "Fire is fire." He said, "I guess it doesn't much matter if someone breaks into your house and you have no gun, because you can be going in to cash your social security check in Oklahoma City or riding a bus in Tel Aviv, doing what you have to do to get through your lousy day, taking the subway in Madrid, and that's it. You're done, you're cooked, game over."

"I hate to admit it," Carlo said, "but I agree."

Robbie was compact again, knees pulled into his chest.

Carlo said, "We can eat brown rice and swim an hour a day, but we've either got the mutation for lung cancer or we don't. We can choose to walk instead of drive to work and be crossing the street and get slammed by someone running a red because he's late for a hot date. So why live any safe way in particular? Why worry about anything?"

"Because the city finally put in that traffic light," Robbie countered, "and because the odds are very good anyway that you won't get hit by a car when you cross the street."

Tom sipped his wine, and was he grinning?

"Robbie and I have this argument every so often," Carlo said. "Fires happen, earthquakes happen. Plagues out of nowhere suddenly in the population happen, devastating plagues—"

"We're not having this conversation now, thanks," Robbie said.

"Apparently you are," Tom said.

"Robbie will tell you that progress is possible. We change the world by *believing* in that progress. Never mind whether we do anything about it—"

"Cut it out," Robbie said.

"There is a genocide in Europe. We say never forget," Carlo said.

"Then we forget," Tom said.

"Oops, genocide in Africa," Carlo said. "Ethnic cleansing in Europe again."

Robbie said, "You know, if your father heard you—"

"If my father heard me *what*?" Carlo snapped.

"And you guys have never even had a threeway," Tom said.

The two men stared at their guest.

"What does that have to do with anything?" Carlo asked.

"Never hired a hooker at a resort, never gone out together to a sex club? I've had so much sex," Tom said, "and it's a miracle, but I'm clean. Not everything comes down to fate, that was my next thought. There's proof someone is watching out for us. Someone is certainly watching over me."

"No one is watching over you," Carlo said. "You've been careful is all."

"Oh believe me," Tom said, his stare hard on Carlo, "I haven't."

Carlo realized he was clasping his hands tightly.

"Then you've been lucky," he said. "We've all been lucky about something at some point."

Tom stood up and wobbled and fell back into the couch.

"I think someone is watching," he insisted.

"I don't think so," Carlo said.

"Carlo," Robbie intervened, "you can't deny someone his faith. That's cruel."

Tom bit his lower lip. "Maybe you're afraid of being alone," he said to the two men. "Twenty years."

"You know, you're kind of drunk," Carlo said.

"So are you," Tom said.

"A little," Carlo admitted.

Nothing was said for a few minutes. Then Tom, staring at the ceiling with his head resting on the back of the couch, unbuckled his belt and unbuttoned his fly—

"Whoa," Carlo said and leaped up from the floor.

"Sex would make it a perfect night," Tom said, and started to shove down his jeans and boxers but couldn't lift up his butt sufficiently to make this happen.

Carlo managed to grab Tom's wrists and hold them in place. For a moment, Tom didn't budge. Carlo stared at him. Tom stared back, his smile ebbed. Carlo released his grip. Slowly Tom rebuttoned his jeans but didn't buckle his belt. He tried and failed to push himself up.

"I need to go home," he said.

"I don't think so," Carlo said.

"I'm embarrassed," Tom said.

"You don't need to be," Carlo said.

"You've been so kind to me and I'm embarrassed," Tom said.

"It's all fine," Robbie said. "But we can't let you drive. You'll sleep here."

"I can drive fine," Tom said. "I …"

"Tom?" Carlo asked.

"You said you believe, right?" Tom asked Robbie.

And Robbie answered, "I think something connects us, yes, something has to."

Tom stared at him like he wanted more.

"There are things science will never explain," Robbie added, "that I don't necessarily want explained."

"It's a miracle," Tom said, and he looked at Carlo: "Someone watches."

"Sure, someone watches," Carlo said.

The two men on either side of their guest sat him up, then got him up on his feet. He was heavier than Carlo would have guessed.

"I can drive," Tom protested.

"I'm sure you can," Robbie said, "but you're not going to."

The three of them shuffled toward the guest room but stopped when Tom tried to step away and speak.

"I'm sorry," he said. "You've been so kind and I made you fight."

"No worries," Carlo said. "Robbie and I don't really fight."

"We have disagreements," Robbie said. "Not to worry."

They made it to the guest room, where Tom fell back on the bed. He pulled off his sneakers from the heels.

"'Your kid or your eyes,'" he said weakly. "It's just so awful, isn't it?"

"It is," Robbie said.

"What kind of world," Tom said.

"I know," Carlo said. "It's sad."

"Maybe you're right, maybe," Tom said to Robbie.

"About?" Robbie asked.

"Any two people. They talk long enough. If I could believe that."

He slipped off his sweater and shirt. His pants fell off, and he was only in his boxers and socks as the two men pulled back the blanket.

"I'm not sure why you've been so kind to me," Tom said, rolling onto his side.

And then his head was on the pillow and he was out. The two men stared at Tom while his breathing took on added weight. The room seemed quieter than it normally did. Their guest was asleep. They left the dishes for the morning. They retreated to their own bedroom and shut the door.

"Signor, signor," Robbie said.

Carlo stifled a laugh.

"He's a bit of a pistol, isn't he?"

"Speaking of gun control," Carlo said.

They stood next to their bureau, facing each other, taking off watches, emptying pockets of keys and coins. They unbuttoned each other's shirts. They unzipped each other's pants. They had a guest and took care not to make noise, which brought economy to their movement, which brought on a rush of furtive heat. And then they held each other first above and then beneath the blankets and they, too, began to fall asleep in the quiet house.

Carlo never had dreams, which was to say he never recalled his dreams, and neither did Robbie, although that might be because he dreamed all day long and so his sleep went storyless, Robbie who was an untroubled sleeper, the first always to drift off. Tonight was no different than any other in their two decades together. One long sigh, and Robbie was out, and he made sleep look so deeply gratifying. He was like a cat this way, Carlo thought, and a cat's sleep was a thing worth guarding.

IT WAS LATER THAT SUNDAY MORNING then when Robbie awoke with the uneasy sense something was wrong, that some volume of air was displaced, something fixed had been moved. He was cold and shivering, even in bed, whereas Carlo, a pillow pulled over his head, exuded warmth like a bread oven. Robbie inched closer to feed on this heat and noted the vial of sleeping pills on the night table. Their policy was that if Carlo took a pill during the night, he was not supposed to return the bottle to the drawer but leave it out so that in the case of a medical emergency, Robbie (who mistrusted all narcotics) would be able to inform the paramedics what was in Carlo's system. So apparently Carlo had been unable to sleep—he would be out a while now.

The alarm clock was also on Carlo's side of the bed, and while it was only seven, there was a guest in the house. Knowing Tom, he would expect a proper breakfast and want bacon and eggs and toast and black coffee. There was no need to interrupt Carlo's slumber, not that Robbie could at this point, so he eased his way out of bed and found his boxer-briefs on the floor. He stepped into loose jeans. The T-shirt he reached first and put on was Carlo's. He remained barefoot and tried to keep his step as light as possible until he was outside the bedroom.

The guest room door was ajar, and so Robbie assumed Tom was up, but he wasn't sure and avoided the hallway floorboards of known creak. He stopped short of the guest room and leaned forward, peering through the open door. Tom wasn't in bed, he wasn't in the room. The bed looked only moderately slept in, and Tom's clothes were gone. Had he woken up still intoxicated and driven home after all? They should have taken away his keys. Next to the bed on an octagonal table, there were three books Tom must have pulled from the shelves. The one on top was the classical architecture tome he'd picked out.

The guest was not in the guest room, nor was he in the main room, although at first Robbie thought he saw him lying on a couch because the couch cushions were still in a state of disarray. The hearth threw off heat even as the embers were ashes and the ashes were white. The corky aroma of the dinner Tom cooked hung in the air.

Out front, his car remained parked in their driveway, blocking their wagon. He had not driven drunk, good—maybe he'd called a taxi.

Robbie rounded the corner into the kitchen and noticed immediately that the dishes had been washed and dried and stacked on the counters. The pots and pans had been scrubbed and also left out to be put away by someone who knew in what cabinets everything belonged. Tom had cleaned up, which was generous of him, and it could be he wanted to apologize for his brasher behavior. Truth be told, by the end of the night Robbie wasn't sure he was eager for Tom's continued friendship, but this minor act of etiquette returned Robbie toward a fonder feeling. He turned around and looked beyond the dining table toward the sliding doors that led out to the patio and saw one was wide open. No wonder the house was as cold as it was—

Robbie caught a chair with his hip as he vaulted across the room. He was out on the patio in seconds, his heel turning against the damp slate.

Tom was hanging from a noose tied to the lowest branch of their neighbor's tree.

His body made a quarter turn toward the lake. A thin rope wound tightly under his chin pulled his neck inhumanly long, his chin resting against his collarbone, his legs long, his arms loose, his eyes wide, mouth agape, jaw aslant. Spit drooling from one corner of his mouth had turned to ice. A patio chair lay on its side beneath him, his baseball cap on the ground. High up the limb of the Liquidambar to which the rope had been knotted, the branch had snapped halfway but not broken free. Tom's body turned back toward the house.

His feet were bare and hanging a yard off the ground, plumb like the rest of him.

Robbie became deaf to his own voice but knew he was screaming because Carlo appeared, nearly naked, bounding toward the patio, slipping—but before Carlo could reach the patio, Robbie had already righted the chair and was standing on it and grabbing hold of Tom's waist, tugging him down—and why, when it was obvious his neck was broken?

He pulled at Tom by his legs and Tom's loose jeans indecorously slid halfway down his ass, and the motion caused the branch to break all the way, to snap free from the tree, and Robbie fell over, lost his grip on Tom—Tom came down and landed on the slate. His body was not warm.

Carlo helped Robbie to his feet, and Robbie could not remember a time he'd seen Carlo so white.

First their guest Tom Field had done the dishes, and then he hanged himself. And in the distance was the lake, always the lake, annealed, unrevealing, the water an unforgiving blue in the ante meridiem light.

2

THEIR HOUSE BECAME A CRIME SCENE. The two men received a gentle reprimand from the police for disturbing it by pulling Tom down, although it was considered understandable they thought they might revive him. They were asked to wait in the main room. Carlo, dressed now, sat with both his arms and legs crossed. He'd barely spoken since they found Tom, or rather, since Robbie found Tom. An ambulance was parked out front, strobe off. A gurney had been rolled through the house and out to the patio, a body bag unzipped, yet Tom's corpse had not yet been removed. It was possible the sleeping pill Carlo had taken allowed him to be calmer, Robbie thought, because through it all, Carlo remained seated while Robbie could not stay still. He needed at least to neaten the couch cushions or return a stray wine glass to the kitchen, where an officer asked politely if Robbie would confine himself to the other room a short while longer and then they would ask more questions, although what more could they ask?

Two officers had already run through the previous evening in detail. "Coq au vin has wine in it, doesn't it?" they asked. They inquired about drugs last night and drug use in general and appeared dismayed no drugs were involved. "So then only a fair amount of drinking," they said.

Questions: Did Tom say he owed money? Was Tom in some kind of trouble or hiding from anyone? And precisely how much did Tom have to drink?

Too much, Robbie thought to himself, although when they got him to bed he could barely stand, let alone hang himself, and so maybe he wasn't as intoxicated as he seemed.

"He was alone and lonely," Robbie told the police.

"What kind of lonely?" the lead officer asked.

"What kind of lonely?" Robbie asked back. "Lonesome lonely," he said.

"When you played tennis," the lead officer asked Robbie, "who won?"

"This matters?" Carlo asked.

"We didn't keep score," Robbie said.

"Didn't keep score. So you weren't gambling," the officer said.

The two men were asked if the rope Tom used belonged to them, and they said it did not.

"And before he showed up at your office yesterday morning," the lead officer asked, "you had never met Mr. Field, is that correct?"

"Yes," Robbie said.

The officer looked at Carlo. Robbie looked at Carlo.

Carlo said, "That's right."

Did the two men hear anyone else enter or leave the premises? No. Was it possible someone came inside and they simply didn't hear him? Probably not, but the men had to admit they were sound asleep and Carlo had taken a pill—when did he take the pill?

"Not long after we went to bed," Carlo said, and his frown deepened. He was sitting now with his legs still crossed at the ankle, his hands plunged into his pockets.

The lead officer was needed outside. Robbie listened to her talk with a forensics man wearing surgical gloves, and Robbie wasn't sure whether he and Carlo should have overheard what they did, but then, it wasn't like they were true suspects in any crime.

Details emerged, like about how because Tom was barefoot, he ended up with splinters in his feet, probably from standing on the wooden fence to tie the rope to the neighbor's tree. It was unclear whether he used the chair to step up on the fence and then jumped from the fence or if he stood on the chair and kicked it away. He may have had plenty to drink, but not so much he lost his balance or rope-tying skill.

Details: The rough estimate was that he had been dead for two to three hours before Robbie found him. Tom's car keys were found in his trunk—he must have retrieved the rope from the car.

Questions: When did the branch snap, when Tom jumped off the fence or kicked away the patio chair? Or later after he'd been swinging a while?

An officer carried away the rope in an evidence bag. The lead officer, a detective named Michaels, talked to the two men again while the body in the body bag was wheeled out. She was saying something about removing Tom's car later in the day.

Details: Tom stuffed his socks into his high-tops and left his sneakers by the patio door. Tom folded a dishtowel and left it on the dining table.

What kind of lonely.

The two men were told that the police would be leaving soon but wished to ask them a few more questions, if they didn't mind, and they wanted to put the questions to each man separately. Robbie didn't like this. Would a husband and wife be split up for an interrogation as if they were suspects? But Carlo didn't behave like it was a big deal and stepped into the kitchen with one officer while Robbie followed Detective Michaels into the guest room.

The detective wore a uniform that made her look round in the shoulders and square in frame, probably due to the bullet-proof vest beneath her shirt. The arc of her brow mirrored the arc of her mouth. The guest room window looked out toward the street, and Robbie could see neighbors had gathered, like their next-door neighbors on whose property the aggravated Liquidambar sat as well as some from across the street. The ambulance drove away, lights on for some reason, siren off.

The detective presented Robbie the exact same questionnaire the two men together had already answered. How long was Tom Field known to them. Tennis played weekly. The rope, not from this household, not given to Tom by anyone present.

And then Detective Michaels asked: "So there wasn't any kind of sexual activity last night with Mr. Field?"

"No," Robbie said, and he knew she was doing her best, yet Robbie was irked. He said, "Because that's what we guys do when we hang out together."

Detective Michaels tapped her pen against her pad.

"I'm sorry," Robbie said, and responded more cordially, "Nothing happened, no. I don't know whether Tom would have wanted it to, but nothing did."

Robbie stared at the table by the guest bed with the three books Tom had taken down from the shelves. One was the text on classical architecture, but the two others were monographs on modern artists, not old masters but twentieth-century painters, two painters whom Robbie revered. There had been a stretch of conversation at some point out on the patio when Tom rued what he perceived as the havoc Modernism had wrought, the downfall of figurative painting, and Robbie in defense had waxed on about the aesthetic discoveries one artist made when he painted a landscape and then scraped the surface of the canvas with a squeegee, ruining the landscape but producing an abstraction with mesmerizing striations. Robbie spoke about how his other favorite painter's best work was in fact inspired by the hill streets of Ocean Park as if seen in a squint: abstract, yes, but born from a figurative imagination. And Tom had pooh-poohed Robbie, but then look, he'd been listening. In the middle of the night, Tom Field got up and located the art books for himself, and at least he had enough curiosity to try to figure out what it was that Robbie saw where he, Tom, saw nothing. Tom had wanted to understand.

Detective Michaels was saying something about how shock was often delayed—Robbie realized he was shaking—and it would be best if Robbie didn't try to drive today, today he needed to take it easy, and at least the two men had each other, they would comfort each other, they would survive this together. The detective grabbed the wool throw from the guest bed and draped it over Robbie's shoulders. She took Robbie's hands and had him clasp the blanket.

Robbie rejoined Carlo on the couch. He wanted to tell him about the art books but couldn't because his teeth were chattering. Carlo reached his arm around Robbie and tried to warm him up.

Finally Robbie had to ask: "Because we wouldn't do a threeway?"

Carlo didn't say anything.

"Because then he heard us?" Robbie asked. "Do you think he heard us?"

Carlo tried to hush him.

"He said he was born at the wrong time. Do people kill themselves because they're born at the wrong time?" Robbie asked.

Carlo started to say something but then didn't speak.

"What?" Robbie asked.

Carlo shrugged.

"No, what?" Robbie insisted.

Carlo shook his head from side to side. He said, "Nothing."

"You heard him, all the things he was going to do," Robbie said.

Even then, already that morning, the two men were like boats in abutting berths knocking up against separate piers.

"Don't," Carlo said, and he sounded tinny, ventriloquized. "Don't try to figure him out, Robbie," he said. "You won't."

THAT DUSK ROBBIE SAT on the piano bench by the window and peered out at the darkened lake. He was alone in the house, which he was not happy about.

All afternoon he had shuffled around, still wrapped in the blanket, while Carlo put away the dishes and pots and pans, while Carlo swept, while Carlo stripped the guest bed and laundered the sheets and remade the bed. Despite Robbie's admonition that for all they knew the police might want a second look at the patio, Carlo hacked up the fallen branch and stuffed the debris in the green recycling bin. It was also Carlo who went round the neighbors and told them roughly what had happened. When he returned, he reported that they were sympathetic, as if this sort of freak tragedy in one's home could befall any of them. Then Carlo rode his bike down to the office—but why on a Sunday? To accomplish what beyond getting away from the house, and from Robbie moping about?

The doorbell startled him. Detective Michaels had returned with a police tow truck to remove Tom's car. As they moved the car out, the duct tape binding the front fender to the chassis came loose, and the driver had to leave the truck idling while first he tried to retape the fender before deciding to remove it.

"How are you doing?" the detective asked. "Where's your partner? Did he go out?"

Robbie said, "I don't get it. He was looking for a church to join."

"Your partner?"

"Detective, what will happen to Tom's belongings?"

"We'll head over to his residence shortly. Family will be contacted."

"There's only his grandmother, as far as I know. He didn't mention his parents."

"Mr. Field didn't by chance leave a cell phone here, did he?"

"He mentioned losing it," Robbie said.

Before leaving, the detective asked if Robbie, as Tom's only identifiable friend, could make himself available the next day in case she had additional questions after going through Tom's apartment.

"If we find certain evidence, we might be able to close the case quickly," she said.

"Like a suicide note?"

"Sometimes there are strong indications of a certain plan in place."

"A suicide note," Robbie said.

"If you will," the detective said.

Robbie said he hoped to return to the office, but in fact the next morning, Monday morning, while Carlo got up at the regular time and showered and was good to go, Robbie couldn't get out of bed. Carlo told him to sleep in, it was fine, and Robbie insisted he'd be down the hill in an hour. An hour later, when he did get out of bed, he only made it as far as the couch. He was hung over without having had any alcohol the night before, dizzy yet not fevered. His back ached the way it did when he played too much tennis. He was still wearing pajama bottoms and a T-shirt when Detective Michaels came by again at noon. She was carrying an oversized manila envelope.

Robbie tried to neaten up a bit. He combed his hair with his fingers. He fluffed couch cushions.

"We successfully accessed Mr. Field's apartment," the detective said.

"And did you find a note?"

"Not as yet," she said. "Nor did we find any medications—"

"Anti-depressants?"

"Or anything else, not even aspirin. Or alcohol—only iced tea. I think it was iced tea."

"Green tea," Robbie said.

"That might explain the color. Like pond water," the detective said. "We did, however, find a cell phone."

"He didn't lose it after all?"

"I'm afraid Mr. Field was not the tidiest person. There were some large piles of dirty laundry we had to dig through. There aren't many numbers on the cell phone, a few, and one of them does appear to be Mr. Field's grandmother."

"You called her?"

"We have someone at the station trained for that," the detective explained.

Because she was sitting at the edge of couch, and because the cushions hadn't been completely tucked back in place after Robbie's morning nap, the seat cushion was lifting away somewhat from the upholstered frame. Robbie was going to offer to reposition the cushion to make the detective more comfortable when he noticed something small and black and square wedged between the back and seat frame. There was also a glint of gold. The detective shifted back on the couch, hiding again whatever the little object was—a wallet? A credit card case?

"Mr. Field also seems to have been something of a musician," the detective said. "There was an electric keyboard propped up on a workout bench and then some sheet music."

"What else did you find?"

"Stacks of library books. A suit in the closet, but not much else really. Most of his clothes seemed to be scattered around the floor—"

"What about a tux?"

"Yes, right, also a tuxedo. So you've been to his place?"

"No," Robbie said. "He mentioned owning one."

"We found some art supplies, some pencils, brushes, and whatnot. And then this," Detective Michaels said, "which I brought to show you."

She withdrew a large spiral-bound sketch book from the envelope and handed it to Robbie, who began leafing through it. On each page of most of the pad, there was a single portrait of a man or a woman or a kid, old, young, pretty, less pretty—it didn't appear as though Tom had ever drawn the same subject twice. By far, the majority of charcoal portraits were of men around Tom's age, many full nudes or nude torsos, a few of the guys with hardons, although most not. All of the drawings were dated, the earliest page a year ago, the most recent the previous week.

"I'm wondering if any of these subjects are familiar to you," the detective said. "If you recognize anyone, if you can identify anyone, then we might try contacting him."

Robbie began at the beginning of the sketch book and turned each page carefully. He knew no one. What he could say, however, was that Tom was deft at chiaroscuro. He used white chalk sparingly, and sometimes he rubbed in sienna or umber, which animated his portraits and gave them warmth. He was skilled and he knew it because he had enough ego to sign every page, his name in tight small caps followed by a period, an emphatic statement: TOM FIELD.

"He was talented," Robbie said.

"I'd have to agree. But you can't—"

"All strangers," Robbie said. "To me, anyway, they're all strangers."

The detective removed another smaller envelope from her jacket pocket. The envelope contained snapshots, which she spread out on the table as if she were going to perform a card trick. She said the photos had been stashed in the glove compartment of Tom's car. Again she asked if they meant anything to Robbie, and he began to suspect that the detective was less interested what information he might provide than how he reacted to seeing the photos, all of which were of Tom at different ages, none recent, many of him posed with an older gentleman usually wearing a seersucker suit and leaning on a cane with an ivory handle or with an older woman who sometimes wore an auburn wig. No surprise, Tom was adorable as a little boy and he always seemed to be caught in mid-sentence. The detective herself had to chuckle at the shot of Tom and his teddy bear wearing matching lederhosen. Here was Tom in tennis whites clutching a racket. Tom by a lake, hair wet, a towel around his shoulders, lips blue. Tom as a teenager in the passenger seat of a convertible, arm over the side, too cool for school. Always speaking something and always, it seemed to Robbie, in a good mood.

"Did Mr. Field mention anything that might have been causing him extra aggravation?" the detective asked.

Robbie was tearing up.

"Did he seem at all desperate?"

What kind of lonely, Robbie thought. He couldn't speak, and perhaps the detective knew not to push him. She gathered the photographs back in the envelope and put away the sketch book. She asked if she could step out to the patio for a brief moment to look at something again, and Robbie neither nodded nor shook his head no, but the detective went out back anyway.

He was drenched with maudlin thoughts about how Tom's death took time to stage: time to consider the drop, to tie the rope to the tree, to knot the rope and slip it over his neck. His death took thought, it took preparation, maybe for days, maybe for years. However, the police had not found a suicide note and they were never going to find anything resembling one, no matter how hard they searched. The dead man's motive would remain hazy, and it was possible Tom was only messing around, inebriate, testing himself in a game of auto-brinkmanship. Also possible, he wanted to die, although Robbie could not accept this. It didn't seem right, it didn't fit.

He looked out at the patio, where Detective Michaels appeared to have some interest in the wooden fence. With the detective occupied, Robbie pulled back the couch cushion and removed the black object, which was neither a wallet nor a credit card case. It was a palm-sized, gilt-edged address book. On the first page of the address book, in a somewhat younger hand but in the same firm small caps with which he'd signed his drawings, Tom had written his name. The little book must have fallen out of his pocket when he started to pull off his jeans or at some other point Saturday night.

The pages were soft, worn by a decade of thumbing, and Robbie noted that nearly all of the entries had been struck through with a hard stroke of ink or lead, all of the names and numbers crossed out save only a few.

The detective on the patio glanced up at the tree. She looked out toward the Reservoir, and then back at the house.

Later, if he was going to be honest about it, Robbie would have to admit that his true adultery began here, because it was with a quickened heart and the sudden, switched-on heat of infidelity that, as Detective Michaels came back inside the house, Robbie shoved Tom's little address book between the couch cushions, stood, and saw the detective to the door.

HE WAITED UNTIL THE NEXT MORNING when he was alone again in the house, Carlo having returned to the office. This time Robbie was glad to have him gone. The woman who answered the phone sounded like she'd been interrupted and Robbie identified himself as a friend of Tom's. He was asked to hold a moment.

He held a full minute before a decidedly older woman came on the line and said, "Yes."

"Mrs. Field," Robbie said.

"Yes."

"I'm Rob Voight. A friend of Tom's. Calling from Los Angeles."

"Oh. Yes," Tom's grandmother said. "Hello."

"I wanted to call and say how sorry I am for your loss."

"Yes. Thank you, yes."

"I don't know what the police told you—"

"They told me, yes."

Tom's grandmother sounded as though she were holding the phone at some distance from her face. She may not have been holding the phone for herself at all. Her breathing was arduous, her voice feeble.

"I wanted to say I'm sorry," Robbie said again.

"Yes. Well. Tommy was Tommy."

Tom was Tommy, Robbie thought.

He said, "I don't know what the police may have said but I want you to know—"

"He was being dramatic," Tom's grandmother said. "Wasn't he?"

"Exactly," Robbie said. "Dramatic," he said.

"Always a dramatic child," she said. "We didn't think he'd—"

"No," Robbie said.

"That's not Tommy."

"No."

"Poor Tommy," Tom's grandmother said.

"It's tragic."

"Very unexpected."

"I'm so sorry."

"Well," Tom's grandmother said.

Then Robbie didn't know what to say. He listened to the old woman work at each breath.

"You sound like a young man," Tom's grandmother said.

"Yes," Robbie said, although he was thinking young relative to Tom's grandmother, not young like Tom.

"You have a life ahead of you," she said.

Robbie didn't respond. Tom's grandmother must have thought he was her grandson's boyfriend.

"And you need to live that life, you hear?"

"Yes, ma'am," Robbie said.

"Tommy would agree with me, I'm certain."

"That's very kind of you to say."

"Goodnight, dear," Tom's grandmother said, and hung up before Robbie could wish her well.

He hid Tom's address book his underwear drawer in the dresser and then lay on the couch a long while. He didn't fall asleep, but he was not really in a wakeful state when Carlo returned in the early evening and found him laid out thus. Carlo switched on a lamp and sat down at the edge of the couch.

"Maybe you'd prefer the bed," he said.

Robbie squeezed a corner of the velvet sofa. He'd been under the impression he was in bed.

"What time is it?" he asked. "It seems late."

"I stopped by the police station," Carlo said.

"They called you?"

"No, I went in."

"Oh. Did they ask you if Tom seemed desperate?" Robbie asked.

Carlo was staring at him as if reading words written on his face, text Robbie would be unable to see unless staring in a mirror. Did Robbie look guilty in some way—did Carlo know Robbie had phoned Tom's grandmother?

"What?" Robbie asked.

"Right," Carlo said, "they asked if Tom seemed desperate, but I said you were the one who'd spent more time with him ..."

He reached out his forefinger and gently caressed Robbie's left eyebrow as if flattening errant hairs, then his right. Robbie took Carlo's hand and held it against his heart. Don't move, he was thinking, let's stay like this.

But Carlo stood, said, "How about I heat up some soup for you," and went into the kitchen.

Robbie realized he'd been dreaming, and in his dream, it was Saturday night or maybe another night. He had imagined himself sound asleep in bed when suddenly he awoke and noticed Carlo wasn't lying next to him. Instead Carlo stood at their bedroom window, gazing out at the patio, at the black trees of night and the black lake beyond, the slope of his shoulders in silhouette, handsome, distant. In the dream, Robbie was determined to stay awake until Carlo, apparently unaware he was being observed, returned to bed, but then Robbie yawned—then Robbie fell back asleep. This was what he had dreamed about: not being able to stay awake.

HE DUTIFULLY ATE MOST OF THE SOUP that Carlo warmed up for him, but then Robbie was zonked, and so Carlo put him to bed, the blanket pulled high. Still clothed, atop the blankets, Carlo held Robbie until Robbie fell asleep. Then Carlo retreated to a chair in the corner of the dark room.

He'd lied to the police twice Sunday morning, and initially he wasn't going to correct the record, but then he understood that his perjury might come back to haunt him. This was why Carlo had gone to the police station to speak with Detective Michaels.

As the detective ushered him to a windowless interrogation room where they could chat, she admitted she was not in the most jovial mood because she'd only that hour learned that in another case, a key witness questioned by an assistant district attorney had contradicted testimony he'd originally given the detective, throwing the prosecution into disarray. Which was to say Detective Michaels was probably not going to be amused to learn about a relatively less serious instance of fibbing.

"I thought it would be best if I cleared something up," Carlo started.

The detective pinched the tip of her nose with her thumb and forefinger and held it a moment.

"I said I'd never met Tom before he showed up at our office, but I had," Carlo said.

"Is that so?"

The detective stared at him, waiting, but it was a difficult story to relay and even now, having decided to come clean, Carlo hesitated. The way the detective was regarding him, half squinting, didn't help.

"Yes," Carlo said. "Last April."

One evening the previous April, he had gone alone to a dinner party at friends in Glendale while Robbie stayed home nursing a cold. Carlo left relatively early and was driving along Fletcher and had passed under the 5 and was coming up to the light at Riverside. He was in the right lane and driving at a more cautious speed than usual because he'd consumed a good amount of wine with dinner, which had been rich, all about cream sauces, a cheese course, a chocolate course, gluttony. He was woozy when he came up behind a car at the red light, and there were no other cars at the intersection. The car, a long black sedan, had its flashers on—it looked like maybe it had stalled out. Carlo was about to turn into the left lane and maneuver around it when two men shot out of the back of the sedan, flailing their arms yet making no noise he could hear.

Carlo's first thought was they wanted him to call for help. He rolled down his window as one man approached, and as soon as he had the window part-way down, the man reached in the car and twice depressed the power lock. Before Carlo could react, the second man had opened up the passenger-side and slid in next to Carlo. This second man was pointing a gun at him.

"What do you want," Carlo asked, "what do you want—do you want the car?"

The man with the gun didn't respond.

"Take it," Carlo said and lifted his hands off the steering wheel, and he would have gotten out of the car and bolted if the first man were not standing next to the driver's-side door and preventing egress.

"What do you want—do you want money?"

The man pressed the gun against the side of Carlo's ribs, which hurt, and still the man didn't speak, which only confused Carlo.

"What, my wallet?"

Which was what Carlo reached for—he kept it in his front pocket—but as he did this, his foot began to slip off the brake and he slammed his foot hard against the pedal, which made the man with the gun in the passenger seat jerk forward, his free fist hitting the glove compartment.

"Don't fuck with me," the man said and jabbed Carlo in the ribs. "And don't look at me," he said. "Don't look at me."

But Carlo already had looked at the man, already noted the

way his chin drooped left to right, the way his moustache was similarly angled. Already Carlo had taken a good long look: blue eyes, black hair, young, possibly high school-aged, a constellation of moles by his left ear. Carlo turned instead toward the other man still standing on the street, which was when he noticed that while the man wasn't holding a gun, he had formed a pretend one with his thumb and first two fingers. Bang, bang.

"Put the car in park," the man with the real gun said, and Carlo obeyed.

"Get out," the man with the gun said and shoved Carlo toward the door, again with the gun pressed at, into his ribs, but the second man standing next to Carlo's door still made that impossible—

"Get the fuck out of the fucking car," the man with the gun yelled, and so Carlo opened his door, which irritated the second man, although he moved aside and grabbed Carlo's shirt collar when Carlo did climb out of his car. Also the second man clutched Carlo's right wrist and pulled it behind Carlo's back, angling it up, painfully so.

The man with the gun slid into the driver's seat and tossed his weapon to the man now twisting Carlo's arm, who guided Carlo swiftly in front of the headlights and back toward the freeway underpass. No one drove by on Fletcher, no one on Riverside, although cars could be heard thrumming across the freeway overhead, useless. They stood in a damp dark space, which was when the second man pushed Carlo against the wall.

He said, "Don't look. Don't you look."

Again too late because Carlo and the man restraining him had made what could only be described as extensive eye contact.

He could describe both perpetrators, similar in height, weight, youth, eye color, haircut—although the one with the gun now had a smoother shave and no mustache.

"Did he look?" the man back in the car shouted.

"He fucking looked," the second man shouted back, and he tugged Carlo's wrist up against his back, which sent a charge down through his elbow and up his shoulder.

Other men got out of the ambush car, its flashers still pulsing, two more men, one from the driver's side, heavy, gesticulating at the guy behind the wheel in Carlo's car, and the man from the passenger side, now strutting over to the underpass. There were many men against him and the only way not to look at them would have been for Carlo to close his eyes, but he didn't want to close his eyes and not know what was happening.

"You shouldn't have looked," the second man said, and he pressed the gun against the base of Carlo's skull. "You fucked up big time, looking."

If Carlo closed his eyes, he thought, it would represent some kind of capitulation, inaugurating the worst scenario. He didn't move. His forehead was pressed against the concrete wall. He ached everywhere.

The man who had walked over from the ambush car was saying something like, "Let's go," or "Let him go," or "Go at him," or "Let me go at him."

Carlo couldn't hear well because his head was buzzing, and didn't dare turn to look now, nor did he close his eyes, and he wanted to throw up. All the rich food. Everything was catching up with him and he became pretty sure he was either going to vomit or defecate.

"He fucking looked," the man holding the gun said to the man from the ambush car.

"Fuck the fuck, and let's go," the man from the other car said.

Carlo was thinking Robbie would never understand what happened tonight, and Carlo never wanted him to know. All that mattered in the world was being held in bed at night—everything else was inconsequential. He wanted to close his eyes. Acid ran through his esophagus into his stomach and his thighs were weak, his knees, calves, and ankles weak, giving in, and he wanted to throw up or shit.

The man holding Carlo was possibly going to break his arm, and also he was lifting his right knee up into Carlo's buttocks.

Behind them, there was shouting. Behind them: "Let's go."

And Carlo let his eyes close. His forehead and cheek were scraped up from being pressed against the concrete. His arm was numb.

"Oh man," the guy holding him shouted. "Oh man," he shouted again and released Carlo's arm and stepped back. "Oh man."

Something had to give.

"He fucking shitted," the man who had the gun said.

"Let's go," the other man shouted.

"Oh man. That's disgusting."

Indeed, Carlo was thinking, disgusting it was. Warm, wrong, infantile, weak.

"Fuck," the man who had the gun shouted. "He almost shitted on me."

"Let's go."

Carlo didn't turn to look, but he heard the men running back to the cars. He heard car doors slamming and engines revving.

And he did finally turn when the man with the gun and the other man both jumped in the ambush car and the ambush car, the long black sedan, its flashers still on, lurched forward and tore off right onto Riverside, zigzagging as it picked up speed. Then the man who was in Carlo's car followed them. He shifted the car in gear and he must have hit the gas hard, but the road was slick with drizzle, and as he tried to take Carlo's car around the corner, he drove directly, definitively into a telephone pole, smashing the right side of the car, the hood folding back like an accordion, small bits of glass flying everywhere.

From where he was standing beneath the underpass, Carlo didn't have a good view, but he could see the airbag deflating, a flower in time-lapse decline. There was some smoke in the air.

The ambush car skidded in reverse. Then there were three men on the street, opening Carlo's car on the left, pulling the man out from behind the wheel like the car might explode— Carlo was waiting for an explosion. The man looked injured the way he held his shoulder and limped over to the ambush car, dragging a foot, and then all the men were in the car and they zoomed off again, doors shutting while the car was in motion.

Carlo doubled over and wanted to throw up, but now nothing came. He waited a moment. No one drove by. He wasn't sure he wanted anyone to drive by because he was wet, he was fetid. He hobbled over to the wreck. No way could he drive the car. The right side looked like it had been welded to the telephone pole. It was wrecked.

His cell phone was in the car, its red light blinking. The message was from Robbie, feeling worse, running a fever. Could Carlo pick up some ginger ale on his way home?

The police came. They called a tow truck. They began to take Carlo's statement, enough information to post an all-points-bulletin. Every time a cop took a step toward Carlo, Carlo took a step back. He was mortified. They wanted to take him back to the station. He said he didn't want to stink up their car, how could he ride with them? They said don't worry about it, it wouldn't be the first time, they had some plastic. Carlo wanted to change his clothes. They said they'd give him something to slip into at the station.

At the police station, in the men's room, Tom Field stood at a sink, washing his hands, leaning toward the mirror, staring into his own bloodshot eyes.

However, this wasn't when they spoke. First Carlo cleaned himself up and changed into the one-size prison overalls he'd been given, and then he went to look at albums of mug shots and iden-tified no one. The car was dusted for prints, although Carlo knew his assailants would never be found. He was told there might be a few more questions for him, if he could hold on, and then he'd be given a ride home, but it was a busy night for crime in the city and he might need to wait. If he wanted fresh air, he could step out back, which was where he saw Tom again, smoking a ciga-rette. Tom offered Carlo a drag, which Carlo accepted. Carlo coughed as he handed the cigarette back.

"What are you in for?" Tom asked, gesturing toward Carlo's prison fatigues.

Carlo's arms were crossed tightly across his chest as if he were also wearing a straight-jacket.

"Oh, what's wrong, baby?" Tom asked.

Carlo had the sense he was crying but no tears came. The back of the station was a rudely illuminated patio enclosed by a

cinderblock wall. There were two metal chairs and a pail of sand
for butts. He couldn't speak. Tom smoked another cigarette and
waved toward the chairs as if the patio were his parlor, Please.
They both sat. Tom talked. He explained that earlier that night,
he was in the process of being kicked out of a bar and engaged in
a heated discussion with the bouncers when a squad car cruised
by. No charges had been pressed but the police were detaining
Tom until he sobered up enough to drive. Tom talked about
nothing in particular—he was talking for the sake of talking.
About Southern manners versus manners elsewhere in the country. How sobriety was a relative term. The way Los Angeles men
were always looking to see who better was going to walk into the
bar. He hated Los Angeles. Secretly he liked it, too. The old
hound dog hills and the good-natured sun.

"Anyway," Tom said. "So what happened to you?"

Carlo told him. Now he was crying.

"It's over now," Tom said. "All in the past, baby, you'll be fine."

Normally Carlo would have bristled at being called baby by
someone he didn't know (or for that matter by anyone), but at
that moment, there was something calming about it. He liked
the smoked-out tone of Tom's voice. And they talked some more,
Tom relating some story of his own about how once a long time
ago he'd been mugged or fended off a band of hooligans. Tom
was wearing a green windbreaker with two tan vertical stripes
down the left side. He was fidgeting with the zipper, pulling it up,
pulling it down. Up, down.

Then Tom said, "I bet you wish you'd had a gun."

Carlo gave an automatic response, that he didn't believe in
guns, to which Tom responded guns weren't something you

believed in—guns were something you kept handy to blow away anyone who tried to mess with you. And they talked more about it, and Carlo said he wasn't interested in purchasing a weapon for self-defense, but if he were, hypothetically, how would he, how would one go about it? Tom said he'd looked into it, recently, although he didn't say why. It wasn't that complicated and he knew where to go.

Carlo was still shaking and Tom took the liberty of reaching his arm around him, which like being called baby, under normal circumstances Carlo likely would not have abided. Yet Tom's embrace allowed Carlo to relax.

Because Carlo was shivering, Tom unzipped his windbreaker, took it off, and said, "Here."

At first, Carlo didn't take the jacket.

"Here, here," Tom insisted, and so Carlo put on the windbreaker and zipped it up. It was tight over the baggy overalls, and Carlo felt like he was costumed in a nylon bodice with canvas pantaloons. So be it, he was a little warmer. Tom had been wearing only a white T-shirt beneath the jacket but didn't appear at all cold.

He fired off questions about Carlo's life: Was he born in Southern California? Oh no, where then? What brought him to Los Angeles and what did he do here? How long had he and Robbie been together? No way, wow—there's hope for the rest of us. Did they ever travel anywhere, where? Did they throw dinner parties? Did they garden? Did they read aloud books to each other in bed? And so on. In this way, Tom drew Carlo out. Carlo may have turned the interview around once or twice but mostly he responded to Tom's queries, and gradually he stopped shaking so much.

When an officer at last was ready to take Carlo home, he and Tom stood, and as they stood, hugged awkwardly.

Carlo began to unzip the green windbreaker, and Tom said, "No, keep it for now. I'll give you my address. You can mail it back whenever." Inside the station, he wrote down his address on the back of a flyer for the neighborhood watch.

"Thank you," Carlo said. "And thank you for talking to me."

"No," Tom said, "thank *you* for talking to *me*," and Carlo never knew what he meant.

At home, Carlo slipped out of his overalls in the entry. He stashed them in the front hall closet with the plan to dispose of them the next day. He would hide Tom's windbreaker in the garage until he had a chance to mail it to the Valley. As he got in bed, he noticed the sleep-inducing cold remedy bottle on Robbie's night table. Robbie didn't wake up and in the morning was still sick, and Carlo explained he hadn't seen the phone message about the ginger ale until it was too late. And after only the merest hesitation, he also reported he'd been in a bad accident, thus the scrapes on his forehead and cheek, the red abrasions like bracelets around his wrist. He had been very lucky and was otherwise fine, although the car was destroyed for good. Robbie was alarmed, relieved, fevered. They would worry about the car later, but right now Carlo said he'd take the other one to the store and get ginger ale and so forth and Robbie went back to sleep.

A random act. The wrong place at the wrong time in a life of mostly being in the right place at the right time. Carlo could not undo what had happened to him, but he could protect Robbie from undue worry. Robbie in all his optimism, his trust, his naïve trust, Robbie was Carlo's raft, and Carlo wanted him to remain precisely the way he was, unanchored, buoyant. And so Carlo decided he would live with his secret.

If Carlo had lied to the police Sunday morning, he explained, it was because it seemed neither the time nor place for Robbie to learn the truth about the carjacking and the circumstances under which Carlo met Tom at the police station. The truth could come out one day when there was less to cope with, only the living, not the dead.

THERE WAS OF COURSE MORE TO THE STORY about Tom Field that Carlo could have and should have disclosed. However, while he was offering his account, Detective Michaels' neck reddened and she tapped the table with a steadily increasing tempo, so Carlo chose to stop there, hoping it would be enough.

"Presumably you don't wish your partner to discover certain aspects of the situation here, which is why you haven't been the most forthcoming," the detective said.

"That's exactly it," Carlo said.

"And so you lied to us."

"That's why I came in. And I do apologize."

"Is there anything else? After that night in April, did you ever meet up with Mr. Field again before last Saturday?"

Carlo blinked. The detective waited.

He blinked again and said, "No," and so one more time, he lied to the police. He'd come in to set the record straight but ended up mangling it even more.

"Maybe, say, you had an affair with Mr. Field all summer long," the detective suggested.

"Oh, no, no," Carlo said and chuckled uncomfortably.

"And you certainly didn't want your partner to find out about it—"

"That's not the case, Detective."

"Finally it was more convenient for Mr. Field not to be around any more. He might say something inappropriate."

Carlo's face was hot, he was blushing.

"He was quite intoxicated, you've reported. But not so much," Detective Michaels said, "that he couldn't tie a rope to a tree *and* tie a rope around his neck, jump, and hang himself. Unless, of course, he had help with all of this."

Again the detective pinched her nose.

Sunday the police had asked if the men heard anyone besides Tom in the house and they had not because they were asleep, and Carlo was asked when he took the sleeping pill, and he'd replied, "Not long after we went to bed." This was the second lie he was hoping to shed, but now, given the detective's line of inquiry, he didn't think he should. It was best to keep the matter simple.

"Perjury is not a good thing to be getting into," Detective Michaels said. "Obstruction, et cetera—not good at all."

Carlo crossed his legs. His arms were folded, which looked defensive. He unfolded his arms, uncrossed his legs.

"You've nothing else to add," the detective said.

"No," Carlo said, perhaps a little too quickly.

"You realize you've made more work for me. We'll need to corroborate your statement, you understand. As if I don't have enough on my plate."

Carlo apologized again, but shouldn't he be given some credit for coming in to the station voluntarily? It didn't matter. If you lied to the law once, chances were every subsequent statement you gave would be sieved through the original prevarication.

"You're free to go," the detective said, standing—free to go, as if Carlo had been run in and detained. "And as you can imagine, we'll be in touch."

Carlo left the police station feeling rattled, and while he'd had every intention of going home and confessing at least as much as he did to the detective, he found Robbie beached on the couch—he who never napped, napping, Robbie's forehead mottled by the velvet fabric—and there was no way Carlo could be honest right then. Now Robbie was asleep again, although his sleep was restive at best. His leg twitched, he flipped around once, then back the way he was.

The deeper truth about Sunday morning was that Carlo's guilt had been immediate and stupefying. If he had lied, it wasn't only to keep Robbie from learning what he didn't need to know, but also because Carlo himself couldn't yet deal with the ways blame came back to him, and he didn't know how Robbie would react. For who knew how long—months, years—Carlo would bear the burden of proving his integrity and goodness to his disenchanted boyfriend, or to be even more blunt about it, given all the compound secrets, it was iffy Robbie would ever trust him again. What if Robbie never forgave him?

Something else was happening while he sat in the dark and watched Robbie sleep. His initial guilt was turning into a kind of anger. For what Tom did, Carlo was beginning to see, was a cruel act not only against Tom's own being but also against the two men, especially Robbie, who had recognized Tom as the lonely soul he was and attempted, if only for a day and a night, to make

Los Angeles a less alienating city. All anyone had to do was look at Robbie these last two days to register the toll of Tom's carelessness, his malice.

And so it was with the coagulation of this fury that Carlo resolved not to tell Robbie anything the next morning, nor probably the morning after that, maybe never. No, never. Carlo needed to nurse Robbie back to his old sanguine utopian self. The two men had made a great life for themselves, and they would ride this out, this *aftermath*, that was all there was to it. Carlo would hold it all together the way he always did—their finances, their office, their home. Hopefully he would get a house built for the television producer. He would find new work. He would meet the police in their queries until they closed the case. Of course he would continue to suffer remorse for what happened to Tom, of course, but in the same way Carlo could not go back to the intersection of Riverside and Fletcher and swing out wide and zoom away untouched, Tom could not be brought back. Carlo would not let any of what had happened break him, and he would focus only on the future. He had no judge to answer to but himself, and whatever amends he needed to make in time would be private. His atonement, one more secret.

3

BY THE END OF THE WEEK, Robbie returned to the office, where there was work to do because the television producer had agreed in principle to move forward with Stein Voight. In order to build on the site, they were going to have to bring in a structural engineer, but before they could do that, they needed to attend to some of the producer's pending qualms with the overall plan. One task Robbie faced, re-siting a detached studio apartment, was tricky but not complicated, yet after only an hour back at his desk during which he did little more than stare at the street, he decided to take a walk to the producer's property for inspiration. He set out at a brisk gait, yet instead of heading up the hill away from the lake as he approached the Reservoir, he found himself drawn toward the atomic movement of hounds in the dog park. And once he rounded the dog park, for no reason other than it was a lovely fall day, he ended up continuing north and making a circuit around the entire Reservoir.

After walking all the way around, he immediately headed into a second loop because he was finding a lot to look at while on foot that he'd long since forgotten about, or taken for granted. There was the lake itself, for one, with its ever-shifting variegations, the many indigo ponds within the cobalt basin, the lustrous patches of sapphire or circles of matte cerulean no different than the open-lidded sky. There was the white scattering of birds that settled on the lake, like a string of buoys moving up and down with the soft current until they took shape and flew and resettled elsewhere across the water. There were the hills on all sides robed with houses, and the range in the crystal distance, snow-capped, rustic, Western. How lucky he was to live here, he thought. He had the sense he'd been missing out on things, rushing, his world a world seen from a train. He had not been attentive enough to his environment, and now, given what had happened, especially in light of what had happened, he needed to celebrate Life, to cherish Life: Long live Life.

Robbie took a third turn around the lake. He wasn't getting tired, quite the opposite. Each orbit gave him more energy, and at first he might have been thinking about the design problem back on his desk. But he was also looking at all the modern houses he walked past, including some that the two men had renovated and one or two designed from scratch, and then Robbie began lingering in front of the homes built by the celebrated mid-century architects who gave shape to the neighborhood, each house with its own pleasing geometry set against the grain of the hills. On the east side of the Reservoir, he headed up a side street and then down a dead-ended street to a collection of houses he'd originally seen what seemed like a mid-century ago in a coffee-table book (it was the history of this particular architecture in Southern California that drew the two men to Los Angeles after college), houses you could see straight through, front to back, mitered glass boxes riding mitered glass boxes, with broad flat roofs and trusses extending beyond exterior walls, houses surrounded by white-barked eucalyptus, twisted, atilt—several houses in a row, each a variation on its neighbor, movements of a sonata for glass and beam.

He was carrying a pocket-sized notebook and, standing on Neutra Place across from the houses, he began sketching a series of overlapping parallelograms, an approximate perspective, then connecting the planes with vertical scratches of black ink. He looked at his miniature drawings, at the homes up the grade, and turned the page and sketched the pavilions again, his pen grasped more firmly between his thumb and first two fingers, his ink line consequently more taut, as if in the act of sketching he could solve the eternal riddle of how a glass edge could meet a glass edge and make a room appear at once solid and transparent.

"You can drive all around the city," he said, "and come across clusters of modern houses like on this one, and I know, I know—you're going to tell me each of these streets is yet one more failed utopia, and all utopias are doomed. And maybe that's true, but then maybe not. Maybe we start with islands of houses like on this street, and then each of these island-streets expands outward until eventually it meets up with another one like it, until eventually you have a whole neighborhood, and then the neighborhoods run into each other, and then you wake up and your entire city has blossomed into a Modern City—"

Robbie stopped. He'd been lecturing aloud, addressing a skeptic, trying to persuade someone, trying to persuade Tom, as if Tom were with him, Tom who had taken the art monographs into the guest room and who maybe in time could have been sold on Modern, perhaps in time, were there the time, which there wasn't now.

Robbie didn't return to the office. He walked home and then in the declining afternoon, from the main room, looked out back at the fall of tea bushes blossoming with tight red flowers, a thousand ruby blooms strewn amid the cindery brush.

One: a lush landscape.

Two: a house with yawning beams.

Three (later, in bed, his eyes adjusted to the dark and he was staring at the hard shallow trench of Carlo's back): a man's back, a thing of grace according to Tom, and maybe Robbie understood him now in a way he'd failed before. There was too much beauty in the world and Robbie didn't know how to absorb it all, too much to take in.

WHEN HE AWOKE THE NEXT MORNING, however, nothing whatsoever looked beautiful. The man-made lake in the distance was a pathetic folly, obsolete, a blight. Concrete shores girded by a chain link fence, and the water, after all, was dammed water, stolen water. Robbie stared out at the patio and the tree where Tom had hanged himself, and what he would give now not to have been the one who found Tom. He remembered Tom's taxidermic face, bloated and grotesque. The chair on its side, his hat on the ground. The sensation of grabbing hold of his thighs and waist and losing balance and falling and semi-stiff Tom falling, too—as if that was what finally killed him, the fall. The dampness of the slate patio, the cold stone, stone-cold, death.

Time passed, one autumn day bled into the next. Robbie could not stay warm—his favorite sweater failed him, his favorite scarf, too. He had little appetite, he was losing weight. He went into the office but left early, without accomplishing anything on the producer's house. Carlo seemed to understand, although he also seemed weary in his own way.

There was one night, for instance, when he came home and headed straight for a bottle of zinfandel, gulping down a full glass before admitting that since Robbie hadn't completed certain renderings, and since the producer had asked for a modification to add a second rental studio atop the one already sketched out, Carlo had decided to open software he hadn't used in ages and make the revision himself, and in the process he'd overlooked something extremely basic, namely that the city would require another off-street parking space to accompany the new unit (and how many times had they dealt with this issue in the past?). Given the grade of the site, this was complicated. Carlo had already informed the client one thing was possible, and now they'd have to double back and offer alternatives, and mark his word, Carlo said, the producer would use this gaffe against them. Carlo drank a lot of wine that night and fell asleep early but claimed the next morning that, no worries, everything would work out. He was glad merely to reveal his goof-up and express some passing angst. Robbie said he'd try to be more available at work, and Carlo replied that, his mistakes aside, he was on top of everything, not to worry.

Robbie made his best effort to perform his regular uxorial role, and when friends invited them to dinner parties or to play doubles (their friends notably never mentioning the Tom Field incident), Robbie went along, although he didn't feel at all social. In a typical autumn, the two men themselves would have been hosting dinner parties because Carlo liked to cook stews and soups when the days were shorter on light, and having friends arrayed on either side of a line of votive candles at their dining table, Robbie knew, made Carlo content. However, this was no longer a typical autumn, and they didn't invite anyone over.

It was October. Robbie helped Carlo groom the plum saplings out front, the boy trees, sprigs akimbo, and yet already elegant even in their youth, with rich leaves as red and clear as claret when the sunlight hit them. He watched the full sequence of French films Carlo rented by mail. He entered into conversation about rescuing some brother kittens, although the two men never made it down to the shelter to check out the cats. He steadied the ladder while Carlo fixed the siding under an eave. He held slats of wood in place while they repaired the fence at the bottom of the property. And the two men were making love the old way, although without the usual leisure. The old passion would return, Robbie told himself, and certainly they'd endured tides of every kind in twenty years, ebb but then full again, in time, in time, give it time.

And yet Robbie recognized that his mood again began to shift. At first he'd been grateful for Carlo's forbearance, for putting up with his, Robbie's, malaise and of course Robbie would do the same for Carlo, not that Carlo would ever lapse into a similar lassitude, which perhaps was a problem in and of itself: Carlo's steely endurance wore Robbie down. Why hadn't Carlo insisted Robbie make the modifications to the producer's house? Was Robbie wrong to sense that Carlo did not even *want* Robbie at the office? Maybe not if Robbie was going to be all dour and deflated, but there was something irritating now about the way Carlo regarded him when

Carlo left in the mornings ahead of Robbie. In his lover's parting glance, Robbie read pity tinged with condescension. This much was becoming obvious: Carlo thought Robbie was weak. Carlo was repulsed.

Finally one night Robbie had to say something. He said, "I don't know how you're simply able—"

"Simply able to what?" Carlo interrupted.

They were reading in bed, or Robbie was pretending to read, and Carlo didn't look up from his book.

"Oh, come on," Robbie said. "You know."

Carlo rubbed his eyes.

"Never mind," Robbie said.

"What choice do we have?" Carlo asked. "We have to move on, and I have. And you only knew him one day, Robbie, one day, one night—let him go."

"But don't you *wonder*?" Robbie asked. "Okay, forget it."

"We'll never know what was going through his mind," Carlo said.

"Yes, I know that," Robbie said, "but maybe …"

Carlo blinked at him a moment, waited, and then returned to his reading. Robbie switched off the lamp on his night table and turned onto his side. Moments later, he felt Carlo's fingers lightly running through his hair, soothing Robbie to sleep. And he did fall asleep soon enough but he was thinking this was the essential difference between them, wasn't it? Carlo ever the rationalist, the mover-on, versus Robbie, a man still trying to read meaning in cold ashes.

In their life together they had never been competitive except time to time playing certain word games or on the tennis court if one of them, say, worked out a snag with his serve into the ad court at the same time the other went through a slump with his toss. And so now, vaguely, Robbie found himself playing Carlo at some unspoken baseline game and losing every rally. Carlo had always had the edge, an unfair advantage in dealing with grief because he'd suffered a grave loss when young, which was to say he'd grown up around death, grown up *on* death. Robbie in the suburbs had known no equivalent. And yet wasn't this precisely what all those years ago in college had drawn Robbie to Carlo?

He'd seen him around campus but hadn't met him, the sexy uòmo in the pea coat, collar turned up. The guy with the long black lashes, his eyes lavender or silver or sky blue or gray—it depended on the weather and how close to the window he sat during lecture. How had Robbie gathered the facts, who had he asked? The roommate who'd gone to high school with Carlo in New York? Cute dark Carlo Stein had a sad dark past, Robbie learned, and yet—this was what was key—he proved from the first meeting to be the least moody, most self-confident, wholly self-sufficient person Robbie would ever meet.

Cut to a dorm room (complete with a dormer window), late at night: Carlo pouring wine into juice glasses. Watch the way he twisted his wrist and never spilled a drop. Look at the miniature landscape painting over his desk, not some poster from the Coop but a real and actual painting, a gift from a family friend. Note that Carlo had traveled around Europe alone as a teenager. Note he could have gone to music school to study piano. He'd had boyfriends (plural) in high school. His parents divorced when he was young and then his Italian-born mother suffered from successive cancers (lung then brain) and Carlo had taken care of her and, until close to the end, obeyed her instruction not to summon his German-born father.

Invite him over to your room, quote-unquote, to hang out and he showed up with a new album, a British-import, and a bottle of sweet riesling, cold wine on a snowy Cambridge night. Meet him in New York and he knew people working at a gallery or in a bistro kitchen. Stay over at his father's place and no matter who was asleep at the other end of the apartment, Carlo would undress you on the persian rug in the living room and you would fool around, no worries, no worries, never any worries. The next afternoon sitting in an Upper West Side cinema, watching a foreign film you could barely follow, he took your hand, and then he held it for twenty years. Cute dark, worldly dark Carlo Stein. All these years later Robbie still couldn't catch up, he would never catch up, and look now at the way he was looked at: Carlo was tired of waiting for him.

WHAT ROBBIE COULDN'T SEE, however, was that while Carlo claimed he had moved on, in truth he had not. Alone more and more at the office, every task, be it paying an electric bill or preparing a spec for the building department, took twice as long as it should have. He was irked by Robbie's fascination with Tom even after Tom was dead and worried where this preoccupation was headed. He told himself to be patient, that Robbie would inevitably return to being his happy-go-lucky self, yet patience was not easily achieved. Carlo was unable to concentrate, and in Robbie's absence, he became the architect who paced, the architect who stared out windows. He walked back and forth across the office as if he were winding himself up to face a blueprint, but only ended up standing in the front window, idly monitoring the traffic.

Which was how one afternoon he found himself gazing at the shops across the boulevard, when a former neighbor boy named Gabriel loped by with another kid who was few years older and who worked in the liquor store. The older kid was long in the sideburns, and both his arms were densely tattooed with imagery including fat fish, the grim reaper, and something likely zodiac. He was friendly enough when you were picking up wine or vodka, but he always stank of cigarettes and sweat, and he couldn't look you in the eye when he gave you your change.

Gabriel, on the other hand, fifteen now, had always been a sweetie. He had lived a few doors down from the two men for the first few years they'd owned their house, but then Gabriel's parents had some trouble (serious drugs, it was said), split up, and Gabriel ended up staying with an elderly aunt in the four-plex adjacent to the gas station. Even though Gabriel currently lived near the office, the two men hadn't spent time with him in a long while.

Gabriel had been slithering along on his skateboard, but once in front of the liquor store, he slipped off it and kicked it up so that the board stood beside him like a younger brother in his charge. Gabriel and the liquor store kid exchanged words, pounded fists in fraternity, and the older boy went in to work while Gabriel dropped his skateboard and glided across the street toward Carlo.

Carlo caught his glance and waved hello, which brought the boy to halt. Carlo opened the door to the office and said, "Hey, stranger."

Gabriel nodded, the cool cat, a silent nod back, Hey.

"It's been, like, an ice age since we've seen you," Carlo said.

"An ice age," Gabriel said. "Brrr."

"What's your friend's name again, the guy who works across the street? Lonny, Donny, Ronny?"

"Something like that," Gabriel said.

The boy smelled a wee bit herbal. His eyes were red.

"I don't know about him," Carlo said. He hadn't meant to say this aloud, but it came out anyway, the subtext: Why are you wasting your time on him?

"Well, there's not all that much to know," Gabriel said.

He had been a cheerful boy, a slow but eager learner, loose-limbed, inquisitive. His parents, when they were around, were decent folk, but they worked in feature production and kept odd hours. They had always appreciated the willingness of the two men to baby-sit Gabriel when he was younger and monitor his whereabouts when he swerved (screeched) into adolescence. The boy had shown an early affinity for drawing, so the two men would loan him books, steer him toward Saturday art classes down at Ivanhoe, and Gabriel sometimes helped the men rake or weed and so forth. He was like a borrowed son.

"Why don't you come in for a drink?" Carlo asked.

"A drink—a drink of what?"

"I don't know what we've got," Carlo said, and headed for the kitchenette.

Since he'd stepped back inside, this drew Gabriel in as well, although first he set his skateboard by the door and wiped his feet on the mat.

Carlo looked in the miniature refrigerator. There was some sparkling water, some organic root beer, organic cream soda.

"Where's Robbie?" Gabriel asked.

"Away from his desk," Carlo said. "Apparently."

He offered Gabriel a root beer, and Gabriel eyed the bottle warily, kid stuff, but accepted it. He scratched his scruff. He had shorn his wavy black hair, and his shaved head looked like it had been dipped in magnetic filings. He wore earrings now, little dangling translucent figures that may have been miniature manga heroes. Gabriel, too, had been tattooed, albeit more tastefully: three red stars ran point-to-point up the inside of his left forearm. His jeans were especially torn, his plaid boxers half revealed, his concert-T torn, as well, and it was odd he was only wearing a T-shirt because although it was a mellow October day for Los Angeles, it wasn't that warm. He smelled like rust, like an old sponge. He'd gained weight, he'd filled out probably by working out, although he was all yoke, his legs still skinny, knee knobs poking through the ripped denim.

"So how's tricks?" Carlo asked.

Gabriel swung the question around: "I don't know—how's tricks with *you?*"

"Fine, fine," Carlo said.

But there must have been something thin about his response because Gabriel said, "Yeah, I heard."

"You heard? You heard what?"

"About that guy who offed himself at your place," Gabriel said.

Carlo felt himself turning red. He sat down at his desk and signaled Gabriel should pull up a chair. What, was the whole neighborhood gossiping about the two men? Of course they were. Silver Lake was a village in many ways. Half of him was curious to know what was being said, and the smarter half didn't want to inquire. But he thought he should at least explain to Gabriel what had happened and maybe that explanation would whisper its way back to whoever was chattering whatever. So Carlo wound through the night in the most cursory way.

Tom as a curious interesting guy they met. On a lark, Tom for dinner. Tom too drunk to drive home, and in the morning, the tragedy.

"What did he use, his belt?" Gabriel asked.

Carlo hesitated, but then he said, "A rope. A rope he had in his car."

"So the guy was, like, a freak?" Gabriel asked.

And Carlo shrugged, although he knew better. It was occurring to him, however, that it might be bad for business, a rumor loose in the hills, and so he nodded, yes, sure, a freak.

"That's fucked up," Gabriel said.

And again Carlo nodded, yes, fucked up. "Anyway," he said.

"Anyway," Gabriel echoed.

One time several years ago, the boy was playing with some kids out in the street and had been trying, helmetless, to perform an aerial trick with his skateboard when he landed on his head, scraping his ear against the pavement. As usual, his parents weren't home but the two men were—they heard the howling—and one man drove while the other man held a towel against the boy's face, the boy stretched out on the backseat. He was never in mortal danger but he'd been shocked, frightened by his own blood, how easily it ran. The two men stayed at the hospital even after Gabriel's grateful parents showed up.

Sometimes Gabriel would tag along on weekends when the two men checked on projects. He used to drop by their office and lie on his stomach on the sisal rug between the men's desks and do his homework. Carlo, good at math, became his best pal. Often Gabriel's parents gave him permission from the set to stay for dinner, and he was a sport and ate whatever Carlo happened to be preparing, no matter the pancetta or fava beans or radicchio involved. But all of this was years ago, and now the boy was growing up and in some ways reminded Carlo of himself at about the same age: alternately sullen and enthused, deliberately hard to reach, elementally alone. In a different way, motherless.

"We never do anything anymore," Carlo said. "We should do something, you, me, Robbie."

"Such as what?" Gabriel asked.

"I don't know. Are the Dodgers at home any weekend soon?"

Gabriel shook his head side to side and kicked his boot toe against the concrete floor.

"Right," Carlo said. "The season is over."

"I'm embarrassed for you," Gabriel said.

"That wouldn't be a first."

"No, sir, it would not."

They sat there quietly in the office. Carlo needed to turn on a lamp but didn't want to, as if any movement on his part might make the kid get up and leave. He had heard a rumor in turn about Gabriel—this was about a year ago and came from Carlo's friend the framer up the street, who knew Gabriel's aunt—a rumor that like his parents, the boy had gotten into some sort of trouble, drugs in the schoolyard, something like that. It wasn't difficult to see the boy's life one day veering off-track into some no-good rail yard. He looked like he had something on his mind, a question he couldn't quite formulate.

"Tell me about the girl whose heart you're breaking," Carlo said.

"Dude," Gabriel said, setting his bottle down on the desk. "Which one?"

"You rake, you," Carlo said.

"Oh yeah, that's me. A rake with his hoes."

Carlo should not have laughed, but he laughed. He tried to redirect the conversation: "How's school?"

"School is school," Gabriel answered, and Carlo didn't know why he'd bothered asking. But then Gabriel said, "I did read a book for English that was mildly cool," and he described the classic Paris novel—the wounded veteran, the gal about town, the bullfighter.

Carlo could almost remember what it was like to be a sophomore and reading the book for the first time.

"I had a paper due on it last week," Gabriel said. "I read the whole book, I totally dug it, I really did, but why do I have to write a paper about it? Why can't the book just *be*?"

"The good news is eventually in life you can read books and not write essays about them," Carlo said.

"No kidding."

"'Isn't it pretty to think so?'" Carlo said.

The allusion made Gabriel smile, and then they lapsed into a silent spell again, the two of them swigging their root beers, one then the other as if to a metronome. Finally the sun had gone down and the office was dark, and Carlo had to switch on his desk lamp. As if exposed, Gabriel stood up and carried his empty bottle to the kitchenette.

Carlo saw the boy to the door. "Seriously," he said, "let's hang out."

Gabriel rubbed his chin again.

Carlo needed to think fast. "Maybe you can help me with a project at the house," he said, although he was improvising and didn't have a project in mind.

"Why, what's wrong with Robbie?"

"Nothing is wrong with Robbie," Carlo said. "I only thought …"

Why was the kid making this so difficult? Carlo sensed something troubling the kid, and he merely wanted to avail himself should the boy need a someone older and wiser and foolish and full of himself to talk to.

"I've been thinking of building a fountain at the bottom of our property, a little hideaway, maybe a koi pond, or maybe no fish—I don't know," Carlo said, and there was some truth to this. "But it's not something Robbie would be all that into helping out on," he added, again true.

Gabriel's expression: Oh, that sounds real fun.

"I'll pay you," Carlo said.

"I'm not sure you can afford me. But you know where to find me," Gabriel said as he stepped out onto the sidewalk and dropped his board. And then with one push, another push, he was skating west toward Sunset.

Carlo returned to his desk, suddenly beat. He rested his arm on his desk, his head on his arm. He remembered a time when he and Robbie were architecture students and on a trip to Italy, specifically driving through the Veneto one day on a tour of Palladian villas with the most famous house still on the itinerary and with the goal to reach Venice by dusk. Carlo had been navigating, and after making a wrong turn, the two men were lost, although they knew they couldn't be too far off track because they were in the right town. It was a mid-autumn Saturday, late in the afternoon—they were zooming along residential roads, houses far apart, unable to see anyone to ask directions. Then they passed a boy riding a bike. He was eight or nine and wearing a red sweater, black football shorts, and red socks. Carlo's Italian was strictly about the accent, his vocabulary as paltry as his ability to express emotion in his mother's language. But he said to the boy, "*Mi scusi. Dove la Rotunda?*"

The boy pointed to his right and offered directions, and Carlo could have pieced together what the boy was telling him, but there was something so lilting and joyful about the Italian, the song of the boy's speech, that Carlo didn't pay attention and was more confused than ever. He looked at Robbie and Robbie shrugged, and Carlo in turn shook his head and shrugged at the boy.

The boy rolled his eyes, silly Americano. He waved at the men, come along then, follow me, made a U-turn on his bike and soon veered off onto another road, the men trailing him in their rental car, the boy pedaling as fast as he could. And there were no other cars or trucks or other people who passed by, it was only the two men behind the boy on his bike, pursuing a long hill, a shallow grade, until suddenly in the distance, the famous villa appeared isolated at the crest. The great white house, the domed roof, the tidy columns and pediments, a paragon of symmetry and order against a backdrop of doom, the gathering nimbus clouds, the anxious trees.

"*Mille grazie,*" Carlo said to the boy, "*mille grazie,*" and the boy grinned again his confident grin and swerved around back the way they'd come and was gone.

The rest of the week they talked about the boy and speculated about what kind of life he led. Football, pasta, ancient history. Robbie kept ribbing Carlo about how he could have had a mother from Bologna yet speak only phrasebook Italian. "That boy, that look he gave you," Robbie would say and giggle. And then after they were back in Los Angeles, they would tease each other: "*Dove* put my sunglasses?" "*Mi scusi.* Could you scratch *mi* shoulder, *mille grazie?*"

The boy in the red sweater who led them on his bike to the point in the road when the great house became visible, he had to be a man. Carlo wondered what had become of him. What kind of life was his life now? Did he have any notion at all how long he had survived in the banter of two American men an ocean and a continent away?

Across the years there had been so many strangers who each in his or her way had become a hero for a day, and lasted a while, and who eventually slipped from conversation, who was forgotten. It was inevitable, and yet each perishing memory weighed against Carlo as it sank. Someone went missing—this was always the sense he had—yet he couldn't say who. He experienced at once a burden to track so many memories and a sense of defeat, a loss, all the people they'd met year by year slipping away. And Carlo also had to wonder if he himself had played the part of the stranger in the lives of other people. If so, how many times a day was he forgotten? Or recalled?

The first time he met Tom, at the police station, as Carlo was leaving, he'd said, "Thank you for talking to me," and Tom had replied, "No, thank *you* for talking to *me*." The second time Carlo saw Tom, Tom didn't seemed at all surprised, as if he'd been expecting Carlo one day to turn up ...

It wouldn't necessarily right anything, and it would hardly constitute any major recompense for the way he'd betrayed Tom, or Robbie—Carlo wasn't deluding himself—but when he sat up and noticed it was evening, he resolved to seek out Gabriel and engage him and make a point of spending time with the boy, if for no other reason than to watch out for him.

ALTHOUGH HE WAS NOT AT THE OFFICE when Gabriel was there, Robbie had gone in earlier and in general was making an effort to show up every day, refusing to give in to his malaise. However, there was no avoiding that he didn't want to be at his desk, and he jumped at any opportunity to run an errand, the longer and more involved, the better.

He drove, for example, over to the hardware store on Tracy to pick up replacement parts to fix the running office toilet but couldn't find what he needed and ended up at a box store in Hollywood, but from the roof level of the parking lot, he gazed out at the ileal ripple of hills in the distance and then before long found himself taking the very long way home, following the arid crevasses, past carports, past stilted cottages, reminded of a time when he and Carlo first came to Los Angeles and would take Sunday drives, peeling off narrow known roads onto narrower unknown ones, pursuing them less to master the city than to lose themselves in this exotic new habitat of mudslides and fire and earthquakes, acclimating fast to the local arrogance: Angelinos built wherever they damn well pleased, no matter the threat of natural calamity, no matter the paucity of water, no matter the unwelcoming carve of the land. Now, even though he knew well enough how the roads ran, he still got turned around and drove in loops, what with no navigator with an open map on his lap in the passenger seat. Remembering the Sunday drives, he was warmed by nostalgia, and yet he didn't quite feel like the same man who made those tours so many years ago for the simple reason that now he was alone.

He went to the grocery store and procured the ingredients Carlo had scribbled out, and at the grocery store, in the checkout line one afternoon, Robbie observed an old woman he'd never seen before (or had he?). She was wearing a formal wool coat and matching navy-blue pillbox hat and walking with cane. Clutching her arm was a middle-aged woman who looked exactly like the older woman—the younger woman could only be her daughter. The daughter's hair was graying and she was wearing a black coat and hat of the same style as her mother—also they had the same sprayed coif and the same unevenly penciled eyebrows, but the daughter walked with a limp and her eyes appeared to focus on nothing, and Robbie guessed she was mentally retarded. The daughter had the mother, the mother the daughter, they weren't alone (quite literally, they looked as though they were propping each other up), yet each in her way certainly looked lonesome. And Robbie wondered what would happen when the frail mother died or could no longer care for her daughter, not provisionally because provisions were likely in place, but emotionally. If the daughter already looked easily frightened, then what would her years be like without the only person on whom she could settle her glance with any modicum of peace?

He knew better than to decide what was and was not going on in other people's lives, but likewise the stooping man shuffling around pots of desiccated plants in the nursery across Hyperion, this man with his trousers belted high, who was going to provide for him when he could no longer eke out a wilting profit? Robbie didn't want to go straight home and headed out on a short drive through Griffith Park but ended up in the Valley at rush hour. It took the better part of an hour to make it back to the house, by which point some of the things he'd purchased, cheese, butter, frozen yogurt, were getting soft or melting.

In the morning he would tell Carlo what errands he would take care of, sometimes in lieu of heading in to the office at all, and Robbie did fulfill each mission, but after selecting new sheets and towels at a white sale in West Hollywood, he continued driving west toward the ocean, thinking he'd scoot up the Coast Road a-ways, except the traffic became overbearing once again and he ended up buying a cultural history of cats in a Brentwood bookstore and sat in a coffee shop reading the book, or pretending to read it while instead surveilling all the other readers and computer-tappers who sat solo at tables-for-two. He couldn't help himself: he kept ascribing to them the same smallness-in-the-world he was experiencing. Everywhere he looked now, no matter where he was, he saw lonely people, as if for years he'd been wearing sunglasses that filtered out anyone in unwanted solitude, anyone filling his or her day with tasks that should have taken a quarter the time to complete, all the loiterers and lingerers and blank-starers of the city, whose legion apparently he had joined. For didn't the woman leaning back in her chair, both hands gripping an unsipped cup of cappuccino, not really reading the *Weekly* open on the table, didn't she notice Robbie and think, He's just like me? We could disappear and it would take a month for anyone to notice. We can go an entire day and the only thing we say is, Medium non-fat latte, please—oh sure, whipped cream. We confide too much in our dogs. We sleep in the middle of the bed.

Robbie stroked his chin with his thumb and forefinger and was reminded he hadn't shaved in days. He looked at the book he was holding, of which he'd apparently digested a good third, except he had no idea what he'd read. He glanced back at the woman—she looked away.

What kind of lonely.

In truth Robbie lived a life nothing like the one he was playing at, nothing like it whatsoever. Every night a bright handsome
man came home to him and asked, "What are you in the mood
for—pasta, chicken, fish?" Robbie was *not* alone in the world,
not remotely. He was neither divorced nor widowed nor abandoned, nor for that matter unloved, nor unloving, however he
would have to admit that pretending he was single brought him
perverse melancholic pleasure. And he had to wonder if he would
ever return to his old self or if this was who he was now, audi-
tioning for a role he feared he might someday play.

THEN ONE AFTERNOON one month after Tom died, a turn:
Robbie returned home from his meandering at around five, and
because Tuesday was trash day, there were emptied square bins
up and down the street, the containers at jocular angles, the lids
thrown back—nothing unusual. However, as Robbie pulled into
his driveway, he noticed first that his own trash bins had been
marked up with an indecipherable white graffiti, while none of
his neighbors' containers appeared similarly marked, and then,
in a much more violent act of vandalism, it appeared the taggers
(or someone else?) had dragged the tied-up trash onto his front
lawn, ripped open the bags, and strewn the rotten content everywhere. Fruit rinds and banana peels and squashed cartons and
wadded tissue and discarded mail, a week's worth of putrid gunk,
lay scattered all around the plum trees and pepper tree and across
the grass and lavender beds. It was disgusting.

The wind was blowing the looser detritus toward the house,
and Robbie did his best to step on envelopes and torn plastic be-

fore it all flew up into the trees and eaves. He bolted after a page of newsprint flapping off toward the neighbors. He plucked a water bottle that had somehow flown up into the fork of the tallest plum tree. He shoveled up what he could and dumped it back in the tagged bins still out by the curb, but the task became sisyphean. He thought he was making headway, but then he spotted a damp half-full coffee filter, a cereal box. Was someone trying to draw attention to how much trash the two men generated? Because they certainly had made a lot of it.

After Robbie had been cleaning up a good half hour, Carlo arrived home. He had Gabriel Sanchez with him. Robbie couldn't recall the last time he'd spoken to the boy.

"Well, hey," Robbie said, but declined to shake Gabriel's hand since Robbie was holding a tomato can in one hand, a banana peel in the other.

"Hey," Gabriel said. And then, stating the obvious: "Whoa. Your trash got messed with."

"What the hell," Carlo said.

"It was worse when I came home," Robbie said.

"What the hell," Carlo said again.

Robbie began rolling a bin back up the side of the driveway toward the garage. Gabriel waited a beat but then helped haul in the remaining bins.

Carlo looked confused, a scowl forming. "This is so foul," he said.

"What brings you by?" Robbie asked Gabriel.

"Your boyfriend," Gabriel answered.

"Is that a gang tag?" Carlo asked—he directed the question at Gabriel, as if the boy would know.

"Why are you asking me?" Gabriel asked.

"Do we even have gangs up here?" Robbie said.

Carlo walked out to the street and back to the stoop. "It's not like anyone else had their garbage messed with, as far as I can tell."

Robbie knew what Carlo was considering and said, "We're hardly the only couple on the block."

"I know that," Carlo said. "You think it was random?"

"Of course," Robbie said, and truly he did.

In a blink it was night—the clean-up would need to be finished in the morning—and so the two men and the boy went inside. As was his habit of late, Carlo poured himself a tall glass of wine.

"It's just—," Carlo started to say.

"Just what?" Robbie asked.

"Because of what happened," Carlo said.

Robbie rolled his eyes, Oh please. As if they were what, marked?

"All I'm saying—," Carlo started to say again, but cut himself off. Silence. Then, "Whatever."

"We'll have to finish cleaning up in the morning," Robbie said. "I'll take care of it."

Carlo had gone mute. He sipped his wine.

"It's nice to see you," Robbie said to Gabriel. "Did you miss the old neighborhood?"

"Kind of," Gabriel said.

"I thought I'd show him the spot where we'd talked about putting a fountain," Carlo said.

"Oh," Robbie said—and now it was his turn to be confused because they'd decided against the fountain at the bottom of the slope, hadn't they? And why would a teenager be interested in a fountain?

"Follow me," Carlo said to Gabriel and led him out to the patio and then down the side of the hill where there was a loose stone path.

Robbie poured himself a glass of wine and stepped outside as well, but he stayed up by the house. It had been Carlo's notion to create a little hideout down where the plot flattened out and there was some shade by a rotting fence. Robbie thought that while they could create a pleasant enough oasis that would be nice to look at, they'd never use it, and Carlo countered that the sound of trickling water would be soothing and audible everywhere on the property, and maybe they went back and forth for a couple of months, but this was ages ago. Robbie heard Carlo explaining to the boy what brush would need to be cleared out, where a pipe might be tied in to the house plumbing and buried and run down the hill. Also he mentioned rigging a hammock. He sounded like he was selling the kid something, and Gabriel, for his part, kept issuing an encouraging, "Cool."

Back up on the patio, Carlo said to Robbie, "If we get the fountain in now, we'll be able to enjoy it next spring. What do you think?"

It was as if they had never discussed the project before, but honestly Robbie didn't much care. "I don't know," he said. "Sure."

"Gabriel is going to help me," Carlo explained.

"Gabriel is getting paid," Gabriel said.

The boy had his hands in his back pockets, his elbows out wide. He'd changed, Robbie thought. In the dim light, the kid was gaunt, his eyes sunken—he was a teenager, probably up all night. Nevertheless, he didn't look great.

"What's new in your world?" Robbie asked. "How is your aunt?"

Gabriel didn't answer, or what he said was a mumble. And then, out of nowhere but as if in response, he asked, "Do you guys believe in ghosts?"

"Why?" Robbie asked.

"You remember my dog," the boy said.

"Oh sure. He was a fun dog," Robbie said.

"I keep seeing him wandering around."

"Oh really?"

"He's been dead for years though, but I keep seeing him and he's panting, tongue hanging out, wants to be wrangled, nuzzled, wrestled."

"Can't find his way home," Robbie said.

"I *know*," Gabriel said.

"Dreams are strange that way," Carlo said.

"I don't see him in my dreams. I see him during the day," Gabriel said.

"In your daydreams," Carlo said.

"No, for real. I see him for real, but he runs away before I can catch up with him."

Neither man spoke.

"Maybe you should drop by the shelter and rescue another dog," Carlo suggested.

His comment seemed misguided. Robbie glared at him.

Gabriel motioned to run his fingers through his hair and stopped, his hand in midair, maybe remembering his once long hair was now short. There was something setting the boy on edge, and he pointed at the Liquidambar and said, "So this is where that guy offed himself, right?"

That burn, that grade-school burn that comes when you realize people have been talking about you made Robbie uncomfortably warm, and the word offed—there was something snide about it, as if a life could be switched on or off like light.

"It was all very strange, and very sad," Carlo said. "We'll always be disturbed by what happened."

This statement floored Robbie more than Gabriel's remark. He wanted to ask, If you're so disturbed, then why don't we ever talk about it?

"He used a rope, you said?" the boy asked, and he made a comic gesture, bringing his thumb and forefinger up around his neck, sticking out his tongue to the side.

Carlo said, "He'd had it in his car. He probably used it to strap his belongings to the roof when he moved here cross-country."

Again Robbie was flabbergasted: They thought that, did they?

"And when he hanged himself," Gabriel asked, "did he, like, piss in his pants?"

"That's enough," Robbie said.

No one spoke.

"What?" Gabriel asked.

Robbie didn't respond.

"What?" Gabriel asked again, looking first at Robbie, then Carlo, then Robbie again.

"It was tragic," Robbie said.

"Okay," Gabriel said.

"Unspeakably tragic when you think about it—"

"Okay, whatever."

"That guy—*Tom* was his name. And Tom didn't mean to kill himself," Robbie said.

Carlo squinted at Robbie.

"It was an accident," Robbie said.

"An accident," Gabriel echoed, dismissive.

"Wait," Carlo said, "what are you saying?"

"With the rope, with the time it took to form a noose," Robbie said, "to rig it, the rest—" He drew a deep breath. "I'm saying he was taking his time, hoping we'd find him and stop him."

Gabriel was standing with the heel of one boot atop the toe of the other, his fists in his pockets.

"I don't think we can be sure what really happened," Carlo said.

"It had to have been an accident," Robbie insisted, and of course he'd thought this all these weeks but never come out and said it.

"We didn't know him really," Carlo said.

"Tom was always very dramatic," Robbie said to Gabriel. "His grandmother told me."

"His grandmother," Carlo said. "Tom's grandmother."

"We spoke," Robbie said.

"You spoke," Carlo said.

Perhaps sensing a spat in the making, Gabriel led the way back inside the house. "There's a good chance I have homework," he said.

Carlo offered to give him a lift, but Gabriel said he wanted to walk.

"We'll get started on clearing the brush down there soon," Carlo said.

"Roger that," Gabriel said, and half saluted the men, pivoted like an enlisted man, and slipped out the front door.

"Didn't we decide against the fountain?" Robbie asked. "Not that I care a whole lot but— What?"

"You called her or she called you?" Carlo asked.

"He wanted us to find him and stop him," Robbie said. "You're right, we can't know for sure, but maybe it was autoerotic asphyxiation—"

"You know we didn't see signs of that."

"You heard him that night. All his plans—"

"Robbie," Carlo said softly, "what Tom did …"

"It had to have been an accident, Carlo. It's the only explanation."

Carlo was staring at the floor.

"I don't know why you have to pursue this," he said. "But if that's what you need to believe—"

"I don't *need* to believe it, I *do* believe it."

"Robbie," Carlo said again, not so soft now, "what Tom did was an assault against us, but mostly against you—look at you. You called his grandmother, you bothered that poor woman? What have you done with my boyfriend?"

Then Carlo took a deep breath and said, "I'm sorry."

Robbie wasn't necessarily sure about what he'd declared, but on some level he knew he had to be right. If only he had proof that Tom never really meant to kill himself, then he would have a strong enough stroke to break the tide that held him from the shore. Or it wasn't so much proof—proof per se would always elude him—but he wanted what Carlo for some Carlo-reason, born perhaps in his faithlessness, his grimmer side, would not give him: if not verification, then the validation of an idea, an alignment in thinking, a telling of the same story the same way. This seemed important to settle, like the only urgent matter in Robbie's life right now, the only way he could move on—couldn't Carlo see that? No, he could not. Carlo would not help him.

"I'm going to go change," Carlo said, gentle now, his hand on Robbie's forearm, sliding down his wrist, taking his hand, swinging his hand. "Then what, do you want fish? Or chicken? Or pasta maybe? Pasta, yes?"

Robbie may have nodded but he was no longer listening because he knew what he needed to do, what he should have done weeks ago.

THE NEXT MORNING, he didn't deal with the rest of the trash the way he said he would and stayed in bed while Carlo completed the chore. When Carlo came back in the house, Robbie pulled the covers up to his chin.

"I finished cleaning up that mess," Carlo said. "I'm worried though. I'm worried this might only be the beginning of something."

"It's one isolated incident," Robbie said.

"Well, you say that now, but—"

"You worry too much," Robbie said and changed the subject: "Do I have a fever?"

Carlo placed his palm over Robbie's forehead. "Not really," he said.

"I think I may stay in bed a while longer. Do you mind?" Robbie asked.

"No, of course not. I'll check in later," Carlo said.

"I feel a little weird," Robbie said. "I want to see if I can sleep this off."

"We'll have to spray-paint over the graffiti. I do hope you're right—no more pranks."

Carlo took a shower, dressed, and left for the office. Only then did Robbie get out of bed and retrieve Tom's address book from where he'd stashed it in the dresser.

Tom had crossed out names two ways, either with a gouged scribble of barbed wire—these entries were entirely illegible—or with single arrows of ink shot through the names and numbers and/or email addresses, which were less illegible. Sometimes Tom had used a pencil to eliminate someone from his life, which to an extent made the expulsion reversible, although often he'd also used graphite to record the person in the first place, so erasing the strike-through risked eliminating what Robbie wanted to salvage.

He dialed several wrong or disconnected numbers before a listing from the B-page answered. The man was driving and upon hearing Tom Field's name said he needed to pull over. Then Robbie said he didn't want to alarm him, but—and the man interrupted, "Oh shit"—and Robbie continued, reporting Tom's suicide and—another interruption: the man had heard Tom was dead and asked if Robbie was truly a friend or in actuality a clinic worker notifying Tom's sexual partners that Tom had been infected. "No," Robbie said, "oh, no. A friend, only a friend," he said. The man on the phone sounded relieved. He'd only known Tom a few weeks roughly a year ago, he explained, and all they had done was fool around a bit, all the while drinking more than the man was accustomed to, bourbon, wine, gin, whatever was handy. That was that, but Tom had been, how to put it, literate, and the man had hoped the two of them might become friends once the sexual relationship waned (which it did when the man wouldn't get drunk with Tom in order to have sex). Friendship didn't blossom and the man regretted that because Tom, he said, had been so vital and quirky and curious—"Exactly, *exactly*," Robbie said, now the one interrupting. And then Robbie asked the looming question: "I know it's speculation, but do you think Tom Field meant to kill himself or do you think it could have been an accident?"

A long silence followed, and Robbie thought the man had either lost his cell connection or didn't want to engage on the subject, but then the man said he hadn't known Tom well, and despite the fight they had the last time they got together, he remained inexplicably fond of Tom Field and thought about him surprisingly often. He'd run into someone else with whom Tom had a fling, who had heard about Tom's death and who had relayed the rumor. And no, the man did not think it was (for lack of a better way of describing it) a straight suicide. There must have been an extenuating circumstance, some other intention now masked by the tragic outcome. He'd heard the news and it hadn't computed. But of course, as noted, this was speculation, nothing more.

The second man, surname beginning with C, whom Robbie reached, he found at an ad agency in New York. This second man, too, had heard how Tom died but didn't believe it, and Robbie offered confirmation. The man said they'd dated a month and he thought it impolite to swap bedroom stories with any of Tom's exes. Robbie made it clear he hadn't dated Tom. The man said, "You must be the only one." He took for granted that the suicide was alcohol-related or drug-related. He didn't know the details but assumed all along it was an overdose, which was to say likely an accident. One great date they'd gone on was to see an old master retrospective and Tom had revealed an obvious passion for the paintings. Tom had black moods and no doubt thought about killing himself, but the man couldn't see Tom actually going through with so ultimate an act. "'*Vissi d'arte*, baby,' Tom liked to say."

To live for one's art, Robbie thought. Once he himself might have said he did that, after a fashion, but not in recent years.

On the F-page of Tom's address book, Robbie thought he'd find other relatives, but only Tom's grandmother was entered, hers being one of the few unstruck-through names. Another name not crossed out belonged to a novelist known for over-the-top graphic depictions of urban tawdriness—the writer to whom Tom had alluded but not mentioned by name, his one friend left in Los Angeles. He did not answer his phone.

Robbie continued calling the numbers he could decipher, and at first it seemed odd that Tom's deleted friends had somehow received word of his demise, but then it didn't seem so strange: Once Tom entered someone's life, he never really left it. Tom's lost friends had a way of tracking him from a distance, wondering about him privately and then chattering about him when, say, at a party the discovery was made that some amount of time spent with Tom in the past was a shared adventure. Tom was never forgotten, he became the subject of lurid gossip, and apparently he had left behind an extensive network wired by rumor, fascination, and bitterness.

While speaking to whomever he reached, Robbie paced the length of the house. He knew Carlo would say he was intruding, breaking-and-entering Tom's life, but Robbie didn't care. He was on to something, gathering compelling evidence, building a case, because each conversation ran the same way: An ex-fellow receptionist from the auction house in New York (from the K-page) or another ex-fellow receptionist from the lobbyist's office in D.C. (the N-page), both had experienced (and enjoyed) limited intimacy with Tom, had heard via some faint channel that Tom was dead and more or less how he'd died, and affirmed Robbie's hypothesis (while at the same time asserting the improvability of the conjecture), that Tom in all likelihood was messing around in some bizarre way but never intended to end his own life. True proof remained slippery, but enough people reaching the same conclusion certainly was starting to look a lot like proof.

"Did he ever cook you a meal?"

The question was posed by a woman whose maiden name began with P and who knew Tom in New York. She hadn't heard about Tom's suicide and needed a moment to collect herself. They had met in a weekend life drawing class when they set up their easels next to each other. Both of them had formal training and were trying to keep their eyes sharp. The woman said when Tom's hand moved across the page—she knew this would sound cliché, but whatever—it was as if he were ever so lightly caressing the blushing skin of his subject. They saw each other in class every

Saturday and always sat together and started getting coffee after class, and then one Saturday Tom asked if he could draw the woman and she said yes, if she could draw Tom. He followed her to her apartment. She was unclear whether like the models they drew in class, they, too, would disrobe. Tom stripped everything, and so she did, as well. They drew each other drawing each other. She could remember the sound of the radiator clanking and the sound of Tom's charcoal pencil against the paper, the way he brushed the side of his hand against the page or used his thumb, and she could remember the way they were each aroused a little bit, although that was the extent of any erotic exchange. And the hour during which they drew each other one winter Saturday years and years ago, the woman said, was one of the most beautiful she could recall. They trusted each other and respected each other and knew each other well, even if only for a short time, and in many ways she was always searching for the perfect improvised afternoon like that one, hoping for a surprise in the dwindling white light of winter. Would it be too much to say she began believing in something that afternoon?

Robbie was no longer pacing and instead sitting on the floor by the piano, one arm wrapped around his knees, the other holding the phone as close as possible to his ear.

The woman said, "After we were done drawing, Tom looked around my pantry and asked if he could cook me dinner. I told him I wished he liked girls. And then he whipped up something amazing, boeuf bourguignon or coq au vin—"

"It was coq au vin," Robbie said.

"You think?"

"That's what he cooked for us," Robbie said.

"So he did cook for you," the woman said.

"The night he died," Robbie said. "He died here. At my house."

The woman said, "Oh dear." She said, "You poor dear."

Robbie brought Tom's address book to his cheek, like a flower, the soft pages.

"It wasn't your fault," the woman said. "That's why you're calling."

"More that I want to understand," Robbie said.

"You won't."

"I know that."

"You can't."

"More that I want to figure out if it was an accident—"

"If you're asking the question."

"If I'm asking the question … what?"

"He cooked for you," the woman repeated. "A lot of wine in the skillet. Extra mushrooms. I knew him a while ago, and he may have changed."

"It doesn't sound like it," Robbie said.

"There was that afternoon and then a couple of other outings," she said, "and that was it. I lost touch with him. My very first thought when you told me the news was that it had to be a mistake, an accident. He was full of life. But we can't know."

"Your name was one of a handful Tom didn't cross out in his address book."

The woman issued a round ha. "I held on to his contact information, too," she said, "even though I knew it had to be out-of-date." Then another long breath, and the woman asked, "So how come he and I never tried to find each other?"

THAT MORNING, when Carlo was finishing cleaning up the front yard, he had tried to decipher the graffiti on the trash bins, and while he understood he was likely looking at a tag, a name, he was also convinced if he stared long enough, he'd decode a message, a threat of some kind. He was convinced the vandalism was the work of someone (or some group) who wanted to kick the two men while they were down, make fun of them as if they'd staged an outré orgy and needed to be mocked. Robbie had refused to read the same augury. Innards had been splattered against the pavement, and Carlo would have thought that in Robbie's pensive state, some rare pessimism might be revealed— not so. Robbie remained the naïf, the undaunted optimist, although at the same time, he was still fixating on Tom's death, still puzzling it out, Tom's state of mind, Tom's motive (and how had Robbie gotten Tom's grandmother's phone number?)—what would it take to satisfy him? Carlo had to wonder, given the way his boyfriend appeared to be groping for answers, if Robbie would eventually try somehow to track Tom's death back to Carlo, and briefly then, a moment of paranoia. Briefly, the thought again that he should at least tell Robbie what Robbie would otherwise never know about what happened after he fell asleep that night—but no, too much time had passed. Even a partial confession now would only make matters worse.

Carlo had picked off strands of dryer lint from the lower branches of the pepper tree and the bread crust and chicken bones scattered across the stoop, the lawn clippings amassing against the side of the house, and when he had gone inside, he tried to make more out of the vandalism than possibly he should have in an effort to distract Robbie, to take his mind off Tom. Robbie hadn't taken the bait. He claimed he had a fever, although he looked fine.

A short while later, when Carlo left for the office, he stood at the end of the driveway and stared at (stared down) the drowsy school kids drifting in clusters down the block. All the boys in their low-draped denim, their practiced illusion of disillusion, any of them could be the vandals. They stared back at Carlo as well, meeting his weary gaze with their own wariness. He was about to turn and be on his way when he noticed Gabriel's friend who worked at the liquor store, Lonny, stumbling along amid the group, which was suspect because Lonny should have been out of school by now. He was wearing a baseball jacket that was several sizes too small, entertaining younger kids with some story that, from what Carlo could hear, was laced with expletives and slurs, and Carlo caught him glancing at the house, snickering, surely noting Carlo standing there, hands on hips, and yet Lonny avoided eye contact. The punk knew something, Carlo was certain of it.

From there the day did not improve. He had been calling former clients asking if they had dream projects ready to realize or perhaps friends or acquaintances with work in the pipeline, and he'd hoped maybe he'd find a positive message or email waiting for him. The only message, however, was from the television producer, who had phoned with news of what he referred to as a breakthrough reconceptualization.

Oddly, Carlo didn't mind the prospect of making alterations or rethinking major aspects of the project because an unexpected pleasure in the weeks following Tom's death came when, with Robbie hardly present, Carlo had to exercise his out-of-shape training after so long deferring to his more talented partner. The fact was he enjoyed revision more than any other aspect of the design process, and he was much more skilled at refining an idea than he was at first-draftsmanship. His true calling might have been as a first reader, an editor, but he'd always been shy about acknowledging this even to Robbie, maybe because the redactor enjoyed far less esteem culturally than the visionary, or more likely because Carlo was uneasy with these and the other roles they'd lapsed into over time. It wasn't always that way, he didn't think, not in the early years when there was more parity both in the office and at home. Anyway, despite his mistakes, he'd had fun redrawing the producer's house and would do so again.

The problem was that now when Carlo spoke with him, the producer wanted a joist-to-roof-beam reconsideration, and when the subject of money came up, given the proposed prolonged design phase, the producer said he also wanted to change the fee arrangement so that Stein Voight conceivably might not, as he put it, see another cent from him until principle construction was well underway. As politely as he could, Carlo suggested that they'd signed a contract, and then with considerably less politesse, the producer bounced back that in his business, contracts were only as good as the lawyers who could file suit over breaches of contracts. Carlo didn't follow, or didn't want to follow. The producer was Stein Voight's only current client.

Over the course of the morning, the producer continued to unspool his new thoughts via email, which included elimination of the rental units in favor of a guest house as well as a lap pool on the back patio of the indoor-outdoor genre. The producer said he wasn't running for elected office and didn't need to prove anything with the solar panels on the roof. He wanted another terrace with an outdoor fireplace. He never understood the mitered brise-soleil around the master bedroom level, and didn't he mention before that he was going to need a weight room? Also, his relatively new boyfriend was taking cooking classes and the kitchen was his theater and therefore could they double the center island space and add a half-dozen stool spots for his relatively new boyfriend's future audience? Finally the house was looking a little too severe (the boyfriend's word). Instead of steel framing, wood might be more pleasant. Instead of metal panels, cream stucco. And what about shutters? Not to use, merely an ornamental touch.

The man wanted a villa. He wanted a completely different kind of house and probably needed a different lot to build it on. Not only would the producer's palazzo necessitate starting from scratch, but also the forfeiture of a career-long aesthetic. To remain solvent, Stein Voight had to build the producer's house, and the more garish a pile of stucco it was, ironically, the more Stein Voight stood to reap in fees. This was not who Carlo wanted to be in the world, a toadeater subservient to his clients' ill will and bad taste, but he reminded himself the job was as much for Robbie's welfare as his own, for the two men together, so he replied that he'd work with the producer's ideas and get back to him.

And Carlo did take a deep breath, and he had every intention of launching himself head-first into the redesign, for what choice did he have, when Detective Michaels appeared at the front door.

"If you don't mind, I have a few additional questions for you," she said when she sat down in the chair next to Carlo's desk. "Mr. Voight isn't here today?"

"He's home sick," Carlo said.

"Nothing serious, I hope."

"I don't think so."

"It's interesting the way different couples operate," Detective Michaels said.

Carlo wasn't sure what to do with the comment. "You mean I should be home taking care of him?" he asked.

"I'm thinking about the events of last April that you told me about," Detective Michaels said, "but didn't tell your partner about."

The detective was staring at him without blinking, reading him.

"This interests me," she went on, "because, you see, my husband and I don't keep anything from each other. Of course, I'm married to a fellow cop—different precinct—and he knows me too well for me to keep secrets."

"That's sweet," Carlo said. "To be in the same line of work—I know what that's like, obviously."

"And your line of work? Business is good for you lately?"

"Some clients are easier than others."

Again the detective was reading him.

"It's been slow," Carlo said. "Why, is this related to your investigation?"

"Slow for how long would you say?"

"A while. A year. Longer."

"Mr. Voight hasn't been working regular hours, has he, since Mr. Field passed away?"

Had the police been watching the office? Had they been on
a stakeout this whole time?

"That's correct," Carlo said.

"He's upset."

"He is upset, yes."

"He's having trouble moving on from the incident at your
house perhaps because ..."

Carlo blinked. "Perhaps because what?"

Detective Michaels tapped her pen against the pad.

"Something is troubling him," she said. "Something he
might have recently learned."

"He doesn't know anything more than he did the night Tom
died," Carlo said. "I haven't told him anything new."

"Still nursing your secret."

"The timing doesn't seem right to get into what happened,"
Carlo said.

"Will the timing ever be right to tell him about what happened last April? Or about everything else?" the detective asked,
a question that took a moment to float to the floor.

What did she know? Carlo didn't think he should say anything
more.

"You didn't tell Mr. Voight about the carjacking," Detective
Michaels said, "so I don't suppose you told him that you'd bought
a gun."

Carlo tried not to blink. He blinked.

"You applied for a permit," the detective said. "We can track
these things."

In the days and weeks that followed the attempted carjacking, Carlo couldn't shake what had happened. He was cloaked in

a kind of numbness, isolated from everything, everyone, including Robbie—a numbness, a haze, an unfamiliar self-directed anger because during the crime he'd acted feebly (not that he knew what he should have done). Blame Tom—Tom at the police station was the one who had brought up guns and what might have gone down instead had Carlo been armed (and it had occurred to Carlo that, unbeknownst to Robbie, Tom's story about the woman murdered in front of her child, Tom's emphatic suggestion that the tragedy could have been averted if the woman had kept a weapon in her house, was a private jab at Carlo). About a month after the carjacking—this would have been in May—Carlo located a gun store near the airport and was surprised the store was as pristine and tidy as any sporting goods outlet. A clerk showed him firearms recommended for novices seeking self-defense, and the truth of the matter was that Carlo wanted a gun made for ladies but ended up buying a butch one that still appealed to his sense of style, a square silver ur-gun gun that would make the point should anyone again rush his car at the intersection of Fletcher and Riverside or anywhere else.

"I suppose I should have mentioned the gun purchase when I told you the rest," Carlo said, "but I didn't think it was relevant. It was going to be for self-defense," he added, a stupid thing to say to a police officer—self-defense as opposed to what?

He had filled out the paperwork for the license and background check and signed up for a lesson at a shooting range, but the moment he left the store, he understood his folly: aim a gun at a banger with a gun, and he will blow you away. Wouldn't it be a whole lot easier to avoid that particular intersection for the rest of his life? What had he been thinking? He'd keep the gun hidden in his night table drawer? A secret gun would have eaten a hole through the hull of their house. He'd thought the act of purchasing a weapon would empower him, but instead he'd felt like a complete idiot.

"This gun," the detective started to say.

"I don't actually own it," Carlo interrupted. "I mean that I don't have it because I never went back to the store after the waiting period." This was true.

"You're saying you never picked up this weapon? After spending the money, after making the purchase …?"

"I'm saying I changed my mind. I didn't want it. I don't want it."

He had watched and read enough procedurals in his time to know what was going on. He'd withheld certain information, and now he, the initial liar, the reluctant testifier, a keeper of secrets from his most-loved loved one, Carlo was undependable and capable of any deception. And if doubt lingered about any aspect of Tom's death, Carlo should be the last man trusted on the subject.

"You understand," Detective Michaels said, "I want to clear the case. I'm not saying that, other than a suicide, there was any foul play at your house on the night in question."

Not saying it, but sniffing around for it, Carlo thought.

"Perhaps nothing criminal happened," the detective said, "but *something* did happen, something I'm not fully grasping here. You understand my needs here, Mr. Stein, don't you?"

"I didn't mention that I'd bought a gun, and now you wonder what else I'm not telling you," Carlo said.

"And *now* you've told us everything we need to know?"

Carlo remembered when he showed up at Tom's apartment after going to the gun store. "There you are," Tom had said, ultra-casual, although Carlo hadn't called ahead and if Tom hadn't been home, Carlo would have left the borrowed green windbreaker hanging on the doorknob. "Come in, do come in," Tom said, the gracious host.

"What is it?" Detective Michaels asked. "Mr. Stein—Carlo?"

"Nothing," Carlo said.

"You're not holding on, say, to one last little secret, are you? You'd taken a sleeping pill that night, right? You were out cold. Ah, for all you know, Mr. Voight might have gotten up? Maybe Mr. Voight can tell us—"

"No," Carlo snapped. "No," he said.

The detective straightened her back.

"With all due respect, I think you're fishing," Carlo said. "Robbie is the heaviest sleeper in California. He would have slept through the Northridge quake, if I hadn't pushed him out of bed. No way. No."

"You sound certain."

He looked the detective squarely in the eye. "I am," he said. And: "I apologize if I accused you of fishing."

"That's okay," Detective Michaels said, and then as she stood, she winked. "Maybe I am."

WHEN CARLO CAME HOME THAT EVENING, he found Robbie stretched out on the floor by the window, practically beneath the piano, Robbie looking spent and apparently truly sick. He needed little encouragement to make his way into the bedroom, leaving Carlo alone on the couch, sipping an amaretto sour, staring at the ceiling. After his long day, he was frankly better off alone on the couch than he would have been dealing with Robbie. Carlo didn't feel as though he had his firmest footing, like a muddy hillside was giving way beneath his boot-heels. He didn't trust himself in this too-emotional state. He didn't know what he might say to Robbie, what he might reveal. On the off-chance Robbie might still be awake in bed and want to talk about anything deep, Carlo finished his drink and made himself another and returned to the couch.

After he'd left the gun store that day in May, Carlo had found himself on the freeway heading north into the Valley. He exited and drove along some very flat streets until he found a building identical to the apartment houses on either side, all of them stucco, all baked in the San Fernando sun down to the same over-cooked salmon color. Some sort of black metal decoration affixed to the façade looked like a demented person's idea of a sundial.

Tom's place was on the first floor and on the side, with bars on the one window. And when he answered the door, he was wearing only jeans cut-offs, no shirt, no belt, the shorts low on his waist.

"There you are," Tom said.

"I'm sorry I didn't get this back to you sooner," Carlo said. The green windbreaker was wrinkled and creased because Carlo had been stashing it in a tool box in the garage. He could have and should have mailed it, but after holding on to it a month, dropping off the jacket seemed the more courteous thing to do.

"Come in, do come in," Tom said, stepping back into his dim dank studio.

"I don't want to keep you, if you're in the middle of something," Carlo said.

"Oh right, the *middle* of something," Tom said. "So many middles, so little time."

He had been playing an opera on a boom box, which he turned off.

"Why do I bother? I really don't like opera," Tom said. "Do you?"

Carlo shrugged, yes, no, some not others. He handed Tom the windbreaker, and Tom promptly tossed it atop one of several piles of laundry on the floor. There were dishes stacked in the sink, and the kitchenette cupboards flung open, the shelves mostly empty. There was a jar of murky liquid on the counter and next to the jar, a stack of pocket-sized foreign language dictionaries arranged alphabetically: Arabic, French, German, Greek, Italian, Portuguese, a rhyming dictionary, Russian and Spanish.

"I just wanted to return that," Carlo managed to say, and for some reason now, he could not look Tom in the eye.

Tom scratched his naked stomach.

"Okay, thanks," he said.

"I should be going," Carlo said.

He was staring at the dirty laundry, at boxers and hand towels and T-shirts. A bright-striped cloth belt looked like a tropical snake coiled around a leg of discarded jeans. The bed was a futon on the floor. By the bed, there was an ageing laptop, the Bible, a box of crackers, a jar of peanut butter, lube, and several small towers of beat-up paperbacks. There was a card table pushed into the corner and on the card table a large sketch pad open to a page with a drawing-in-progress of a younger man, maybe a teenager. Under the card table, a pair of dusty duck boots that looked out of place in Southern California. That was it. This was Tom Field's world, and it was a little sad.

"I should go," Carlo said again but he didn't move.

"How have you been?" Tom asked. "I've wondered."

Carlo wanted to tell Tom about going to the gun store and how pathetic he felt about it, him with a gun, but he couldn't speak. Everything was coming back to him.

"Oh, what's wrong, baby?" Tom asked the way he had in the police station, but unlike their encounter in the police station, this time Tom took a step closer to Carlo, and then Carlo was weeping. In the month since the carjacking, Carlo hadn't cried like this, not once—finally he let go.

"It's okay, baby," Tom said, pulling Carlo into a hug.

It was not okay. It was not one bit okay, but Carlo knew on some level that he hadn't mailed back Tom's windbreaker and instead delivered it in person because he wanted to see Tom again. He wanted to see Tom because Tom would understand what Carlo was going through in a way Robbie never could (in a way Carlo would never want his sweet Robbie to), and not because Tom had been at the police station that April night, but because Tom Field comprehended violence, and not only violence in the street but also violence in one's mind, violence in one's heart. Tom was dark, Tom got it.

So Carlo wept, and Tom held him tightly. Carlo's tears dripped onto Tom's bare shoulder. Eventually Carlo cleared his throat and gained his composure, and the two of them sat down on the only place to sit in Tom's apartment, the futon on the floor. This was not okay, but also, curiously, it wasn't so strange, and once again, Carlo found he wasn't embarrassed in front of Tom.

"Feeling better, baby?" Tom asked, and Carlo nodded, he was.

Tom fell back on his elbows. A blue comforter was half peeled back, and Tom's sheets were patterned with sailboats.

Then Carlo lay on his back, too, so that the two of them, side by side, were staring at the ceiling. There was a long crack in the plaster, water damage, the crack branching like a river delta. Now that he wasn't crying, some embarrassment returned, or not embarrassment so much as a rush of some other heat. Carlo rolled onto his side and looked at Tom and noticed specifically Tom wasn't wearing underwear. Tom stroked his stomach, which was flat and hairless, and Carlo wanted to touch it, to trace the arc of Tom's pelvis curving parenthetically beneath the loose denim. Did Tom know Carlo was getting hard? He must have. He took Carlo's hand and placed firmly it on his, on Tom's, belly.

At first Carlo was frozen—he didn't move his hand at all. Then he rotated his fingertips in a tentative circle. Then up, down, and not so tentatively as Tom arched his back slightly, responding.

Tom slipped off his cut-offs, and when Carlo sat up, Tom pulled Carlo's shirt over Carlo's head. Then Carlo's pants were down around his ankles, bunched up around his sneakers. Awkwardly Carlo had to stand and tug off his pants with his sneakers, and when he knelt again on the futon, Tom pulled Carlo on top of him. They didn't make out, or they maybe kissed once. It was all very fast, and in short order, Tom had rolled over onto his stomach. Carlo wasn't sure what to do. He reached for the lube. He looked for but didn't find any condoms. How long it had been since he'd used a condom.

"I'm okay," Tom said. A pause. "And you're okay, I assume?"

Carlo said he was, and he knew he was fine but he also knew better. He was a little clumsy, abrupt, but Tom didn't appear to mind, nor did he appear especially to be enjoying himself. Carlo worked to bring things to a quick end, but Tom said he didn't want Carlo to stop. He wanted Carlo to go on a while and so Carlo went on a while. Tom seemed to want Carlo to be rougher than Carlo was accustomed to. When he came, he didn't come inside Tom. Tom rolled over onto his back, sweaty, and Carlo rolled onto his back again, too, strangely winded, and then thought to tend to Tom's needs, but Tom said it was okay, he was fine, he didn't need to get off.

"You're sure?" Carlo asked.

Tom hummed, yes, he was quite sure, thanks. He was propped up on his elbows again, chattering. Sunlight now poured in through the one window, and the mullions and the iron bars cast a plaid shadow on the brown carpet.

"It's almost summer," Tom said, "and I used to like summer but now I hate summer. I especially am not looking forward to summer in this city. Such a long summer, like a prison, the summer here. Is that the way it is?"

"Is that the way what is?" Carlo asked. He felt as though he were waking from a long hibernation. "I should go," he said.

"No, stay a little while," Tom said.

And Carlo felt obliged then to stay, considering Tom's hospitality, as it were. He lingered, and Tom rambled about something, quite excited about something or other involving the audio-book he'd been listening to a little bit every night, but Carlo wasn't paying attention. His head was clearing, a lucidity returning, a sense of logic—of right versus wrong, too.

Carlo glanced at his watch. Knocking on Tom's door, weeping, fucking—remarkably he had only been at Tom's place for forty-five minutes, although it felt like hours.

"I want to play you some of this book," Tom said. "A few pages—you'll like it."

Carlo sighed.

"I guess you have to go," Tom said, resigned.

"I'll be expected back," Carlo said.

"I suppose you will," Tom said.

Carlo got dressed.

"Hopefully that did the trick," Tom said, and Carlo didn't know what he meant at first, but then of course, as he drove away, as he looked for the freeway, he knew perfectly well what Tom meant.

Carlo had not only cheated on his boyfriend but also used someone, used poor Tom, and yet Carlo didn't experience any remorse, the contrary. As opposed to back in the gun store parking lot when he'd felt helpless and foolish, now Carlo raced east on the freeway with a sense of empowerment—why? Because he'd figured out what he needed and sought it out? Because he'd done something for himself, yes, ridiculous but true, and he was laughing because life was absurd. He ended up exiting the freeway early and driving surface the rest of the way home because he was a bit discombobulated. Over the hills and back into the city basin, laughing out loud—why? Because he felt released from his anxiety, and like he was breathing the air of a higher altitude, and alive again. Life was so very strange, wasn't it? It was when one understood that strangeness, the randomness, the swerves, it was being able to see all that from above that made one feel more perceptive, and thus invigorated, thus vital.

He made it back to the house in one piece, and Robbie wasn't home yet, and Carlo took a long hot shower. All these revelations—he was exhausted, and after his shower he ended up on the couch, which was where Robbie found him. And Robbie kissed him hi and stretched out next to him, and the two men lay there very close and plotted their evening, not that it would be so different from most every other evening, but they had their rituals, the most mundane lovely rituals like discussing what to eat for dinner, whether to go see a movie, or stay in and read, or take a walk, or maybe even drop by a bar. Life was going to be normal again, life prosperous, life good.

Carlo thought he would never see Tom again, and Tom had no way of knowing where Carlo lived. Yes, that did the trick. He was alive and on the other side of something now, he'd thought—wrongly as it would turn out, but that was what he'd believed that night, that a turnaround was inevitable, for him, for the two men: How could it be otherwise?

IN THE MORNING, Robbie again told Carlo he was sick so he could continue making phone calls. Not everyone he contacted, however, was willing to speculate about Tom's suicide, although these tended to be the same canceled acquaintances who didn't sound all that wistful about Tom in the first place. Only one person, a screenwriter who dated Tom last summer and endured a rather bad bar crawl with him on the Fourth of July, during which Tom downed a dozen lagers and made out with two other guys at the last stop—"I didn't ditch him," the man said, "because I didn't want him on the road drunk, less for his sake than the other drivers', but at the end of the night we had a fight when he accused me of thinking he was an escort, and he drove off drunk anyway"—only this man was willing to speak harshly of the dead. He said, "If the sex hadn't been so hot, I'd never have agreed to a second date. Tom Field was the most self-fascinated person I've ever met, and that's what I told the police."

The police, it turned out, had recently contacted this man because apparently Tom still had the man's number in his cell phone. The detective who phoned had more or less run the same interrogation as Robbie.

"This was a Detective Michaels?" he asked.

"Michaels, yeah," the man said. "She said they were looking into different scenarios."

"Different scenarios—what different scenarios?"

"I don't know," the man said. "It was probably an accident because I can't imagine Tom being the kind of person who would think the world could go on without him in it."

There were also several long conversations that never quite wound down to Robbie's principle question. In these instances the people with whom he spoke might have assumed Robbie wanted to trade anecdotes the way one might at a funeral, and while Robbie may not have polled them the way he did others, information nevertheless surfaced:

An older woman who had been one of Tom's high school history teachers (and why had Tom drawn a line through her name? what possible trespass against him had she committed?), recalled the way Tom would visit her after school and sit in her office and talk to her as long as she would let him. Young Tommy always seemed dismayed when she said she needed to go home and feed her family. She taught ancient and medieval history, and in her classroom she kept her own library of texts that she never loaned out, except to Tommy, to whom she recalled lending many reproductions of illuminated manuscripts and in particular a definitive tome on hieroglyphics. She felt a certain duty to him, she said, given his parents. Robbie knew nothing about Tom's parents, only his grandparents, and the old teacher said, "The mother was something of the town floozy, disappearing one day when Tom was ten, never to be heard from again. Tom's father was believed to be schizophrenic or manic-depressive or borderline—something. He self-medicated, you could say, and was never able to support himself, and when Tom was a toddler, his father went off hiking on his own one winter, out into the bitterest of nights. By the time he was located, he had frozen to death."

"Tom loved beautiful things," a different woman said, someone who knew him during his Boston school days. "He bought a cashmere scarf, the palest gray scarf, and from that day forward wore it, all fall, all winter, every day, into the spring, that scarf, which he referred to as his signature scarf. He wound it twice tightly around his neck, then tied the ends loosely in front, never tucking it in his coat. He had a clear image of himself," she said, "or who he wanted to be, which was a portrait painter for good families. A society artist. Did you ever see any of his drawings?"

Robbie was about to ask the woman whether she thought a true aesthete and epicurean like Tom could really kill himself, but he had to end the call early because the doorbell rang. It was Detective Michaels.

"Sorry," she said. "I understand you've not been feeling well."

In pajama bottoms, an old T-shirt, and slippers, certainly Robbie looked like he'd climbed out of bed to answer the door. He invited the detective in. They stood awkwardly in the kitchen. Detective Michaels apologized for not calling first, but she was in the neighborhood. She mentioned that she'd been in contact with Carlo. Robbie interrupted: Wasn't she getting from him whatever assistance she needed?

"Yes," the detective said, "yes. However, I've still got one or two questions—"

"You're considering different scenarios," Robbie said.

"That's my job. Ruling things out."

"You're wondering whether it was an accident? Whether Tom really meant to kill himself or if he might only have been messing around?"

"Is that something you're asking yourself?"

Robbie nodded. The detective waited for him to say more but he didn't. She had her pad out, her pen.

"Awkward question, Mr. Voight," she said. "It's about your relationship with Mr. Stein."

"Oh? Why?"

"Well, you understand. I'm trying to close this case, but I have this funny feeling I'm overlooking something."

"About Carlo and me?"

"Would you say your relationship is solid?"

Solid? For sure, they'd known more solid autumns in the past.

"Like granite," Robbie said, and he tapped the kitchen counter.

"And you and Mr. Stein—you'd say, as a rule, you tell each other everything?"

Robbie squinted at the detective. What was she getting at?

He said, "Everything, yes."

The detective made a note but shook her head in puzzlement. She said, "In a long marriage, sometimes one partner goes and does something the other partner wouldn't want him to."

"Detective, I'm not sure what you're after. And I'm not feeling well—"

"A long marriage," Detective Michaels said again. "Sometimes there are secrets."

"Maybe for some, but we're simply not like that," Robbie said, as if Stein Voight were a nation and his patriotism were being tested. "Carlo and I don't keep secrets."

"Oh, go on."

"Honestly we don't."

"You have nothing, say, you're keeping from Mr. Stein? Nothing about Mr. Field, about what happened that night?"

If Robbie began to form an uncomfortable smile it was because he'd assumed that in querying about matters unspoken or covert between the two men, the detective was wondering if Carlo kept things from Robbie, not the other way around. As a matter of fact, it was Robbie who held a secret at the moment: There was Tom's address book, which Carlo didn't know about and which, Robbie realized, sat in plain view atop the piano. There were the calls he'd been making. There were all of his alien thoughts of the last weeks, each a secret in its way. One of these days, he was going to be found out, if not by the detective, then by Carlo.

"We don't hide anything from each other," Robbie asserted again, "and I'm sorry, but do you think we could talk another time? I should lie down."

THAT NIGHT, a dream, Robbie's now recurring dream, the one in which he woke up abruptly and noticed Carlo wasn't next to him in bed but instead was standing at their bedroom window. Except this time, the dream was different: It wasn't Carlo at the window (Carlo wasn't in the room at all). The man at the window was looser in branch—it was Tom, Tom dressed for tennis.

He stood there, his arms at his side, staring out at the night, and Robbie pulled back the blanket and swung his legs over the side of the bed and ever so quietly crossed the room until he was standing behind Tom, and Tom didn't appear to notice Robbie or let on if he did. Robbie inched close enough so he could feel whatever heat Tom threw off. Robbie was breathing on Tom's shoulder, his neck. Robbie extended his hand out beyond Tom's side, out in front of Tom, and Tom studied Robbie's hand a while, then took it in his, and placed Robbie's hand over his, Tom's, heart.

When Robbie understood Tom was not going to let go, Robbie allowed his head to rest against Tom's shoulder. And this was how he returned to sleep, standing behind Tom, head on Tom's shoulder, hand on his slow-beating heart.

FRIDAY MORNING OF THAT WEEK, Robbie slept late and didn't have to lie again about being sick because Carlo was long gone by the time Robbie got out of bed. He called one or two more people in Tom's address book, as if it were a part of his morning routine, and then wanting some exercise, he went out on a brisk walk, completing two turns around the Reservoir. Back home, skimming the newspaper, he noticed a listing that Tom's writer friend was giving a reading in a West Hollywood bookstore that night. At the end of the day, Robbie left Carlo a note and headed out.

The writer wore a narrow-cut suit. His pink pocket square matched the T-shirt he had on beneath the suit jacket. It was hard to say what the novel was about, Europhile vampires who wore expensive clothes and left messes in hotel suites, or were they pop stars and the vampire motif was metaphoric? The writer read one scene that involved a decapitation at a shoe sale. The store was packed and the audience loved it.

After the reading, Robbie hung back while a line of adoring readers snaked toward the writer, the writer who looked overlarge at the table he sat at and who kept asking a bookstore clerk if he could smoke, expecting an answer other than the one he'd received five minutes earlier. Finally, with a good number of fans still waiting for his autograph, he said he would be right back and slipped out the door to the parking lot. Robbie went out the front of the store and walked around the building. He approached the writer and apologized for pestering him while he was enjoying his cigarette, and the writer said nothing. Robbie thought of something charitable to say about the excerpt read aloud and then he explained he was a friend of Tom Field's, and the writer immediately reached out and squeezed Robbie's shoulder.

"It's hideous what happened," the writer said.

"I left you a message," Robbie said.

"You're not with the LAPD, are you?"

"No. Did they contact you?"

"A black-and-white came to my house. You can imagine the amount of scrambling that went on. It's not the drugs I worry about so much as the porno."

"What did they want to know?"

"The usual," the writer said, and left it at that. "Actually I'd heard about Tom from the maitre d' at the restaurant Tom and I would go to in the Valley, a steak joint we liked, very red-booth, this place. Tom was my third buddy this year to o.d. The shit out there, man, it's shit."

Robbie didn't correct the writer, nor apparently had the police.

"I met him at a club in New York," the writer said, "and I found him kind of vivid. I moved back out here to finish this book, and I ran into Tom in a pharmacy on Ventura—in fact, there's a secondary vampire in the novel based on Tom. Anyway,

I told ole Tom I'd buy him dinner and I did, and then about once a month, I met him at the steak place. He amused me. I don't know if I amused him."

"He had an address book full of crossed-out names," Robbie said, "but not yours."

The writer scratched the side of his nose with his thumbnail, dragged on his cigarette.

"I went away a couple a months ago," he said, "and didn't tell him. I should have told him. Whenever we went out, I dressed like this—"

The writer made a gesture, open-palmed, I'm fabulous, I'm not so fabulous, whatever.

"And Tom wore his gray suit," the writer said. "I ordered steak au poivre and Tom the béarnaise, and we went through at least one bottle of a good red if not two. I didn't talk much. He talked quite a bit. I fed him gossip, literary, music-industry, blah-blah. I made it all up, although I think he knew. He regaled me with sex stories. I am not under the impression he was making them up. He told me he wanted to draw me, but as you may know I don't like being photographed, and I certainly don't want to be *drawn*, and also it sounded vaguely sexual and as you may also know, he was a little old for me. But I said sure, like instead of my next author photo, a Tom Field drawing, nifty. And he left a message last fall about wanting to take me out when I was back in town to celebrate the new novel. When we went out for steak, I always paid because I knew Tom didn't have any money. But he was adamant in the message that this time he would pay."

The writer dropped his cigarette to the pavement, but it rolled away from him before he could stub it out with his boot. "Tom in that gray suit," he said, shaking his head, before heading back inside the store.

Robbie wanted to be by himself and went to a coffee shop, and when he arrived home late, he found Carlo waiting up, stretched out on the couch, drowsy, paging through a magazine.

"How was the reading?" he asked.

Robbie considered making the connection, the writer to Tom, why Robbie had sought him out. He didn't want to be keeping secrets from Carlo the way the detective suggested.

"Interesting," Robbie answered. "It was interesting."

"Well—good. This writer, he's someone you've discovered recently?"

Robbie hesitated but then said, "Tom recommended him."

"Tom recommended him to you or someone else?"

Robbie didn't understand the question. "To me," he said, and he expected an immediate dismissal, a write-off, but Carlo only nodded, only blinked.

"And you're feeling better?" Carlo asked.

"I am."

Robbie sat at the edge of the couch. There was so much he wanted to say and nothing he thought Carlo would want to hear. They talked about how cold it was that night. A belt of constellations sagged low in the sky. They were being pleasant with one another—how practiced they were at being pleasant with one another.

"What are you looking at there?" Robbie asked.

"Nothing really. There's an article on fountains. Oh, my father called today," Carlo said. "He's definitely coming this year."

"Good," Robbie said. "That's good?"

"We should start the drinking now."

"Oh, he's not that bad," Robbie said.

Carlo sat up on the sofa and glanced around the main room. "There were all these things I wanted to get done before he got here," he said.

"Make a list. I can deal with it."

"No, there's a lot to do—"

"For crying out loud, Carlo, make a list. I'll take care of it. Actually ..."

"Actually what?"

Robbie looked at him and Carlo appeared to read his mind.

"You want to take a little break from the office," Carlo said.

"I feel guilty about it," Robbie said.

"Don't. Take a week."

"You need me on the producer's house."

"We're fine. Take two weeks—take whatever time you need. I'll make the list."

Then Carlo launched into a monologue about the fountain he had in mind, the slate he wanted to use, and Robbie hummed when appropriate, although he'd drifted. He was thinking about Tom, imagining him cleaning up and putting on his gray suit, waiting for the writer at the steak place, ordering a martini, dirty, three olives. Watching the door and when the writer sat down, Tom would have an anecdote warmed up and ready to go. They had played tennis that afternoon in September and Tom had shouted across the court at Robbie that they could play Saturdays all year long. It might have become another ritual, stitching together all the other hours, Tom's lost hours, into a readable sequence of days.

CARLO HAD ASKED ROBBIE if he was feeling better, although he already knew the answer, and not because Robbie had driven himself to a bookstore. That morning, Carlo had spotted his boyfriend out on a hale and vigorous walk around the lake. Carlo had been late for an appointment with an engineer up at the producer's property, but as he was driving north on Silver Lake and was about to turn left, he noticed Robbie in a fast stride headed

west, coming down past the dog park and rounding the basketball court. Carlo made the left turn, but rather than stop and
wave hello or roll down his window and call out to Robbie, he
continued on, making another left and pulling over to the curb.
He turned around and watched Robbie approach through the
back window of the car—Robbie, it would seem, was too deep in
thought to notice Carlo or their car, too preoccupied, elsewhere.

What a rare phenomenon it was to run into one's spouse out
in the world. Maybe now and then the two men might run errands separately, and, say, unexpectedly cross paths in the shared
parking lot of the dry cleaners and supermarket, or perhaps they'd
overlap at the gym, one entering as the other was leaving—but
that was not running into each other really, because each always
knew what the other was up to, where (at all times) the other
was. Until recently, at any rate.

Robbie walked directly opposite the cross street and Carlo
pivoted in the driver's seat so that he was less obviously a man
spying, although he did continue to watch Robbie in the rear-
view mirror, which he angled as Robbie proceeded up the hill.
And what was that expression on Robbie's face, that intentness
as if he were drawing in his notebook or listening to music
through headphones? Although he wasn't wearing headphones,
and he also seemed unaware of anyone coming toward him, a
dog walker, a couple with a stroller. Robbie looked sealed off
from the rest of the world, and for some reason this left Carlo
suddenly very blue.

Once Robbie was out of view, Carlo swung into a U-turn
and drove up the hill slowly, and once again, at the point where
Carlo should have swerved off to the west, he paused and looked

the other way down the street at Robbie, at his back as he headed around the Reservoir at an eager pace.

And Carlo let him disappear again, but why hadn't he pulled up alongside Robbie and stopped him and shouted, Hey, handsome! Why hadn't he pulled up alongside his boyfriend and asked how he was feeling? Why hadn't he asked, What are you thinking about, Robbie? It wasn't a mystery: Carlo didn't actually *want* to know what Robbie was thinking about. His latest notions about Tom—Carlo didn't want to know, and he also didn't want Robbie politely asking the same of him. And what's on your mind, signor? What's *your* latest obsession?

The engineer called Carlo on his cell phone—he was running late, too—which left Carlo sitting in his car by a slope of weeds and remembering how in college, he and Robbie used to study at the GSD, but Robbie wasn't nearly as engaged by design as Carlo was, not initially. When graduate school first came up, Robbie derisively labeled an MA a creative person's law degree, a default course of study when one didn't know what else to do with one's life. He changed his mind about architecture and ultimately proved an abler student than Carlo, but Carlo suddenly found himself besieged by what-if's, like what if Robbie hadn't attended graduate school with Carlo, and what if they hadn't gone into practice together? Robbie had been talented at so many things—would he have pursued film? Would he have followed an academic plot and gone into literature or anthropology or philosophy? Would he have become the better chef and gone to culinary school? Would he then have wanted to open a restaurant? Or would he maybe have become a psychotherapist? Because Robbie the avid listener would have made a good therapist. Would he have become a school teacher? Patient, enthusiastic-about-everything Robbie would have made a good teacher. And then would he have wanted children? What would Robbie's life have been like if had he fallen out of love with Carlo? In what city would Robbie live? Would he still be back East and closer to his family? Would he have a boyfriend? Yes, of course he would have a boyfriend, but what would this man look like and would he be smart? Yes, of course he would be smart, but about what kind of things?

Carlo jumped when the engineer rapped his knuckles on his windshield. He hadn't seen him pull up to the site or get out of his car. Carlo had managed to agitate himself greatly, although he wasn't sure which was more disturbing, that he could fluidly imagine alternate lives for Robbie or that he wasn't inclined to ask the same questions about himself. Without Robbie, what would *his* own life look like? Carlo had no idea. He had no idea at all.

It was strange enough to spy on Robbie walking around the lake and strange, too, when Carlo came home in the early evening and found Robbie's note saying he'd gone to a reading, but it was beyond strange, it was disconcerting and unsettling when Carlo went into the bedroom to change and noticed a slim black object atop the dresser: an address book, an old address book of soft pages and years of notations—Tom Field's address book.

Which explained how Robbie had located Tom's grandmother. Carlo left the address book where he'd found it and decided not to mention it to Robbie, but he had to wonder, why did Robbie have this thing in his possession and did the police know he did? What was Robbie up to, what kind of sleuthing? Had

Tom said something to someone about his encounters with Carlo? Was Robbie now trying to trace Tom back to Carlo? Could he?

HE TRIED TO CONVINCE HIMSELF he was becoming paranoid, but Carlo couldn't stop fretting and during the night got up and went into the kitchen, where he drafted an ambitious to-do list, improvising extra tasks because keeping Robbie busy, especially if he wasn't going to come in to work, might prevent him from over-pondering Tom's death, or Tom's life, from looking into matters Carlo did not want Robbie looking into. This way, too, Carlo could keep better tabs on Robbie's whereabouts if Robbie was home polishing the silver et cetera and not at large in the city. Not that this would work, but it was the only thing Carlo could think of at the moment to move Robbie away from Tom.

Saturday morning Carlo went into the office because there was plenty of work to do on the television producer's house (the producer phoned twice while Carlo sat at his desk letting the calls go to voicemail), yet he found himself thinking about his fountain, which he now envisioned as a slate square pool amid a little slate patio, with moss growing up at the edges, and some wildflowers, and maybe grasses, maybe a row of hopseed bushes to screen the neighbors on the property below. What he was picturing was a neat hideaway that you wouldn't be able to see from the house or even the upper patio, a retreat where he would, well, retreat. What he imagined was taking a very long nap, with a pond gurgle in the background, a rejuvenating bise brushing down the hillside, rocking him in his hammock.

He pushed aside the specs he'd been working on for the producer's villa and began doodling what he had in mind for his secret garden, and his doodles gradually became more composed illustrations. He had

some pastel pencils in his desk drawer, and he began adding color.
He lost himself in the movement of his pencil-gripping hand and
there was something delightfully familiar about the emerging in-
dentation in his index finger, the soft pencil against his skin. He
used to draw, once, and he used to paint in oils, and painting had
brought him such an unabashed joy. He was never so very brilliant an abstractionist, but he liked mixing color, juxtaposing
fields of color, dense saturated color. He'd stopped making canvases when he and Robbie bought their house. When they were
moving, he'd either given away or sold all of his paintings. Why
had he given up something he loved doing? Because painting was-
n't serious and he needed strictly to engage in serious endeavors?

As was his habit lately, he ended up standing in the front
window, pensive, staring at nothing in particular. When he saw
Gabriel coast up to the liquor store across the street, Carlo
stepped out to the sidewalk to shout hello, but before he did, he
fell back against the door because a car drove past, coasting toward the lake, a long black sedan. It didn't slow down, but Carlo
could see them, the men in the front seat, the men in the backseat, dark hair, scruffy, trouble.

It was the ambush car, it was the carjackers, the fuckers, it was
them.

Or not. No, of course it wasn't them, how could it be them,
he was being silly. The car sped up the hill toward the lake. Who's
a silly man? It wasn't them, he told himself again, even as a part
of him held on to that possibility.

A short while later, Gabriel emerged from the liquor store. By
this point, Carlo was sitting on the shallow stoop of his building, his elbows on his knees. Gabriel looked at him a moment,

weighing, it seemed, whether to cross the boulevard, which he did on foot, his skateboard tucked under his arm. He stood in front of Carlo a moment.

"What's wrong?" the boy asked.

Which was what Carlo was about to ask him—Gabriel was squinting as if he had the sun in his eyes, which he didn't. Something was eating him.

"Nothing," Carlo said and stood and locked his office door. "Come with me," he said, and hooked the boy's arm, guiding him around the side of the building to his car parked in back, indicating the boy should get in.

"Where are we going?" the boy asked.

"Nowhere special," Carlo said, and for some reason the boy did not question him and obediently slipped into the passenger seat with his skateboard resting against his knees, although when they turned out onto the street, he did sink low in his seat, very low as if to avoid being seen.

"This is kidnapping," Gabriel said. "Help," he said. "Help, help."

"Oh, be quiet," Carlo said.

"Help."

Carlo's first stop was the hardware store to pick up a pair of heavier-duty shears, and while he was at it, a new shovel to replace a rusted-out one. Then he drove the boy back to his house.

"You aren't, like, expecting to put me to work or anything," Gabriel said.

"The thought had occurred to me," Carlo said.

"It's supposed to rain, you know."

"It won't."

There was a pause in the conversation and Gabriel looked the way he did when he stepped out of the liquor store, acidic, without bearings.

"Do you want to tell me what's troubling you?" Carlo asked, expecting to be rebuffed.

"It's complicated," Gabriel said.

Pause.

"How so?" Carlo asked.

"Well, for starters, I owe someone something."

"Owe who what?"

Gabriel didn't answer.

"Who, Lonny?" Carlo asked.

Gabriel said nothing.

"What, money?" Carlo asked.

Again nothing.

Carlo tried and failed to contain a sigh.

"You owe Lonny money. For what?"

Gabriel gazed out the passenger-side window.

Never mind for what, Carlo thought. He didn't want to know for what.

"How much are we talking about, a hundred?" Carlo asked.

Which elicited a laugh.

"Two hundred? More? Five? A thousand?" Carlo asked.

Gabriel shrugged.

Carlo shook his head and said, "Okay," although he didn't know what he meant when he said okay. "Maybe you can work it off—I'll pay you."

Gabriel shot him a look: Oh, right, work off a grand working for you.

"We'll figure something out," Carlo said. "Don't worry about it right now," he said.

"You'll loan me the money?" Gabriel asked.

"I said don't worry about it," Carlo said.

And Gabriel relaxed his frown, grinned, and said, "Thanks."

Carlo nodded. Had he just offered to loan a teenager a thousand dollars to pay off a drug debt, money he didn't have in the bank to give away, which is what it would amount to, a gift? However, the boy was smiling and that was worth something for the time being.

Robbie wasn't home. Carlo led the boy through the house and out back, the new shears and shovel in hand, collecting work gloves and trash bags and other tools on the way down to the bottom of the property. Most of the area he wanted to clear was covered with a gnarled mass of unfruited ficus, all the stalks heavy with rotting leaves. Where there wasn't the ficus, there were menacing patches of bearish acanthus. Carlo handed the boy the shovel and a pair of gloves, saving the shears for himself, which he held in front of him like a divining rod. His only instruction was, "All this comes out," before he began hacking indiscriminately at some acanthus vines.

Gabriel leaned on the shovel, watching.

"What are you waiting for?" Carlo asked. "Start digging."

"You're paying me for this, right?" Gabriel asked.

"Oh, for crying out loud," Carlo said. "Dig."

The boy hesitated a moment longer, but then he went at the vines, too, pulling at them, throwing his heel against the shovel head, while Carlo chopped and tugged at the waxy plants. They said nothing and worked like this for the better part of an hour, only eradicating a minor patch of the bear's britches, not making any progress on the ficus or other weedy matter, but it was a start, and the physical work had done

Carlo some good, probably the boy, too. That hour removing the vines, Carlo had thought about nothing of consequence.

Meanwhile, the clouds assembled overhead, and it became cooler and windier. Robbie came home while Carlo and Gabriel were taking a breather, and after he'd made his way down the hill, he nodded in approval, although he didn't say anything. Carlo wanted to ask him if he'd been wandering around the Reservoir or rifling through Tom's address book, which notably was no longer atop the dresser, but didn't. Robbie picked up the shears and meekly hacked at a vine. Then Carlo took the shovel and tried to dig at some ficus roots. And Robbie clipped another vine with a little more gusto, and Gabriel gathered the trimmings and packed them into a trash bag, and the three of them worked like this another half hour before it began to drizzle. Quickly the drizzle turned into rain, and they scrambled back up the hill and into the house, kicking off boots and sneakers and tugging at damp socks. In the kitchen, Robbie took various things out of the refrigerator and set them on the counter, olive tapenade and roasted peppers and tuna fish and baba ganoush and cherry tomatoes. He sliced wheat bread. And they made sandwiches and barely spoke, and given recent events, it seemed illicit how content Carlo was at that moment. If he wanted proof that he was worrying too much, here was his proof.

The rain began to taper off, although he wished it would continue. A glass house was its most spectacular against the threat of inclement weather. All around you outside, the elements were uncharitable, unpredictable, moody. Yet inside, enclosed and dry and safe, nothing changed, you were secure. Nothing in the world could go wrong. It was then that Carlo had the vaguest premonition that his troubles, the troubles the two men faced, even whatever was bothering the boy, might be taking a turn for the better. The past would recede quietly into the deeper past. The winter ahead would be a good winter.

Later he would think back to this rainy Saturday afternoon and see that all he'd done in allowing himself this momentary satisfaction was push his luck and, even though he did not believe in such things, jinx himself.

AS PROMISED in the days that followed, Robbie worked his way down Carlo's list of tasks. He waxed the dining table. He cleaned lighting fixtures, the hood over the stove, the tool table in the garage. He recaulked the bathtub spigot. He thinned his wardrobe and packed clothes to be given away. A full pile of firewood rose up by the hearth. The silver gleamed. He seemed to be tapping a new font of energy, and at night he fell asleep with ease. He wasn't spending all that much time with Carlo, who was either at the office or working with Gabriel to clear brush for the new patio and fountain, yet Robbie thought this separation was temporary, and he found himself actually looking forward to his father-in-law's visit, to their Thanksgiving, the full stride of the holidays one can fall into when the meter of one's life for whatever reasons has fallen off tempo. Two months had gone by since Tom killed himself, and while Robbie had never been searching for exculpatory evidence—whether the two men should have cut off Tom's drinking would always be something he would turn over—the fact remained that after speaking with two dozen people who one way or another knew Tom, after a certain consensus had congealed around Tom's intent, or probable lack of intent, Robbie did feel unshouldered of some responsibility and ready, at last, to move on with his life.

And yet, that said, he still awoke in the morning with the nagging sense that some definitive discovery about Tom's true nature could still be made, and because he hadn't exhausted all the contacts in Tom's address book (which he took better care to hide deep in his sock drawer after leaving it out in the open—Carlo hadn't mentioned anything, so Robbie assumed Carlo was none the wiser), since there were still a few more names and numbers, Robbie continued making his cold calls across time zones.

One morning after Carlo went to the office—this was the Tuesday before Thanksgiving—Robbie opened Tom's address book from right to left to the XYZ-page, deciphered a struck-through number (although not in another time zone, but local, the same prefix as Robbie's number), and spoke with yet one more man whom Tom had dated, in this case the previous spring.

"It's amazing you'd call today," the man said. "I thought I'd lost it, but last night I found the drawing Tom did of me, which I sort of hid from myself when we broke up. I couldn't throw it out. Apparently one doesn't throw out a Tom Field drawing."

"He let you keep it," Robbie said.

"Didn't he let you keep the drawing he made of you?"

"Tom never drew me."

"So you didn't date?"

"No. No, we didn't."

"It was part of his seduction MO. Everyone naked, the sketching."

There was something about the man's voice uncannily Tom-like, or not so much his voice (his timbre was more the cello to Tom's violin), as a similar crescendo of enthusiasm with each statement.

"My weeks with him were wretched on the one hand," the man said, "but also wonderful, and then I have to say he sort of saved me. But that's a long story. We were both artists, that was part of it. I mean that we were both artists in that if someone came up to you in a grocery store and asked, 'Hey, so, what do you do?' We'd say, or I'd say, 'Artist.'"

"Tom mentioned he dated a painter," Robbie said. "He also indicated that there were some arguments—"

"Like ever I got a word in," the man said. "Tom has to be the first and only guy I've split up with over art, and I guess that's oddly cool on some level, but mostly it was oddly odd. He called me a dilettante—*he* of all people called me a dilettante. But he did have a sweet side. It's horrible, not only that he checked out, but how."

It occurred to Robbie possibly he'd reached his limit as to how much he wanted to consider Tom's death, and he thought about exiting the conversation.

"At the bar where I met him," the man said, "there's a bartender who looks after me and who also found Tom amusing, and then for some wacky reason fixated on the idea of the two of us together, poured us free bourbon. The bartender had to call the police on Tom once or twice apparently, after Tom and I were finished, and he was also the one who told me Tom hanged himself. I mean, how awful. Apparently you die from asphyxiation— it's like drowning."

Robbie was sitting on the floor, propped up against a window. The pane was cold against his shoulder blades.

"I wish I'd done something to stop him," the man said.

Robbie sat up. "What do you mean?" he asked.

The man hesitated, and then he said, "He wanted us to do it together.

"You have to understand," he went on, "I had no money, I'd stayed in a ghastly relationship with a guy a year too long. I'm a little younger than Tom, and maybe he wanted me to see myself in him, like I would become him. We were drinking of course, and he brought it up, ending things together, the world be damned—I cut him off. I said, 'No way.' I said, 'No matter how hard it's been, no thanks. I want to live forever.' And do you know what Tom said? He said, 'Be careful what you wish for.'

"Then one of the last times I was with him, a month later but before he accused me being a dilettante who would amount to nothing, Tom said he was burned-out all the time and wasn't sure what the difference was between being alive and being dead. I didn't want to get into that conversation again. I didn't say a word and he changed the subject as if he were embarrassed, like he thought we were the same person with the same experience and realized finally we weren't. Which must have made him feel lousy, and lonely. Obviously I've thought a lot about this. I should have, I don't know, *said* something."

"But,"—Robbie had to clear his throat—"but what could you have said?"

"It's difficult. Someone who is always over-the-top talks like that—how *do* you respond? But I was selfish. I was thinking no matter how much I struggled, living this impractical impossible life, I was in better shape than Tom."

"This is how he saved you."

"Kind of. And no, it's more complicated, and a little personal."

There was a pause and then the man said, his voice slightly more baritone as if sharing a secret, "My bartender friend told me Tom killed himself at a trick's house—"

"It wasn't a trick," Robbie said.

"Then at some stranger's place. And I thought, that was Tom. Make sure there's a story people are telling about you."

The word *stranger* sank like a stone in Robbie's chest.

"I think Tom was waiting for the right time," the man said, "the right place. I know this sounds twisted, but I think he was looking for a peaceful place to die, and maybe he found it."

Robbie got up on his knees and pivoted so he was facing the lake, all ten fingertips against the glass.

"Hello?" the man asked.

"It is very peaceful up here, I will say that," Robbie said.

Another pause.

"Oh no," the man said. He said, "I'm sorry. What did I say? I'm trying to remember what I said."

"I have his address book," Robbie explained. "I've been calling people."

"It never occurred to me— I'm so sorry."

"I'm fine," Robbie said, "I'll be fine," but he was thinking, yes, *strangers*—in the end, they had known each other only a day and remained strangers, Robbie and Tom, no different than Robbie and the person on the other end of the line, tenuously linked by a hanged man, yet disconnected, distanced as they listened to each other breathe. The man's name was Jay.

"You don't sound like you'll be fine," Jay said. "You found him?"

"I did," Robbie said.

"You found him, and you were all alone," Jay said.

He'd made a leap, but Robbie chose not to correct him.

"I'm sorry, the way I was talking—I should have been more careful. Is there anything I can do for you?" Jay asked.

"No," Robbie said at first. But then he looked again at Jay's address on Waterloo Street and added, "Or maybe we can meet up sometime and talk more. We live in walking distance."

"Anytime. You can come over."

"Right now?"

"Right now," Jay said, "my place isn't very tidy."

"I've been deluding myself about Tom. I'm a fool. I've been selling myself a story—"

"Give me fifteen minutes," Jay said.

Robbie stood slowly, muddled with vertigo but clearer now. If he had continued contacting Tom's friends, it was because he never completely bought what anyone told him. All along he'd been waiting for confirmation of a blacker doubt. Tom in his gray suit at the steak house with the writer, Tom looking for a peaceful place to die—both habits sustained him in different ways, and one ultimately won out over the other. Nobody should be alone, and they had left Tom alone. Tom's whole life, everyone had left him alone.

To walk to Jay's place, Robbie headed down his street to Duane and down the hill away from the Reservoir toward Glendale Boulevard, a steep pitch made unpleasant by the wind. He clutched his scarf over his nose. Jay's address was difficult to locate because the street number was both scraped from the curb and missing from the building, a triplex with one unit tucked in back and upstairs, which turned out to be Jay's apartment. At the end of the street was a freeway on-ramp, and directly opposite Jay's building there was a triangular park, a baseball diamond on which at that hour, a man stood on the mound side-winding pitches at a boy-catcher who dropped every ball.

Robbie climbed a staircase rising over trash bins and knocked on the metal door, but no one appeared. He waited, knocked again, and Jay did not answer. When he knocked a third time, the door swung open wide, and Robbie took a step back and hit the railing. What kind of weird trick was this?

Jay extended his hand, the open cuff of his half-buttoned, wrinkled shirt falling away to reveal the raised vine of veins in his forearm. Cold hand, firm shake. He bounced a bit off one foot as he ushered (pulled) Robbie inside.

His apartment was a studio, longer than it was deep and surveyable in a blink. It was, yes, a bit of a mess, and yet also a calm forest because the walls had been painted a mossy color and the partially drawn matchstick blinds were a dark wood. An upright piano stood in one corner, sheet music open, sheet music scattered across the bench and spilling onto the floor. A guitar was propped up against the wall like a cowboy enjoying a standing siesta. In the opposite corner, piles of books banked up against a bed like cottages set into the foothills. There was a small writing desk, a shallow kitchenette, empty wine bottles on the counter, a bathroom with dated tile. In the center of the room was an ornate upholstered couch, a burgundy brocade, an atlas open on the couch to a map more lake than land.

Jay was barefoot and wearing paint-streaked jeans, which, as he asked Robbie if he wanted some tea, as he bounced across the studio to turn on the kettle when Robbie didn't respond, he had to hitch up because they were more or less falling off his narrow hips.

The wind rattled the glass as if a train tore past.

Also in the studio, in the vicinity of the couch, Jay had set up an easel (presently unoccupied by a canvas) and another wooden table layered in squeezed-out tubes of paint, jars of ratty brushes and crusted palette knives. The long wall across from the window wall was covered with small unframed square canvases that at first looked like monochromatic color field paintings, one black, one brown, one deep gray, and so on, although as Robbie's eyes adjusted, he could see they were more complex. The darker colors had been painted over grids of brighter hues, although not completely, and here and there cadmium lines of orange and red, electric blues and greens, all very fine-lined, emerged, suggesting a hidden heat source.

Robbie sat down on edge of the couch, and Jay was saying this or that—Robbie was finding it difficult to concentrate. Eventually Jay sat down on the couch, too, handing a Robbie a mug of black soap-scented tea.

Two differences. One: Jay didn't look battered like Tom did nor scratched up like he'd been in a fight. And two: Jay was blond and Tom had been a brunette with a only a few blond streaks when he first appeared.

"How are you doing now?" Jay asked, half standing and tucking his right foot under his left thigh, sitting again.

A brief curtain of steam off the tea gave Robbie cover. He stared at the open map but couldn't identify the featured peninsula by its shape alone.

"Tom told me I should be embarrassed I didn't have a world atlas handy," Jay said. "Everyone should have a world atlas handy, and also he was appalled I didn't properly stock my pantry, not—as you can see—that I have a pantry, and not that I'm sure I would know what a properly stocked one looks like. After my Tom weeks, once I started working at the bookstore, I used my employee discount to buy this atlas and now I can lose half a Saturday flipping through the maps— What's wrong?"

"Jay, you look like Tom. Am I crazy? You look an awful lot like Tom."

Jay tipped his head to the side (like Tom), and threw off a giggle (like Tom).

"My friends called me a narcissist, dating him," Jay said, "and I told Tom that, and Tom being Tom went and got his hair dyed so we'd look even *more* alike. Actually he dyed his own hair with something store-bought, and it came out white. You wouldn't have recognized him. He looked more like a ghost of himself."

Robbie set his mug down on the floor and crossed the room to get a better look at Jay's paintings. He studied an umber canvas, umber mostly but not entirely covering patches of viridian, that looked like a plot of rural fields as seen from a plane.

"It's pretentious but my idea was to start out with a pencil sketch of someone on the canvas, and then build up color, the color of the clothing the guy was wearing, his complexion, and so forth, and then add the colors I felt as though the person was throwing off, layering fields over that, until you have the final painting," Jay said.

"A mood portrait," Robbie said.

"You're looking at Tom. He reminded me of an old growth forest. I guess I thought he'd be happier living in a cottage in the woods, a hermit. Like I said, it was a pretentious project."

"No, I get it," Robbie said and turned back toward Jay, startled once again even though Jay was more Jay and less Tom now. "I like your work," Robbie said, which he did.

"I haven't painted much lately."

"Because of Tom's criticism."

"No. Maybe. No. Well, he was right, or it's not so much I'm a dilettante as I don't really stay with anything."

"Neither did Tom, I'm told," Robbie said and sat back down on the couch, his knee under his leg the way Jay was sitting.

"If it weren't for Tom though, I probably wouldn't be apply-ing to grad schools," Jay said.

"Oh? For what?"

"I can't decide. I'm choosing between art, geology, and library science."

"That's a good range," Robbie said, trying to sound encour-aging. And then he asked, "So you really don't think it could have been an accident? Tom only goofing around? Tom tempting fate?"

Jay didn't appear to want to contradict whatever Robbie be-lieved. "I can't imagine what that was like for you," Jay said, "find-ing him. And to be alone in that situation."

Once again Robbie opted not to correct him.

"But you think it was deliberate," Robbie pushed. "You're convinced. Did the police ask you about all this, too?"

"They did, and I'm sorry to disagree, but I think a rope is pretty deliberate. I don't think he was playing games."

"I'm convinced now, too," Robbie said. "I don't want to be, but …"

He recalled the horror story Tom told by the fire that night. Your kid or your eyes. Robbie formed a visor with his thumb and forefinger, shielding his brow as if the lamplight were the sun dur-ing an eclipse. Abruptly he began to sob.

Jay slid across the couch so he could pull Robbie toward him awkwardly. This wasn't right, Robbie thought, they didn't know each other but then, two surprises: one, he wasn't all that embar-rassed to be losing it so openly in Jay's apartment—and two, the way Jay held Robbie, he exhibited unexpected strength for some-one as thin as he was, and Robbie didn't want him to let go. But Robbie stopped crying and pulled away and, even if it may have been unnecessary, he apologized for his outburst.

"I'm sorry," he said. "I don't know you."

"You do now," Jay said.

He crossed the room to the writing table and shuffled through what looked like sheet music, although what he withdrew to show Robbie was Tom's charcoal drawing. Robbie noted the way Tom had captured Jay's veiny forearms and hands, the same veiny forearms and hands now holding the broad page. In the sketch, Jay was reclining on his couch with one leg up on the cushions, the other knee bent, his foot on the floor, fingers laced behind his head, gleefully nude, which made Robbie blush. In the corner of the page was Tom's familiar all-caps declarative signature: TOM FIELD, period. And after the signature, a date from last April.

The uphill walk home wore out Robbie, especially given how windy it had become. It was late, the far edge of dusk. He wanted to make it inside and collapse, but Carlo was home and out front, kneeling, tending to the plum sapling closest to the street. Robbie didn't want Carlo to see he'd been crying, but if Carlo noticed, he didn't comment, perhaps because he was preoccupied. The skinny trunk of the tree had snapped halfway up, revealing a blond youthful pith, and the purple bough dangled upside down over Carlo's shoulder. The sapling was partially uprooted, too, and pulled away from its stake, although the trunk hadn't been completely severed.

Then Robbie noticed that a second tree next to the first had also had been snapped, also uprooted.

"What happened?" he asked.

"I found them like this," Carlo said. "Your car is here—where were you?" he asked—he seemed especially upset. "Walking around the Reservoir?"

"Yeah, around the Reservoir," Robbie said. "These poor trees."

"I know," Carlo said, he winced.

The two damaged saplings looked liked a pair of beaten mendicants, stooped over, each extending an open palm without great hope.

"This wind," Robbie said. "It's crazy."

"This *wind*?"

"Wind, yes. Why, what do you think happened?"

Carlo grasped the fractured bough and stood, trying to lift it back into place.

"Maybe we can tie the trunks together where they splintered and they'll, I don't know, self-graft," he said.

When he let the tree fall back, the wood cracked deeper along the break.

"Who the fuck would do this?" he asked.

"*Who*?" Robbie asked. "You're saying it wasn't the wind."

"Oh, come on. The wind snapped *both* of these trees?"

Robbie looked out at the street and sighed.

"Someone came along and tugged up the stakes and lifted up his boot against the trunk," Carlo said, "and the trees gave—"

"Seriously?"

"Robbie. This is not the work of the wind."

"Nor an axe," Robbie argued.

"I didn't say an axe, I said a boot."

"Honey, I don't think so—"

"I warned you we'd have more trouble. First the trash, now this—although this," Carlo said, gripping the tree, "this is much more callous."

A terrier sauntered by out on the street, long-leashed, the dog walker far behind. The walker paused a moment and stared at the broken trees but didn't engage the two men, as if they might be in the middle of a marital spat that had gotten out of hand.

"You don't see a pattern," Carlo said.

"The trash was a month ago. I don't see a pattern," Robbie said.

"The wind?"

"Why would anyone target us? What have we done?"

The pepper tree was agitated by an uneasy draft. There was a thickening mist in the air. Carlo knelt again and tried to tamp the root ball back in the soil.

"Maybe I can save them," he said. "Saw the trunks at the break, hope they stand the shock. Maybe there will be new buds, branches. What?"

"You're not serious," Robbie said.

"It can't hurt to try," Carlo said.

"I mean that because Tom killed himself at our house, you and I are now somehow undesirable and—what—need to be scared out of the neighborhood?"

Carlo pressed his palms flat against the soil. The knees of his jeans were damp. "There are six trees here and someone picked on two," he said.

"This is crazy talk."

"A tree for each of us."

"That's absurd. That's crazy paranoid talk. Why would anyone do that?"

"I don't know, to threaten us like you said—I don't know."

Some neighbor children carrying instrument cases wandered past the house. They lingered longer than the dog walker.

Robbie was too tired to argue. However, he could see that Carlo was not himself, and so Robbie tried to be kind and said, "Look, you know more about trees than I do, so do whatever you think will work. If you can save them, sure, then it's worth a shot." And then he went in the house.

THE NEXT MORNING, he was aware of Carlo moving through his routine and leaving the house. Robbie pulled a pillow over his head and pretended to sleep, then fell back asleep. It was eleven when he got out of bed, and when he did, he had the sense something was wrong, that some extra warmth had been added to the air, as if an intruder had entered, watched him sleep, and left. He stepped out into the hallway and avoided the floorboards that creaked and approached the guest room warily, its door ajar, and peeked into the room. Nothing looked amiss. He turned to the main room and the furniture stood where the furniture always stood, the couches, the coffee table, the piano as ever, unplayed. The bookshelves were neat, the dining chairs symmetric around the table. He went into the kitchen and the only evidence of life was some crumbs on the counter from Carlo's breakfast. Robbie turned back and looked out at the patio. He went so far as to stand at the sliding door but didn't go outside. A low-slung breeze caught the brush running down the slope of their property, sending the tea bush and sage into ecstatic prayer.

Usually the sky was a paler blue than the Reservoir, a grayer blue, but today it was different. The daytime sky was two shades darker than the daytime lake, pressing against the lake with new weight. Or maybe it was not the case that today the sky and lake were different fields than the day or days before, not the case that the landscape had changed, but rather that Robbie was seeing what he could have seen all along and never did.

Fire is fire, Tom said, and he would probably look at Robbie now and say, A lake is a lake. Tom would tell him the world as Robbie wanted it to be was not the world as it was. The world as it was was what he now needed to see.

So he thought about the two damaged plum trees in front, and he honestly did not believe anyone was out to get them, not that he necessarily thought the wind was the sole culprit, not that he had an explanation. But more troubling to him this morning than the vandalism itself was Carlo's reaction. Why had he immediately read a pattern of malice and, without hesitation or doubt, connected the trash on the lawn with the snapped trunks? Did he have a special reason to be suspicious? What was he not saying?

Not for a moment these last weeks that Robbie was aware of had Carlo paused to dwell on why Tom killed himself. Maybe Carlo simply didn't want to know or care. That was what Robbie had assumed, but now what Detective Michaels said was beginning to eat at him—a long marriage, sometimes there were secrets—and for the first time, Robbie was considering another possibility: perhaps Carlo did not *need* to ask the ultimate question about Tom because, in fact, Carlo knew something all along that he'd kept to himself.

Robbie wasn't sure what he was looking for when he pulled open Carlo's night table drawer. There were Carlo's sleeping pills and a never-worn, tarnished silver bracelet, some euros in a money clip, lotion, his passport. His mother's watch, her wedding ring. A pocket moleskin journal. Robbie knew better. He definitely knew better, but he slid aside the black elastic band, and turned to the last page of writing, expecting to find what, he wasn't sure. He found nothing because Carlo hadn't made an entry in over a year.

He put everything back where it was and shame alone should have halted him there, but he kept going and rifled through their dresser, specifically through Carlo's sock drawer, his underwear, his old T-shirts, nothing. He looked through Carlo's side of closet, slipping his hand in and out of trouser pockets. He looked behind the old tennis rackets, even in the ankle boots Carlo rarely wore—nothing, but then what did he think he'd find? A billet-doux? Questionable credit card receipts? A hidden diary in round, unfaithful cursive? He was being silly, and what he was up to was absolutely wrong, and yet he couldn't shake his suspicion that Carlo was hiding something from him.

In the foyer closet, Carlo's coats, the velvet-lined pockets, nothing. Amid his cookbooks, nothing but the usual bookmarks. Back to the guest room, which Robbie rarely had set foot in since Tom stayed the night, the guest closet: Amid the extra pillows and blankets, nothing. There were file boxes, taped since the last move, the seals unbroken. He looked in the built-in linen closet in the hall, slipping his hand into the stack of sheets and pillowcases. The extra toiletries, a basket of hotel loot, nothing. He opened the smaller second cabinet built-in above the lower one, and there on the left per usual was the book box packed his grandfather's tin toy soldiers, which had some value but which Robbie had never had the heart to pawn. There on the right was Carlo's wooden art supply kit with all the tubes of oil paints he no longer used. Nothing was disturbed, nothing out of place.

Robbie had reason to be embarrassed. Carlo was the most remarkably reliable man Robbie had ever known or would ever meet. On the one hand, he wanted to atone for his temporary loss of faith and go buy his lover a box of dark chocolates. What's this for? Carlo would ask and Robbie would answer, No reason, signor, an early Valentine. And yet, he couldn't help it, his suspicion lingered. He needed to get out of the house to clear his head.

A dense piano étude emanating from Jay's apartment stopped when Robbie knocked.

"Hey," Jay said cheerfully. He had on the same jeans as the day before, although today he was wearing a faded blue T-shirt, ripped along his collarbone.

"Sorry to disturb you," Robbie said.

"No, it's cool," Jay said.

Robbie took one step inside and said, "I want to thank you for yesterday."

Jay flapped his hand, think nothing of it.

"No," Robbie said, "listen, thank you." ·

Jay dug his hands in his pockets, which had the effect of pulling his jeans lower down his waist and revealing a sliver of underwear.

"If you're not too busy …" Robbie started to say.

He glanced down at the floorboards and noticed two dark nail heads, close together, serpent eyes staring back.

"If you're not too busy, can I buy you coffee?"

4

THERE WAS NEVER ANY QUESTION in Carlo's mind that whoever had thrown the trash around the yard had come back to commit another act of vandalism, this time to do more harm, and no matter Robbie's denial—what kind of wind could partially uproot the saplings *and* their stakes *and* snap the trunks!— the near-felling of two trees was unambiguously symbolic: two broken trees, two broken men.

In the morning he tried again to lift a fractured bough back in place, wondering what magical regrafting might occur were he to secure the split wood at the break. He was kidding himself. He retrieved the handsaw from the garage, got down on his knees, and pressed the roots of the tree back in the earth, patting down the mud into a berm, all the while trying to hold the trunk steady. He began sawing the trunk beneath the break, but it had rained overnight, making the bark slippery, and he could see he was doing more harm than good, not so much cutting through the wood as scarring it. He tried again at a different angle because he thought maybe if he cut the trunk cleanly, and the roots were reestablished, then the tree might survive the shock and continue to grow and eventually develop new buds, which would yield new branches, and with proper nurturing, one day the tree might look no different than its siblings.

For about fifteen minutes, this was a potent fantasy. However, he couldn't saw the tree the way he wanted, and also, the root ball was more disturbed than he was admitting. He told himself he was doing the right thing when he went back to the garage for a shovel, and dug at the roots and uprooted the sapling (which proved to be more of a chore than he'd imagined), and dragged the ruined thing around to the side of the house, out of sight. Then he went at the second tree and removed it, as well. He kicked what mud he could into the cone-shaped craters where the trees had stood.

The yard work had been messy and he had to take a second shower of the morning, and meanwhile Robbie slept, which maybe was best. Carlo didn't want to talk about the plum trees, he didn't want to argue about where to lay blame, and while Robbie's inability to perceive a blatant threat was infuriating, Carlo also didn't want to drift back into conversation that would bleed into a larger meditation on Tom—blessedly, Tom hadn't come up at all recently, and Carlo wanted to keep it that way. It was better not to involve Robbie and handle things on his own, and besides, any further back-and-forth about why anyone would harass them was pointless: action was required.

All morning at his desk, he pondered what to do, and one thought was to drive over to the nursery and pick up two new saplings. Like whitewashing graffiti the morning after it was sprayed (not that they had done anything about the tagged trash bins), they would get the new trees in the ground immediately so that whoever was attacking them would see that the two men refused to be intimidated. But then planting new trees, a kind of digging in (as it were), could be perceived the wrong way. Challenged thus, the vandals might be inspired to attack once more. Another thought was to call the police, but Carlo didn't want the police up at the house again anytime soon, and anyway, he'd already disturbed the scene of the crime. He would need to pursue his own leads, and he did have one idea.

He marched across the street to the liquor store, where Lonny was minding the register. No one else was in the store and Carlo stood at the counter, tapping his fingertips, until Lonny managed to lift his head from his motorcycle magazine and ask, "Help you?"

"Well, yes actually, Lonny," Carlo said, "yes," and he recognized he was starting off at too sharp a pitch. "Perhaps you can."

Lonny made a sour-fruited face.

"You see, we've had a couple of incidents up at our house," Carlo said. "You know our house, don't you? Of course, you do. Well, first there was garbage thrown all over our front lawn, and then yesterday, someone took an axe to *two* of our plum trees."

Lonny looked over his shoulder, toward the back room.

"Or maybe it wasn't an axe," Carlo said, and he couldn't help himself, he was getting louder. "Maybe *someone* snapped each tree against his boot," he said, "one then the other. Robbie says it was the wind, but I seriously doubt that."

Carlo stared at Lonny—Lonny stared back at Carlo.

"Why are you asking me?" Lonny finally asked.

"Because you're the top dog on the block," Carlo said. "I've seen you give the other kids rides, cigarettes—who knows what else."

The phrase "who knows what else" did not appear to sit well with Lonny. "I don't know what you're talking about, Mr. Stein," he said and returned to his magazine.

Carlo knew he was approaching the matter entirely the wrong way but couldn't correct his tone. "I am asking you, Lonny, who you think might be behind this nastiness up at our house. What can you tell me, Lonny? What do your sources say?"

Again the sour face, a cover—he did know something, and Carlo was not going to stand there while this dumb-ass punk pretended he had no clue what Carlo was talking about.

Lonny looked up and asked, "Do you need to buy something?"

"I need you tell me who is trying to scare us," Carlo said.

"Can't help you out there," Lonny said.

"Can't help me out."

"Look—"

"I think you can."

"I don't know who is messing with you, okay?"

"Oh, so you would agree someone *is* messing with us."

Lonny didn't respond and glanced over his shoulder again, like he hoped a buddy would emerge and then Lonny would ask, Can you believe this asshole? What a freak.

Carlo reached across the counter and with both hands grabbed Lonny's flannel shirt, pulling him forward.

Lonny blinked, startled.

"Tell whoever it is to lay off," Carlo said.

"What the fuck," Lonny shouted.

"And while we're at it," Carlo said, "whatever business you've got going with Gabriel, it needs to stop right now."

"What the fuck are you talking about?"

"Forget about whatever he owes you—"

"Let go of me."

"I said, forget about—"

"Let go."

Carlo looked at his fistfuls of Lonny's shirt.

"Jesus. Shit. Whatever," Lonny said when Carlo released him.

Carlo took a step back. "Sorry," he said.

"What*ever*," Lonny mumbled, blushing.

Another young guy, this one wearing an apron, emerged from the back room. He was holding a case of beer. He asked, "You okay, Lon?"

Lonny seemed more flustered than irate. The redness of his fists made him look like he was wearing mittens.

"Sorry," Carlo said again and waved his hand in the air, Peace, as he turned and left.

"I don't know what the fuck you're talking about," Lonny said. "Fucking weirdo."

Out on the street, Carlo was shaking. He needed a glass of wine, or to take a sleeping pill, several pills and sleep a year. What had come over him? What was he doing? Who did he think he was?

HE DIDN'T HAVE MUCH TIME TO RECOVER. Given the holiday traffic, he needed to head out to the airport right away, but at least he was able to channel his anxiety elsewhere when his father did not appear among the other first-class passengers from New York making their way toward baggage claim carousel number two. Carlo stood as close as he could to the down-escalator and suffered his usual frustration at not being able to greet his octogenarian father at the gate in this, the new security age. Silver-haired men bobbed among the passengers and were greeted by family, half of them still wearing their overcoats or parka vests, but none in tweed or camel's hair, none sporting a ribboned fedora tipped at a jaunty angle.

Carlo saw his father only a few times a year and never knew what to expect. Would he finally look frail? Would his light blue eyes, always darting this way and that, suddenly reveal less acuity? Would he still be able to solve the crossword in ink in about the time it took to twist apart, spread almond butter across, and eat his morning croissant?

Lo and behold, Henry Stein emerged at the top of the escalator, his hair as white as his pocket square, his overcoat a cape. The brim of his felt hat ran parallel to the slope of his nose. He did appear to be walking with some difficulty, talking to a woman around Carlo's age and leaning into her for support. The woman in turn held the hand of a young girl, who dragged a child-size backpack with some kind of fuchsia animal-doll creature affixed. Carlo's father's suit looked loose on him. He did not appear to be scanning the crowd for his son—the woman had his complete attention. However, when the escalator had borne him all the way down, he stepped off the disappearing tread with an agile skip, one step ahead of the woman so he could help her disembark. Carlo realized his father wasn't leaning on the woman and that it was the other way around, she relying on him.

"Hi, son," his father said to Carlo and clutched his arm (with a fit grasp) and kissed him. Then, adoringly, he gripped the back of his son's neck, his cold wedding band sending a shiver down Carlo's spine. "Hi, hi," his father said, and despite their continental drift, Carlo was aware the old man loved him.

Carlo's father introduced the woman. "Her poor silly foot, you see, fell asleep over the Rockies and never woke up."

"My first mistake was taking off these shoes," the woman said. "I could barely get them back on. Your father has been telling me about all the houses you've built all over Los Angeles."

"All over," Carlo echoed. "My father tends to exaggerate."

His father said to the woman, "You should see them, all glass. Glass, glass, glass, like it's going out of style."

"It sort of has," Carlo said.

"I love the term the realtors use to describe these houses," his father said. "Son, what do they call them in their listings?"

"Architectural," Carlo said.

"Ha," his father said.

The woman smiled politely and said good-bye as her daughter tugged her toward the baggage carousel.

"She is some kind of university professor," Carlo's father said. "What did she call her field, comparative geographies? She's lovely, but the daughter is a little alien. What? You should have seen the thumbs on this girl, playing some mindless electronic game the whole flight. Would it have been too much to ask she open a book for an hour?"

"No luggage?" Carlo asked, and relieved his father of one suede carry-on, weighted by, Carlo imagined, a bestseller, walking shoes, one change of clothes, and toiletries.

"You know me," his father said, and they headed for the car.

As they worked their way through the airport traffic, Carlo asked if his father had completed the new acquisition he'd talked about weeks ago when they last spoke. He had. The drawing was especially unusual. It was Dutch, of course, another church interior, more graffiti in the nave. Yet the shadows were exquisite, the varying expressions of the churchgoers …

Henry Stein had come to the States from Germany in 1946, having floated around Europe for a year after the liberation. He was able to make some connections in New York, had limited family resources he could tap, which he parlayed into a minor fortune distributing medical supplies. Carlo was a late child and by the time he was born, his father had already sold the company and worked part-time as a consultant, mostly devoting himself to collecting art. Sunday brunch chez Stein became a salon for local and visiting scholars, who would inspect the latest procurement and then enjoy bagels and lox and a smidgen of sturgeon. For a while, Carlo's father was a dealer, as well, working out of their apartment, and Carlo remembered their dining room (lined with drawing cabinets) after his father had seen a client and retrenched to his study: The crumpled white gloves on the table, the magnifying glass askew in its velvet box. The empty cordial glasses, the tart rueful smell of sherry.

"But I may flip it," his father said.

"Sorry?" Carlo asked.

"You weren't listening."

"Yes, I was."

"I was saying my group and I, we're thinking of going in on a twenty-by-thirty ice-scape. On canvas. It comes up in London next month."

"You'd part with a new drawing so soon?"

"You have a point," Carlo's father said. "That's unlikely."

They coasted down the highway in silence and didn't say

much again until they were back on surface streets, as if speaking on the freeway was unsafe.

"You've lost weight," Henry said.

"I don't think so," Carlo said.

"You're trying to lose it or busy running around?"

"I weigh the same I weighed the last time you saw me," Carlo insisted.

"Weight loss in young men—"

"I'm fine."

"Son, is it stress?"

"Everything is fine, Dad," Carlo said, although he probably had lost weight—he'd not been paying attention.

His father gazed out the car window. Los Angeles had a way of making him sigh slowly and frequently, as if breath were being drawn from him like a tire leaking air through an imperceptibly tiny puncture. In less than forty-eight hours, he would be gone, Carlo consoled himself. He needed to pace himself. Two days he could do, two days was nothing.

They arrived home at the same time Robbie appeared to be returning from a walk, yet another walk around the lake, Carlo figured.

His father greeted Robbie in the driveway: "My true son!" he shouted, and two days seemed like a very long time.

To Robbie, Henry had seemed old for twenty years. Spry and sharp and urbane, but white-haired at the same time, coarsebrowed, prone to halitosis. He walked up the front path with a senatorial stride. He did not care for Los Angeles—"So untested as a city"—and he loathed the holiday—"What kind of ersatz palliative history is this Thanks-giving *story* anyway?"—and yet, he was nothing if not a traditionalist, and families saw each other at holidays, and they were still a family, and so, depending upon auction house schedules, the father came West with the proviso the son did not cook a turkey.

Once in the house, Henry unzipped his carry-on and removed several items. About a square bottle of cranberry relish, he said: "This is not the day and age to be seen as unpatriotic—I am an American citizen—long live cranberries!" About the half-pound bag of coffee he produced: "I'm requiring this in the mornings. It contains a measure of cocoa," he said, "which is good for my blood pressure."

"Is that new? You've never had high blood pressure before," Carlo said.

"Well, I don't now because of this coffee curative," Henry replied.

Then he removed a wrapped gift, a book. Usually he brought the two men the biography du jour, but this time what Carlo unwrapped was an exhibition catalogue for a show in New York the two men had missed, a retrospective of an artist who had died the year before and who was an old Stein family friend. The artist-friend began his career in abstract painting but ended up making video installations, which he referred to as paintings kids today would look at.

"That's lovely, Dad," Carlo said. "Thank you."

"Beautiful," Robbie said, leafing through the color plates.

"You know the story," Henry said to Robbie.

"Of course," Robbie said. "It's famous."

Henry told it anyway. One rainy day when Carlo was about four or five, his mother set him up with some art supplies in their kitchen. He sat at the butcher block table and made a series of tempera paintings, a bright zoo of images, and then took them back to his bedroom, where he promptly disobeyed the house rules and used scotch tape to hang his art on the walls. He came out into the living room where the adults, including the artist-friend, were enjoying cocktails and beckoned them into his gallery. He charged a nickel admission and the art was for sale at a quarter per painting, forty cents for the diptych landscape ("It was a tennis court seen from above, not a landscape," Carlo interrupted), and the artist-friend was so amused, he bought the entire show in one swoop.

"I was precocious," Carlo said. "This isn't exactly breaking news."

"But that's not the point," his father said, and continued: The family friend told Henry and his wife in front of young Carlo and then again privately that he thought their boy should be encouraged in his artmaking, that beyond his entrepreneurialism (not to be discounted), he had all the promise of a serious colorist. Note the way Carlo had juxtaposed different shades of the same color, the different weights of green. Note his preference for inebriated blues and lovesick reds—the way he took *risks* with color, that was what was exciting. The artist-friend kept after Carlo's parents until finally they enrolled Carlo in a private art program intended for older children.

"My friend had faith, and he was right," Henry said.

Robbie chuckled appropriately but also glanced sympathet-
ically at Carlo, for the subtext of the story was that Carlo had
given up on painting when he became an architect, which was to
say an applied artist, which for Henry Stein was tantamount to
retail work. The story was not dissimilar to others Robbie had
heard Henry tell over the years, always implying Carlo hadn't
achieved his greatest personhood, and time to time, Robbie found
ways to interrupt and sing Carlo's praises, specifically citing whatever recent project Stein Voight had seen through. But on this
particular occasion, there were no projects to extol, not really, so
no praise was sung.

Robbie patted his jeans pocket and removed his cell phone.
Carlo and his father waited. The phone had beeped and the red light
was flashing. He had a text message. Who sent him text messages?

"Who sends you text messages?" Carlo asked.

It was from Jay. He said he enjoyed their time together—
they'd spent two hours in a café, chattering, two hours that could
have been fifteen minutes. Jay was headed down to his parents'
for the holiday but wanted to know if Robbie was free to hang
out again over the weekend.

"It's nothing," Robbie lied. "A phone company promotion,"
he added and then quickly replied yes to the text. "There. I told
them to go away," Robbie said.

"I do miss that old coot," Henry said, referring to the artist-
friend. "We're dying off, the old gang."

"Now, now," Robbie said.

"Don't you now-now me," Henry said. "It's fine. It may even
be natural. We're here a time, we do what we can, which isn't
much, and then we rot and are forgotten."

One didn't challenge the old man. Robbie had learned this early on in his career as a son-in-law.

"I'm in the guest room?" Henry asked, and headed into the hall with Carlo in tow, although Carlo hesitated at the threshold.

"What is it, son?"

"No one has slept in here since …"

Robbie slipped past Carlo into the room and drew the curtain. Henry sat down on the bed, slid his hand under a pillow.

"It was a vexing episode, no?" he asked.

Both men nodded. They were avoiding each other's gaze, focusing instead on Henry.

"Eerie," Henry said. "Mystifying."

Outside, there were abrupt gusts of wind that rattled the glass. Not a storm approaching, but something of the East Coast early winter brought along with the guest.

Then Carlo looked at Robbie but addressed his father. "Mystifying, definitely. This man, Tom—he said all sorts of things, and who knows if any of it was true."

Robbie wrinkled his brow, What? Why was Carlo saying this—where was this coming from?

"I think he could be trusted just fine," Robbie said.

"You yourself said he was prone to exaggeration," Carlo said.

"No, I didn't."

"Very dramatic, you said."

"Well," Henry said, standing, intervening, "I am always more than happy to be the one to break a curse. And I am quite certain I shall sleep well. Robert, you know how I prefer a martini."

"Yes, sir," Robbie said.

They wore jackets and had their cocktails outside, but it was too chilly to serve dinner on the patio, as well, so they ate à table, a light supper, trout, lentil salad, red wine. The night was cold yet the sky held few stars.

The old man removed the rubber tip from his epee when he drank. His latest diatribe was on the failure of the political parties to effect lasting growth: "I mean boom-or-bust-resistant change. I mean progress irregardless of a fickle Street." Also he held forth on free trade, the admission of certain countries into economic unions, and the ethics of war journalism. Also the use of force by the police. Also how bored he was the other evening at the ballet.

He asked after Robbie's parents and sister and demanded news of them, though there was none of significance.

"We must do that thing where we all meet up in the City," Henry said.

"I'm sure my folks would love that," Robbie said.

"There must be some show on the *Broad*-way they're all dying to see—"

"Dad," Carlo said.

Robbie looked at Carlo to say, It's okay.

"What?" Henry asked. "What?"

Carlo sighed and asked, "Another drink?"

In Germany, Henry Stein had married very young and had a son, and two years later the family was split up and sent to different camps. Henry never again saw this wife or this son, and he also never talked about them or showed anyone photographs (if photographs existed). It wasn't until Carlo's mother was dying and Carlo told her he'd invited over his father who had begged to see her, not until then that Carlo's mother said: "Poor Henry—to lose two wives—poor Henry." Which was how Carlo learned of the existence and demise of his father's first family. He didn't tell Robbie about this the entire first year they knew each other, and whenever Henry was around, the past remained a taboo topic.

Robbie had always wanted to interview his father-in-law about the years between arriving in America and marrying Carlo's mother, about how he found life again and made life again. Was it necessary to avoid remembering his first wife and son, which was why he kept them secret, at least from Carlo when he came along? Or did Henry think about them every day? And what then: If he revealed his secret and spoke about what and whom he'd lost, did he worry that details about them would dissipate in the telling and he would begin to forget them? With each public recollection, his memory would lose a dram more vapor until one day that precious memory was little more than an ethereal fiction.

The old man was arrogant, an elitist, he always had been, but Robbie always read these traits as necessary to a kind of survival he could never fathom. Nevertheless, Robbie knew Carlo tired of his father. How could Henry be so certain about everything? So many opinions. His utter doubtlessness became oppressive. Sometimes Robbie marveled at Carlo for making it through his youth with this man. Whatever had caused Carlo to get riled up about Tom before—Robbie decided to let it go.

Later in bed, he reached his arm around Carlo, and Carlo, as if surprised, as if caught off guard, waited a beat before taking Robbie's hand and pressing it against his, Carlo's, chest. They'd not had sex in a fortnight nor discussed that fact. Then they were facing each other, and Robbie was frisky, but Carlo seemed to want to slow things down. They were off tempo. Carlo nuzzled his cheek against Robbie's neck and shoulder, grateful, and he was on top of Robbie, with Robbie's knees moving up, Robbie's thighs against Carlo's ribs, Robbie's calves against Carlo's back, a familiar story. There was something in the way Carlo stared at Robbie—what?—solicitous, trusting, apologetic. How are you doing there? he was asking. Fine—and you, signor? Quite good at the moment, quite good indeed. And for better or worse they agreed upon a meter, or their bodies did the way bodies do, and they belonged to each other. When they fell back to their respective sides of the bed, Carlo yawned and drifted off first as was the new norm. Robbie was restless and didn't sleep well at all.

NEITHER DID CARLO. His father's presence always made him think about his mother. For a long while after she'd died, Carlo had only been able to conjure her at the end of her life with straw-like hair, half herself, her cheekbones too big for her face, her reading glasses sliding down her nose. Then time passed and when Carlo thought about her, he retrieved a deeper memory, a boyhood nightmare. At a school assembly, a police officer had screened a cautionary film about how to move through the world safely, not talking to strangers, looking both ways before crossing the street, and so forth. At one point in the movie, a woman ran across Fifth Avenue toward the Park and was hit by a taxi. The impact wasn't depicted, only the running into the traffic and the aftermath. What Carlo learned was that apparently one's shoes came off when one was hit by a car. A woman dead in the street, both sneakers yards away from her body—this stayed with him. Carlo's mother was a world-class jaywalker, and so in his dream, Carlo was strolling home from the bus stop when he noticed there had been an accident outside his building, and when he was closer and could see it was his mother lying in the street, he wanted to reach her side where paramedics were attempting resuscitation but first needed to retrieve her favorite black velvet pumps from the gutter. He could actually feel the square heels, one in each palm—he awoke and was gripping the wood rails of the headboard.

Then this nightmare receded, too, and what he thought about when he remembered his mother (what he pictured as he lay awake now) was her at the stove pinching spices from bottles with cork stoppers, stirring bolognese in a sauce pan all across the span of a winter afternoon, opera on the stereo. Carlo had been a reluctant reader and his mother heard about a young-adult serial and got him hooked. Each night after dinner they read passages aloud to each other. A prairie girl, her blind sister, a house roofed with sod. In those days, Carlo told his mother he was going to become a writer and she said, "Wonderful, but don't mention it to your father. You know he believes you should be an artist, or if not an artist, worst case scenario, a concert pianist."

Also he remembered sitting in the backseat of an idling car with his mother behind the wheel. They were out by the train station of the town where they had their country house. His father's train was late and his mother appeared tense, and it was possible she'd been crying, but Carlo couldn't see his mother's eyes behind her dark sunglasses, which she was wearing even though it was past dusk and dark out.

When Carlo, extra-groggy, served his father breakfast Thanksgiving morning and made him his special coffee with the cocoa, Carlo felt as though he'd been conversing with him all night. After breakfast, he showed his father where the new fountain would be, and then the three men took a walk around the Reservoir, even though the wind was brittle. The ever boatless lake looked forbidding, almost icy, a mirror longing for something bright to reflect.

"I come to Los Angeles for this kind of bone-chill," Carlo's father complained.

"Los Angeles heard what you said about her the last time," Robbie said.

"My true son."

When they got home, Carlo sautéed apples for the dressing and set about stuffing the goose. His father removed his cuff links and folded back his shirt sleeves and reached around Carlo to tip the goose so Carlo could finish the task. Henry handed his son skewers and then the string. They worked without chitchat, the one seemingly anticipating the other's next move and stepping aside or handing over what was needed. Carlo rubbing the goose with salt and pepper. Henry piercing the skin with an unused skewer.

Carlo asked Robbie to put on some music, and Robbie chose a requiem. His role as sous-chef had been supplanted, but he hung around the kitchen while Carlo and his father turned their attention to preparing dough for an artichoke-and-pea pie, to baking a chocolate torte. Whatever disdain the old man held for the holiday-like manufacture and consumption of a big late-afternoon meal was not in evidence, and Carlo found himself slipping into a good humor, as well. He winked at Robbie. That they'd made love the night before certainly helped, the recharge of sex. However, Robbie seemed preoccupied, and at one point he touched his pocket, his cell phone going off again. He answered, grinned, said, "Oh, hey, hold on a second," then grabbed a pair of garden shears from a drawer. He didn't say anything

more until he was out on the patio with the door closed behind
him, and then once on the patio, he continued down into the
yard a-ways and out of view.

Carlo glanced at his father. Did this seem strange to him,
Robbie receiving random phone calls on Thanksgiving Day?
No, why would it? What his father didn't know was that Robbie had already spoken with his family back East. Carlo's paranoia flared up. He wondered if the caller in some way was
related to Tom, and if so, what information he or she might be
feeding Robbie. Carlo tried to read Robbie's expression when he
returned a short while later clutching a bundle of tea bush
branches and long sprigs of sage and lavender, which Robbie
then put together in an unwieldy arrangement that was far too
tall as a centerpiece and instead positioned at one end of the
table. His expression: goofy, giddy about something other than
his oversized arrangement.

"Brilliant," Carlo's father said. "The way things grow out
here. Disquieting, but brilliant."

THEY SAT DOWN AT FOUR. There was the goose and its
dressing and the artichoke pie and also zucchini with oregano,
stewed pearl onions and sautéed carrots with fennel—all the
recipes (save the goose) came from Carlo's mother's cookbook.
Robbie played his accustomed role, leaning in toward Carlo's father and nodding at one story or another about some near-miss
with a forgery, feigning shock, even though his father-in-law had
been telling the story for a decade. Robbie kept Henry's goblet
full, served him another sliver of pie. Carlo watched the old man

carve some food on his plate then set down his knife. His fork hand quivered a bit, his browned, hairless hand all blood vessels. Earlier, Carlo had heard his father talking to himself: "You forgot to tell the maid to take the tux to the dry cleaners." "What do you need with another rug in your house? Where will it go?" Ah, maybe he had aged. Maybe he'd lived too much of his life alone.

"The Italians always knew what to do with peas," Henry Stein said, referring to the presence of the peas in the artichoke pie.

"The same could be said about fennel," Robbie said.

"Very true. Oh, my word—"

"Whoa," Carlo said.

Out of nowhere, Gabriel had appeared at the sliding glass door to the back patio. The men hadn't seen him come around back and were startled. Robbie waved him in.

"I didn't mean to interrupt your dinner," Gabriel said.

"Why are you coming in the back?" Carlo asked. "Did you knock in front?"

"I was on my way down to do some work," Gabriel said.

"All by yourself?" Carlo asked.

"It smells good in here," Gabriel said.

"Aren't you with your aunt today? Or your parents?" Robbie asked.

It was obvious the question made Gabriel uncomfortable. "Things didn't work out as planned," was all he said.

"Such pressure," Carlo's father muttered, "to all get along. It's too much really."

"Are you hungry?" Carlo asked. He set Robbie's flowers on the floor.

"I had a cheeseburger," Gabriel said, although he sat down at the table.

Robbie brought him a plate, utensils, and a napkin.

"You remember my father," Carlo said.

"You are looking very much the model of youth today," his father said.

Gabriel seemed uncertain what to make of the comment, although his response was to take off the leather jacket he still had on and drape it over the back of his chair. He filled his plate with food.

"We've been speaking about the Italians," Carlo's father said.

"Them again," Gabriel said.

"What they can do with peas," Robbie said.

"Give peas a chance," Gabriel said.

"Clever," Carlo said.

"Tell us," the old man said. "What does one study in school these days?"

Gabriel was working his way through a drumstick like he hadn't eaten in three days. He blinked at the two men—was he required to answer this question?

Carlo winked back: He's elderly, humor him.

"This is the year everything is American," Gabriel said.

"Heavens," Henry said.

"American history," Gabriel said, "American English."

"American English?" Henry asked.

"I mean in English class, it's all American lit," Gabriel said.

"American biology?" Henry asked.

"Clever," Carlo said.

"Just history and literature," Gabriel said.

"American trigonometry?" Henry asked, trying for a double.

"The history part is decent," Gabriel said.

"History better than literature?" Robbie asked.

"Keeping it real, you mean," Henry said.

"Something like that," Gabriel said.

"Here's what's interesting," Henry said, pushing aside some carrots with the side of his fork as if to clear a place on his plate for whatever was interesting. "I've lived long enough to have read several different accounts of what I lived through, what I experienced firsthand, accounts that contradict each other. The German citizens knew x or y but not z. Then suddenly the German citizens knew perfectly well x *and* y *and* z. I have a point, it's this: *History* has a way of changing, young Gabriel, it isn't fixed. It's no better than memory. And as such, you see, it's as malleable and faulty as the literature you don't prefer."

Gabriel's jaw went slack—he was puzzled.

Carlo was watching his father. He could tell the old man was agitated about something and followed his gaze first to Gabriel's earrings, then to the tattoo on the inside of Gabriel's left forearm.

Robbie walked around the table filling wine glasses.

"Don't forget me," Gabriel said, and Robbie decanted a third of a glass.

"It's a terrible idea," Carlo's father said, "to separate American history from the global rest. What that breeds. The myopia, the jingoism. For the record, I brought the cranberry relish all the way from New York."

"You were born in Germany," Gabriel said, "but you don't have an accent."

Henry nodded and said, "I was twenty-two when I emigrated and worked my tail off to get rid of it. I still avoid phrases like *wagon wheel.*"

"At twenty-two, how did you lose the accent?" Robbie asked.

"I took a class. It was necessary to move forward in business. Jewish or not, I sounded like the enemy."

"Was that really true?" Robbie asked.

"I suppose not. But I wanted to be scared it was the case."

"You *wanted* to be scared?" Gabriel asked.

"It was a better thing to be scared about that than all the other things that disturbed me," Carlo's father said.

Carlo was startled and could see Robbie was, as well. The old man seemed to be broaching the forbidden subject. How much would he allow? He was still carving away at some goose, but Gabriel had stopped eating.

"What was the worst thing you saw there?" the boy asked.

"*There,*" Carlo's father said, mocking.

"I'm not sure that's appropriate, Gabriel," Carlo said.

"*Appropriate,*" his father echoed, riding his son.

"I'm not trying to be disrespectful," Gabriel said.

Carlo's father did not look the boy straight in the eye when he waved his knife toward him and addressed him: "That tattoo of yours, three red stars. Are you now or have you ever been a member of the Communist Party?"

Gabriel was not easy to embarrass, yet with his right hand, he gripped his left forearm and then let go.

"Dad," Carlo said.

"Because, ha, do you know what these stars remind me of?"

"Careful," Robbie whispered. "It's not like he can go in the bathroom and wipe if off."

"They remind me of the neon stars atop all the towers around the Kremlin," Henry said. "Originally there was religious statuary, but of course that had to come down. Don't look so upset, young man—"

"I'm not," Gabriel said.

"Because these neon stars at dusk, they way they hover at the center of the city, it's breathtaking. No really, it is. To Muscovites, it's a warming sight. They see them, they're home. Mother Russia and all that."

Dinner was finished. More wine was drunk, mostly by Carlo's father, although Gabriel slipped in a little more and no one stopped him. The topic changed to tennis, which the old man still managed to play in the country and which was the only sport he'd ever followed. He longed for a return to wood rackets and serve-and-volley and tournaments on grass. The chocolate torte was oohed at and served.

Carlo's father was holding his wine glass an inch above the table, twisting it around, swirling his wine.

"Tell me, young man," he said to Gabriel. "What's the worst thing *you've* ever seen?"

"Henry," Robbie started to say, "I'm not sure this is the best—"

"People holding hands and jumping out of the burning skyscrapers," Gabriel said. "I still can't get it out of my head."

"But you didn't actually *see* that," Carlo's father said, "did you?"

"On television," Gabriel said.

"For some reason, his sitter at the time thought it completely appropriate for a nine-year-old to watch the coverage," Carlo said.

"You're very hung up on what's appropriate, son," his father said. "Did I raise you to be so concerned with decorum?"

"Yes, actually," Carlo said.

"I have this nightmare," Gabriel said, swept along in his own associations, "where I'm in a burning skyscraper, except it's here, downtown, and the fire is getting closer and closer, and the windows are all blown out, and I have to decide whether I'm going to jump or not."

"That's terrible," Robbie said.

"Not really though," Gabriel said. "Because I end up jumping and it's—I don't know—it's crazy, it's fun, I'm out of breath, I can't breathe at all. It's a total high. I mean, you know, it's not like I splatter—I wake up before that. But on the way, I'm this human kite."

Carlo's father hummed. To Gabriel, he said, "The comparison, one atrocity to another, is a faulty rope bridge, son, we shouldn't ever walk across."

Once again Gabriel didn't understand the old man.

"It's better," Henry suggested, "that we think about root causes, eh? Where all this hatred comes from, no? You don't get at that in school, do you? No, of course not, not during your American year."

"I don't know," the boy said. "All I can say is I have that nightmare a lot for a month, and then not at all. Then it comes back. It's not really a nightmare. If I know I'm dreaming, I try to make it happen."

Gabriel was having some kind of bad family day. Carlo and Robbie traded glances: What to say to make him feel better?

"Mr. Stein," Gabriel said. "I've noticed that you wear a wedding ring, but I thought Carlo told me you weren't married."

"Gabriel," Robbie said.

"Let the lad speak, for pete's sake," Henry said. "You're perceptive. The ring is especially strange given that Carlo's mother and I were no longer together when she died twenty-four years ago. We never divorced but we were headed that way when she fell ill."

"I see," Gabriel said, his voice small.

"But I hadn't gotten used to the idea that we were not going to be together, which was largely due to my—what?—my *excesses*, and so I hadn't yet removed my wedding band."

Henry turned the ring once around his finger.

Carlo slumped back in his chair. He pictured his mother sitting at the kitchen table, her unfiltered cigarette unattended in an ashtray, the broken spine of the Italian text she was translating, a blank pad in front of her—his mother staring out the window at the airshaft, at a fluttering pigeon, at nothing.

"First of all, she was beautiful," Henry said. "A curtain of dark hair like Carlo's, which one would find her invariably sweeping back with her hand—like so—one side then the other, combing all that hair behind her ears, which was futile because it would only cascade back across her brow. Then she was astonishingly quick—what a mind. She was working as a translator when I met her. She could read Carlo in a way I never could. I'm sorry, son, but it's true."

Carlo managed a wan grin. For twenty-four years, his grief came and went, came and went according to a tide with no almanac. What kind of friendship would he have had with his mother, if she had lived? Close, his mother as his diurnal confidant—but of course, it was impossible to know. What if his mother discovered the truth about her son, that he was a betrayer and a secret-keeper like his father—would she still love Carlo then? If she knew how Carlo had behaved the night Tom died—she'd disapprove, wouldn't she? Her disappointment would be crushing.

"She was a saint. Santa Giulietta, I called her," Henry said, again twisting the gold band on his left hand. "I enjoy thinking about her, it *calms* me. Yet I broke her heart. I regret that profoundly and hope that she forgave me."

Carlo knew he could say that of course his mother did, but he chose to remain silent. The house became still, very still.

Gabriel turned toward the old man. "Do you believe in ghosts?" he asked.

"Ghosts?" Henry Stein asked back.

"Gabriel has seen a ghost of his late dog wandering around," Carlo said.

"I'm just asking," Gabriel said.

"I can't say I do," Henry said, but then he changed his mind: "Or maybe yes. Maybe I believe people have a way of hanging around after they're dead."

Gabriel chuckled.

"What?" Henry asked. "Oh dear. Poor word choice, eh?"

"So you wear your wedding ring so Mom can see it," Carlo said.

"I wouldn't go that far," his father said.

"That's interesting," Robbie said.

"Oh, *very* interesting," Carlo said.

Robbie was glaring at him, signaling him to be nicer, but Robbie didn't get it, never got it, and so Carlo glared back. Then he noticed that Gabriel was watching him, watching the two men closely. And Gabriel became fidgety, tapping his thumbs against his placemat.

"I suppose then I don't believe in ghosts like you mean ghosts," Henry said to the boy, "but I believe in haunting."

"There's a difference?" Gabriel asked.

Carlo's father stroked a patch of gray scruff. Everyone was looking at him, waiting for him to be wise.

"Do you mean something within as opposed to something observed?" Robbie asked, he tried to help.

Still the old man didn't speak.

"It's okay, Dad," Carlo said, gentler now.

"No," his father said, addled it seemed, "no."

"Anyway," Gabriel said.

"A haunting *presence*. Very solid, very troubling …"

Again the table waited for the old man to elaborate, but he merely sighed and raised his wine glass to his lips with a quaking hand.

"I don't know what I think," he said. "I have absolutely no idea what I think. Ghosts. Oh, why the hell not? Why not?"

The conversation continued—tennis may have been discussed again, music, the boy's preference in music—but Carlo didn't participate. He was shocked. He'd never seen his father hesitate to render his verdict on any subject. After the boy left, Robbie cleared the table and Carlo made a fire. His father slipped off his shoes and with some difficulty hoisted one foot, then the other up on the coffee table. The old man was old. He'd been left out of sorts.

"That boy," he said when the two men returned to the couch. He tapped his sleeve with his finger. He said, "I don't understand *who* would allow a child to burn a tattoo on the inside of his forearm, to brand anything there."

He'd had his own mark removed from his arm, leaving a scar in the shape of a caterpillar.

"It's obscene," he said. "Does anyone *not* know what it conjures? Does it *not* matter to anyone anymore? Shouldn't there be some kind of moratorium on tattoos on the inside of anyone's forearms for at least a hundred years? Please. Tell me. Am I all alone in thinking this? Obscene."

THE NEXT MORNING when Carlo stepped out to get the paper, he saw something hanging from a low branch of the pepper tree, but he did not understand at first what he was looking at. There was a white nylon rope and then what appeared to be a tattered flannel shirt hanging from the rope, the blue-and-green fabric damp with dew. When he did understand, Carlo beckoned Robbie out to the stoop. His father came out, as well.

It was Henry who said, "It's an effigy."

"It is?" Robbie asked. "An effigy of whom?"

"Who do you think?" Carlo snapped.

The shirt was limp like a flag without wind, and not packed with anything to give it body. There was nothing corporeal about it whatsoever, and no person obviously mocked.

"Wait. How is it an effigy?" Robbie asked.

"Dad, it's cold. Maybe you should go inside," Carlo said.

"Savage," his father responded, shaking his head.

"I don't see it," Robbie said. "It's a shirt. On a rope. It's weird, but …"

Carlo rubbed his eyes. "How can you *not* see it?" he asked, exasperated.

His father intervened. "Because of that business. You know, Robert. With your acquaintance."

Robbie walked across the wet lawn in bare feet to the tree and pulled at the shirt and rope. In three tugs, the knot gave and the whole thing fell to the ground. Robbie picked it up. The shirt had been fitted over what appeared to be a partly deflated tetherball, the kind one found in a schoolyard.

"Savage," Henry said again, and the old man was pale. He didn't like this at all, not one bit.

"It's not helpful to exaggerate, Dad. Go have your coffee."

"So you're saying this is Tom," Robbie said. He lifted the rope in the air, drawing up the shirted ball. "A headless, legless Tom?"

"I'm not saying it's Tom exactly," Carlo said. "But it's a hanged man. Because people hang themselves at our house, and someone thinks that's funny."

"This sort of thing," his father said but didn't add more.

"If that's true, it would be really cruel," Robbie said, "really low."

"Low, I agree," Carlo said, and he took the shirt and tethered ball from Robbie and chucked it into one of the still-tagged trash bins.

Robbie stood on the front path, hands on his hips, scowling.

"We can talk about it later," Carlo said to him. "Dad?"

"It's so unnecessary," his father said. "The thought, the creativity, if you want to call it that, the *expression*. So wasted on absolutely nothing."

"Come on, Dad," Carlo said, passing his father on the way in the house. "You have your plane."

Robbie went in, as well, but the old man remained on the stoop a moment longer, gazing at the pepper tree as if he saw something else hanging from its limbs.

CARLO HAD DRIVEN HIS FATHER most of the way to the airport before his father spoke: "It's these idle children with too much time on their hands," he said. "No place in this world."

Carlo gripped the top of the steering wheel with both hands.

"Last spring," he said, "I was driving back from a dinner party. I was alone because Robbie was home sick. Two guys rushed my car at a stoplight."

His father shifted in the passenger seat. Carlo told him most of the rest, although not about meeting Tom at the police station, none of that or what followed.

"Son," his father said. "You told me it was an accident."

They had entered the airport and were working their way around the horseshoe of terminals. Carlo signaled and maneuvered toward the curb.

"When I made it home later, Robbie was already asleep," he said, "and the next morning I didn't tell him. I never told you, I never told him."

His father bit his lower lip.

"You've been through an awful lot lately," he said, "haven't you?"

Carlo put the car in park.

"I don't know. Maybe," he said.

"Maybe? I should say so," his father said.

His furrowed brow was easy to read: Why was his son giving him this news right as they were about to part company? In doing so, Carlo was being unkind. He got out of the car and grabbed his father's bag from the backseat along with his hat and helped the old man out of the passenger's side, waiting while his father smoothed back his hair with his palm and threw his overcoat over his arm and took the bag, the hat.

Father and son stood there a moment. A plane lifted off. Henry gripped Carlo's arm. It was clear he didn't want to leave him, not like this.

"Dad, your flight," Carlo said.

His father kissed him on each cheek and a second time on the left before moving toward the automatic doors and heading off, turning once to wave. Carlo leaned against the car.

When they were alone in the kitchen that night, Tom had said, "And yet you believe all there is is the ground beneath your feet. Nothing more than that? That's it?"

Maybe their house was cursed, maybe Gabriel was on the right track. Ghosts of beloved dogs, of sad young men rambled around Silver Lake. Tom as a ghost strewing trash; phantom Tom hacking the plum trees; Tom the poltergeist taunting them with a minimalist effigy. Tom was behind the pranks, insisting in some spectral way that finally he be understood for who he was, in trouble, lonesome: unseen.

If only he could subscribe to something alongside hard science, Carlo thought, a complementary unempirical system that made working sense of the proofless: Against what was known, faith in the balance. To find a place for skepticism or doubt or cosmic ambivalence was a yearning as fast-spun, unexpected, and perplexing as any Carlo had suffered that autumn, and for one brief moment, the mere prospect of belief and, perhaps more significantly, the prospect of commune with others holding belief, left him light.

"Sir," an airport police officer on a motorcycle said. "You can't park here. You'll need to move your car, sir."

A plane descended toward the airport, lumbering, hesitant, as if it had hoped to remain airborne longer and landing were a defeat.

HE DID NOT HEAD STRAIGHT HOME because he did not believe in ghosts or restless spirits. He believed in real people, unknown but real, their malevolence real. Even though he hadn't been back since May, he found the place near the airport easily enough, the acre of a parking lot, the store itself as unremarkable as any in the city except that there was an armed guard posted out front who opened and closed the door for each customer.

Carlo made his way through the racks of rifles and hunting gear and approached the counter, itself a vitrine of handguns. All the pistols on glass shelves looked like reptilian specimens in a natural history museum: even inert and lifeless, a snake looked capable of harm.

All these months, he'd kept the claim check in his wallet. He slid it across the counter. He wasn't sure what the procedure would be, if another clearance would be required. Maybe the weapon had been resold.

A sales clerk looked at the claim check and pointed at the date. His eyebrows bounced up and down twice, as if to say, Oh my, oh my. Or. Why now, why now? He indicated he would be back in a moment, and then, as if he thought Carlo might disappear again for another six months, the clerk added, "This shouldn't take long."

And it didn't take long before he returned with what could have been a shoe box. Although there weren't shoes in the box, but rather, fitted into a foam bed, a fat, square, silver L of metal, pug-nosed, unfed, brutish: a gun.

5

AFTER CARLO AND HIS FATHER left for the airport, Robbie was dumping coffee grounds down the trash disposal when he became stuck on a thought, or less a thought than a question: If challenged by the same tragedy in their home as the two men had been this autumn, and if then subjected to the same sequence of unsettling vandalism, wouldn't most couples, in seeing each other through the ordeal, be brought closer together? The morning Robbie found Tom, Detective Michaels had suggested as much would happen, but that had not been the case. And now this sketchy effigy hanging from the pepper tree—Robbie did not want to talk about it later. He had no desire ever to talk about it with Carlo.

He decided to change what he was wearing and put on a pair of jeans he hadn't worn in a while, more frayed than what he usually went around in, a tighter fit in the seat. He undid an extra button of his shirt. When he headed out, Robbie noticed the shallow craters of mud where the lost plum trees once stood. It wasn't until that moment that he realized Carlo had apparently given up on the saplings.

Jay giggled when he answered his door because he and Robbie were dressed alike, their torn jeans, their faded black shirts. He offered to switch into something else, and Robbie said he hardly cared if they looked like twins, which they didn't, and never could, he pointed out, not with their age difference. Then Jay said something along the lines of, Oh please, you look like you're turning thirty, not forty.

Their afternoon together was loosely structured around Jay's quest for a new belt buckle, thus drawing Robbie in and out of stores (and not only clothing stores) he wasn't sure he'd ever set foot in on Vermont, on Hollywood, down Sunset a-ways. Instead of the elusive belt buckle, Jay bought inexpensive opera CDs and a set of pastel pencils. He bought two used cowboy shirts, while Robbie purchased none, although he did try on several, and when he did, Jay slipped through the curtain into the changing booth with him to assess the fit. They became familiar, easily physical, or Jay did; he had a way of tapping Robbie's arm, shoulder, or back as if to italicize a comment or add an exclamation point. They made a date to hang out again after the weekend.

That night at the house, the two men read, one in the main room, the other in the bedroom. When Robbie came to bed, Carlo let his open book fall against his chest.

"I'm sorry if I was angry this morning," he said.

Robbie nodded. "It was strange, I admit. Hard to read. But it will stop."

"You think?"

Again Robbie nodded.

Then Carlo was staring out the window, not looking Robbie in the eye when he asked, "Do the police know you've got Tom's address book?"

Robbie burned with blush. He said, "No," and he explained how he'd found the address book in the couch. So Carlo had noticed it on the dresser after all, and yet all this time had gone by and he'd said nothing. That fact aroused a different kind of burning, one deep beneath Robbie's sternum.

"You wanted something of Tom's, a keepsake?" Carlo asked.

That sounded good, so once more Robbie nodded.

"Or were you hoping to discover … something?" Carlo asked.

Robbie surprised himself with his frankness: "That, too," he said.

"I see. And what did you hope to learn?"

Carlo seemed extra-nervous, extra-tense, like he was wearing a stiff, cringing, papier mâché mask of his face over his true easy-grinning face.

"What have you discovered?" he asked, impatient.

Once upon a time, Robbie wanted to talk to Carlo about Tom, but now Tom was a place Robbie had journeyed to on his own, and he found he didn't want to relay his adventures in Tom-land, what he saw there, what he carried away from that trip. Tom belonged to him alone, not the two of them together.

"I can't say I discovered anything," he said, and his voice sounded thin, he knew.

"Do you feel, then, that you're over Tom?" Carlo asked.

Over Tom! As if these past months Robbie had been lovesick, and perhaps it was fair to say he'd suffered an infatuation for a

dead man, for an acquaintance whom he never got to know as a
true friend, but that seemed so far from the core of what he'd felt.
How misunderstood he was in that moment, he thought. How
monumentally misunderstood, yet to explain why meant surren-
dering what he wanted to guard, so he remained cool.

"I suppose," Robbie said, an easy exit. "Sure."

Carlo propped up his book but didn't read it. This was when,
unplanned, Robbie asked how Carlo would feel if Robbie extended his break from the office.

"Oh," Carlo said. "For how long do you think?"

"I'm not sure."

Carlo didn't blink. His mouth was open, a thought forming.

Make a demand, Robbie thought. Tell me to come to work. Say
to me, Earn your keep. Say, Be my best friend. Say, We don't talk—
talk to me.

"No worries," Carlo said. "Everything is fine. I can manage."

And Robbie thanked him with a cursory kiss on the cheek
and then switched off his night table lamp.

EVERYTHING WAS HARDLY FINE, and not for a moment did
Carlo believe Robbie had moved beyond Tom or the tragedy at
their home, nor did he think they were done being taunted by
whoever wanted to prolong the aftermath of that tragedy. A liar
knows when he's being lied to, and Carlo was certain he
was being misled. He regretted raising the address book but he
couldn't stand wondering any longer. Robbie knew something,
and he wasn't admitting it. Or maybe he knew nothing, and there
was nothing to admit.

The only remedy for Carlo's anxiety seemed to be working out back on his fountain. He spent that weekend digging a trench for a pipe from the house to the fountain and in the process made a muddy mess. He had to pull out some lavender that had been allowed to shrub and gather cobwebs, and dead irises, and withered flax, and then the dead plants had to be bagged and carted off to the conservation center. Also he was working on hoeing the dirt down where the fountain would go, leveling the plot. As long as he was engaged physically, he could be level. When he stopped to rest and leaned on his hoe, dark thoughts returned, although he tried to soothe himself with this thought: The holiday season was always a kind of mountain pass—make it through, and the flat valley ahead would be easy to traverse. The holidays were a time of joint-survival, and the New Year this year, he hoped, might occasion renewal and rededication. The two men would find their way. So he had to hold on. He had to hold it all together for the two men, and he could resent that burden all he wanted, but it remained his to bear.

At the office the Monday after Thanksgiving, he calculated which bills not to pay but quickly lost his focus. He made fountain doodles, cascading water doodles. He gazed out at the street. There were ten phone messages from the television producer, and so finally, reluctantly, Carlo called him back.

"Where the fuck have you been?" the producer asked. He was on a ski slope somewhere out of state. "Did you see what I got in the mail? Did you fucking *see*?"

Carlo had not yet opened the envelope that had been messengered from the producer's office but did so now, skimming what turned out to be a letter from a neighborhood association.

A complaint had been filed with the buildings department protesting the scale of the producer's house (and these were for the old non-villa plans), in particular its height, which citizens of a street up the hill claimed would obstruct their view, and which citizens across the street said would effectively block sunlight. Carlo was inclined to side with the neighbors, and the new villa scheme would be much, much worse.

"Does this happen to you often," the producer asked, "one fuck-up after another?"

Carlo began to compose a temperate response.

"Fix it," the producer said.

"Fix it?"

"Maybe I should have my attorney file suit to recoup the money I've wasted on you so far, not to mention you being in breach," the producer said.

In breach? This was rich. "I wouldn't worry. With the new materials, the upgrades, the neighborhood association will like your new plans much better," Carlo said.

The producer didn't respond. He probably could tell he was being played. It was what he did professionally, play people.

"With the revisions we're making," Carlo said, "you'll end up with a more traditional home. I promise you, everyone will be happy."

"You promise—"

The connection was lost. Moments later, the phone rang again, the producer calling back.

"I'll take care of everything," Carlo said before the producer could speak.

"When am I going to see these new plans? What the hell do you do all day long?"

"You enjoy your skiing, and I'll speak with you when you're—"

"When are you—"

"Next week," Carlo said.

"Next week what?"

"A full set of new plans will be ready for you to review next week," Carlo said. "We'll pull the new permits. We'll break ground in January."

Silence.

"You'd best not be fucking with me. Do you know who you're fucking with, if you fuck with me?" the producer asked.

"See you next week," Carlo said, and of course nothing he'd said was true, his word worthless. And considering his worth, he called his bank and set up an appointment with a loan officer. The firm had maxed out its credit cards. Hold it all together, he told himself. One month, and then the New Year, and new clients would turn up the way they always did. They would survive and they would survive.

LATER THAT AFTERNOON, Carlo was standing in the front window when he glanced north toward the convenience store at the corner and noticed Gabriel standing in the parking lot next to a squad car. The boy was talking to Detective Michaels, who tapped her pad with her pen and who made the occasional notation.

Carlo's first instinct was to bolt across the street and demand she stop interrogating the boy without a parent or guardian present. Of course, it was possible the detective was asking Gabriel about some other matter beyond the investigation into Tom's death. Maybe the boy's association with Lonny had caught up with him. The detective had her back to Carlo, and so he couldn't quite tell whether she was satisfied with Gabriel's responses, but Gabriel, meanwhile, kept shrugging. With each shrug, he tugged at both backpack straps. Then he nodded and slipped into the convenience store. Carlo half expected Detective Michaels to walk across the street to his office, but she didn't. She got in her squad car and drove off the other way toward the Reservoir.

Carlo waited a moment until he was sure she was truly gone, and then he dashed diagonally across the street, avoiding the liquor store, and heading for the convenience store right as Gabriel emerged, a candy bar in hand.

"Hey," Carlo said, trying not to sound out of breath.

"You're not going to tell me I eat too much sugar, I hope," Gabriel said.

"Oh, gosh no, I don't care. So what are you up to?"

Gabriel nodded toward the liquor store, indicating he was headed there next.

To which Carlo said, "You don't need to be hanging out there, do you?"

Gabriel cocked his head. "What did you do to Lonny, anyway?" he asked.

"Nothing," Carlo said.

"What did you say about me owing him money?"

"Honestly nothing," Carlo said.

"He said you said something."

Carlo hooked Gabriel's arm. "I need to go to the stone yard. Come keep me company."

"I'm sure I have homework," Gabriel complained.

"It can wait."

"Nice."

"I'm lonesome today," Carlo said.

Which was true enough, and maybe sweet Gabriel detected as much and therefore went along for the ride.

As they rounded the Reservoir, Carlo said, "I saw you with Detective Michaels."

"The lady cop?"

"She shouldn't talk to you without your aunt being there."

"It's not like she arrested me. She can ask questions. I know my rights."

"Do you now? And what did she want?"

"She was asking me questions about that guy."

"That guy? What guy, Tom?"

"The dude who offed himself."

"Tom."

"Like had I ever seen him around your place before."

"What did you say?"

"I told her," Gabriel said.

"You told her … what?"

"And then she wanted to know crazy shit. How well did I know you and Robbie, what's your relationship like." Gabriel stopped. He was studying Carlo.

"What?" Carlo asked.

They had turned onto Glendale and were at the stoplight at Fletcher.

"It's not like you guys did anything," Gabriel said.

Carlo's heart beat hard.

"Right?" Gabriel asked. "That dude was a freak."

"Tom," Carlo said again, and maybe he half nodded, sure, a freak.

"You guys were asleep, you said. Only trying to keep the guy from driving drunk, and then he got twisted. That's not your fault."

Was this what Carlo told the boy, that Tom had gotten twisted?

"Is that what you said to Detective Michaels?" Carlo asked.

"The guy was a freak," Gabriel said, "and the cops should leave you alone and go fight crime or something."

All Carlo could do was nod again, and he knew then he should not have distorted the truth about Tom and the night Tom died, and that the misconceptions he'd allowed the boy to believe, the unfair depiction of Tom as a freak, would catch up with him, would wash ashore, soaked and bloated.

"I'm sure someone was murdered somewhere last night," the boy added.

Now they were on Fletcher and heading for Riverside. Carlo kept both hands on the steering wheel. He'd stashed the gun in the glove compartment of this car, the better car, which he drove exclusively, and knowing a loaded weapon was there somehow kept him steady. They approached the underpass, and he wondered, if confronted, would he actually use it? He might. He

Peter Gadol   221

would have no choice. But in front of the boy, would he draw it?
No. Well, if threatened—

"Why are you driving so fast?" Gabriel asked.

Carlo was unaware he was speeding and slowed down.

"So who is Robbie's new friend?" Gabriel asked.

Carlo didn't know about any new friends.

"The blond dude," Gabriel said.

A pickup honked and cut around Carlo's car—now he was
driving too slowly—and he maneuvered into the right lane.

"You have no idea who I'm talking about," Gabriel said.

"This is someone you've seen Robbie with," Carlo said.

"The other day," Gabriel said. "Oh man. Dude."

"Oh man dude, what?" Carlo said. "Robbie can have his own
friends."

"*Friends?*"

"What are you saying?"

"Friends he doesn't tell you about."

"It was only the other day you saw him? Maybe he hasn't gotten around to it," Carlo said, but in point of fact, Robbie always
told him as soon as he met someone interesting.

"People look a certain way. You can tell something is going
on," the boy said.

"And what way is that?"

"Loose."

"You know about these things. You speak with authority
about these matters."

"My mother," was all Gabriel said. "Whatever," he said. "Pretend you don't care."

"I care," Carlo said. He looked at the boy: "I care. But I don't
think there's any need to worry about anything."

"Whatever," Gabriel said, and the subject was dropped.

Carlo turned onto San Fernando and found the stone yard. In silence, he and the boy wandered the yard and checked out all the gray slate. There wasn't much to choose from, but the boy had slipped into a pouty mood and would not express an opinion. Carlo placed an order.

At home that night, he regarded Robbie differently. For one thing, Robbie's hair had grown longer than usual, and given the December wind, was more of a mess. He had started wearing untucked snap shirts open over T-shirts, and a pair of scuffed square-toe boots he hadn't worn in years. If Carlo didn't, say, note a faint wrinkle at Robbie's earlobe, he could have mistaken forty-year-old Robbie for twenty-year-old Robbie. When he was alone in the kitchen or bathroom, Robbie whistled songs Carlo didn't know. Robbie's easy giggle was back, too, although whatever he was laughing about, he kept to himself. He was getting text messages, phone calls. Carlo could ask point blank if something was going on, but Robbie would lie the way he'd lied when he said he was over Tom. Carlo was miserable—this erosion of trust—he felt awful.

They hadn't talked about Christmas. Their policy was that in lieu of major gifts for each other, together they would buy something they needed or wanted. One year it might be a new washer-dryer, and another year, a painting. But so far, they hadn't discussed what (if anything) they would purchase, nor had they talked about getting a tree (which some years they did, but not other years), or if they'd try to have friends over or throw a small New Year's party.

Carlo wanted to dislike him, but he couldn't, the opposite. He remembered how one weekend senior year during the winter reading period, the two men had gone to Provincetown for the day during the bitter, bleached-sky off-season, and managed to get turned around walking back to wherever they'd parked their rental car, which seemed a feat given how small the town was. No one was around and they kept passing the same cottage with the same unseen barking dog. They should have been worried that perhaps their car had either been towed or stolen. They were not concerned, however, and these were not the years when concern came quickly. Their teeth were chattering and they kept walking around and amused themselves with a game they improvised, which later they called Double-Alpha-Meltdown. You took a name and said the name—Carlo Stein—and then the other person removed the first letter from the first name, as well as the first letter from the last name, and then pronounced the truncated formation: Arlo Tein. The name was then tossed back to the first person for the same treatment again, and the mutated words were eventually merged, until nothing was left but a sound: Rlo Ein, Loin, On. Robbie Voight, Obbie Oight, Bbieight, bieght, ieht, et.

It was dumb and it was silly, but they were giggling as if intoxicated, and Carlo's ribs ached because he laughed so hard and the air was sharp to breathe, and they kept playing their little game with the names of friends and relatives and professors and ex-boyfriends and famous architects. They did find their car and drove back to campus, and thereafter the game was played whenever in the dull chill of winter they were keeping themselves warm while walking from Robbie's dorm to Carlo's apartment in Cambridgeport, and vice versa.

When had they stopped playing Double-Alpha-Meltdown? Was it in graduate school when a practical lexicon took the place of their invented language? Was it when they began making presentations to clients? Was it when they took on a mortgage and accrued credit card debt? Or was Carlo being too severe with himself, because in fact, weren't the two men still capable of silliness?

Gabriel Sanchez, Abriel Anchez, Brielnchez, Rielchez, Ielhez, Elez, Lz. It wasn't much fun to play alone.

Even before Tom killed himself, Carlo realized, he'd been in mourning for something terrible that had not yet occurred, as if this was where he had arrived in life: grief now preceded loss.

ROBBIE SAW JAY EVERY DAY. He stopped by the bookstore on Vermont at the end of Jay's shift, and the plan was to see a movie next door, but instead Robbie tagged along while Jay completed some urgent errands, like buying stamps at the post office so he could mail in his bills, like picking up cat food for the neighbor cat Jay was taking care of, like pumping his bike tires with air at the gas station. The most mundane rounds, and yet Robbie was floating.

"This is hardly the movie you wanted to see," Jay apologized.

"I'm fine," Robbie said. "I'm great."

"Surely you have something you need to get done, too," Jay said.

"No, nothing."

"I must seem like a mess to you. All these late bills, no stamps."

"Not the least bit a mess," Robbie said.

And yet Jay didn't appear to take him at his word and bought him a mocha as consolation for dragging him around. At the café, Robbie tried to explain that an uncomplicated ordinary day brought him greater pleasure than an extraordinary one. Venturing to the grocery store and the bank and the dry cleaners was possibly more fulfilling than a museum outing or day trip to the desert, go figure.

"Go figure," Jay said.

"Maybe I'm strange that way," Robbie said.

"Possibly," Jay said. "But it's a good kind of strange."

They spent the next afternoon together before Jay had to be at the bookstore for an evening shift, and then the day after that, and all they did was wander around performing everyday tasks, shopping for tennis shoes, whole grains, guitar strings, hair product. All the while, their conversation was fluent and increasingly intimate.

What did they talk about? About Tom at first, like when they went over to the bar on Fountain where the bartender with the big arms had to call the police when Tom got too rowdy. They talked about Tom's promise as a sketch artist and his autodidactic nature and the way he merrily held forth on any topic. Robbie wondered what Tom was like as a lover, and Jay reminded him that Tom needed to be drunk to have sex. But the kissing was phenomenal, Jay reported, accompanied by mapless foreplay prone to digression because Tom could never really stay on point, as it were. But eventually Tom became less a special topic and more a naturalized presence in the normal course of conversation.

What did they talk about? The European capitals where Jay had lived growing up, his father an economist for world banks. Washington for high school, New York for college. He studied anthropology, he studied film, he studied acting. He'd been engaged in every art form, piano since childhood, painting only recently. He always thought of himself as moody but never perceived himself as classically depressive. He never connected an inability to stay with anything (or anyone) as related to clinical malaise, but clearly there was a link. Jay never questioned why he was perpetually drawn to manic boyfriends—he didn't see them as manic. They were colorful was all.

"You said once Tom saved you," Robbie said.

"We'd had sex, drunken sex, a rare instance of all-the-way sex," Jay said, "and in the morning, after Tom left, I realized we hadn't used a condom. I freaked. I went to my doctor. I did the protocol, kept retesting fine—Tom by then was out of the picture. But with the doctor, I started talking about how sad I was all the time, and I resisted it at first but agreed to medication. It helps. I sleep at night. My doctor tells me I may not have to take this goop forever, and I hope not because I hate the thought of being dependent on anyone. I mean, *anything*. When I say Tom saved me, I guess I mean he was a decent guy to hit bottom with, or skid pretty close."

What did they *not* talk about? About Robbie's life all that much. He disclosed he was taking time off from his architectural practice. After Tom's suicide, Robbie said, he realized how burned out he was. Jay asked how Robbie's firm was handling his leave, and Robbie explained his firm consisted of only him and his partner (he did not characterize Carlo with any word other than partner), who was very understanding. And so Robbie wasn't necessarily lying, although he was hardly being truthful.

"Don't you want to get back to work?" Jay asked.

"I don't know," Robbie said.

"Will you go back?"

The question surprised Robbie—or he was more surprised by his response, a shrug.

"What do you think you'll do?" Jay asked.

"I don't know."

"You don't seem concerned about it."

"I know," Robbie said. "It's weird, but I'm not."

Once upon a time, a confession like this would have been impossible, all too frightening to admit. But in Jay's company, Robbie never had any worries—around Jay, Robbie experienced an old confidence he was unaware he'd lost. It was as if he were the same man he'd been a long time ago, even before Carlo— carefree, upbeat—and also a new man, or maybe a changed man, although changed in what ways he was unable to say.

It was December. A daytime friendship ran into the night. When Jay didn't have to work in the evening, Robbie left notes for Carlo saying when he expected to be home, but not where he was heading, not with whom.

Jay turned twenty-six (twenty-six!). Robbie offered to take him out for dinner but Jay didn't want that. He had a simpler craving: They went to the cramped bistro in Sunset Junction and sat in the corner, bunkered among jackets and scarves, and they shared a bottle of a dry bordeaux and two orders of salty pommes frites. They were seated close together on the banquette, and Jay let his hand under the table rest on Robbie's knee. Robbie extended his arm across the back of the seat. They looked like lovers. Would anyone whom Robbie knew see them? He wasn't sure he cared, nor did he feel reckless when at the end of the evening (and thereafter with every parting), Jay kissed Robbie on the cheek.

They were seen together on at least one occasion that Robbie knew of, when they were walking around the corner from the bookstore and Gabriel coasted by on his low-rider bike. The boy looked back over his shoulder, briefly meeting Robbie's glance. Without noticeable acceleration, the boy rode off down the street and disappeared, and that was that.

One time Jay said, "You never mention past boyfriends."

Robbie hesitated.

"I'm prying."

"No, it's fine. There's a reason I don't talk about it," Robbie said, and now he was laying on a thick varnish.

"When did you break up?"

Again Robbie hesitated.

"Maybe we can talk about it some other time," Jay said.

They rented favorite movies from the video store on Hyperion and took them back to Jay's studio. They each chose French films. The one Jay picked had come out forty years before Robbie's selection, and did Jay sense how much it meant to Robbie to be watching that particular film with him? The impish schoolboy, his day playing hooky. Caught, breaking free, on the run, on the beach, looking back—freeze frame. Did Jay notice Robbie holding his breath? Robbie was staying out later and later, beyond when he told Carlo he'd be home, but Robbie accepted a glass of wine. Jay improvised something on the piano, a strain he'd picked up from the film. "I should go," Robbie kept saying, and yet he didn't go, not until midnight, and when he got home Carlo was asleep, awake briefly when Robbie climbed into bed, asleep again fast.

In the morning Carlo noted how late Robbie was getting in, and Robbie apologized, and he waited, he waited a good long minute for Carlo to ask him where he'd been. Or maybe Carlo, busying himself making coffee and toasting muffins, was waiting for Robbie to volunteer the information. Ask me, Robbie was thinking, demand to know what I've been doing all these hours away from you, *ask me.*

"I'm sorry if I woke you," Robbie said.

"Don't worry. It's fine," Carlo said, end of discussion, and his response, his apparent lack of concern, at once confused and wounded Robbie. He thought: So be it. He had unspoken permission to do as he pleased.

Later these late autumn days would be difficult to remember, pulling them apart, one from the next. The day he and Jay hiked in Vermont Canyon. The day they went to check out a desk someone was selling online. The evening—this would have been the last evening of autumn—when Jay tuned his guitar and played Robbie some songs he'd written. They were all languorous ballads, which Jay sang in a shy baritone, a suite of songs about two men, doomed lovers. Robbie was moved and profuse with compliments to the point that he worried he sounded disingenuous. Jay was young and according to his own testimony had not yet experienced the life about which he was writing: How had he been able to capture so convincingly the spirit, the longing, the bliss of decades-long love? Robbie asked him this.

Jay blushed, took the compliment, and said, "I think about it all the time, a real relationship. It's speculation, I guess. But it's what I want."

"You want to have your heart broken, too, like in the songs?"

It wasn't a serious question, but Jay frowned.

"You should write more songs," Robbie said. "You could do a whole opera."

"I should," Jay said. "And I should make more paintings, and I need to finish those grad school applications—ergh. I'm all talk. I don't want to be all talk. Am I all talk?"

While they were having this conversation, they were sitting on Jay's sofa, and Robbie felt something under his thigh. He dug his fingers between the cushions and withdrew a stack of tiny index cards bound with a rubber band. Each card had a cyrillic letter on one side, the English equivalent on the other. They were Tom's, from when he was teaching himself Russian, one more item he'd lost in the crevice of a couch.

"I had to quiz him," Jay said, "and so I was learning Russian, too. Or the alphabet at any rate."

Robbie undid the rubber band and flashed a cyrillic side at Jay.

"That's the Y," Jay said.

Robbie tried another card.

"That's the Zh-shound."

Another card.

"Got me."

"That's the D," Robbie said.

Something about the quiz silenced Jay.

"He's here in a way, isn't he?" Robbie asked. He wound the rubber band back around the flash cards. "Maybe *we* should learn Russian," he said.

"In memorial to Tom. I like that, yes."

"I think you mean *da*," Robbie said.

"*Da, da*," Jay said. "*Spasiba*."

Robbie glanced at his watch. It was late again.

"Robbie, why don't we ever spend time at your house?"

"Oh," Robbie said. "I like getting away."

"Why don't you want to tell me about your boyfriend?" Jay asked.

Robbie said nothing. Then: "Oh." And: "Right."

Jay had seen the name of the firm stenciled on the office window on Silver Lake Boulevard and then consulted the white pages and, as he'd suspected, discovered that a Stein also cohabitated with a Voight.

"The man I was with before Tom, that awful relationship I've told you about," Jay said, "it was with a married guy, and I'm not doing that again—"

"No, no, of course not," Robbie rushed to say. He knew he was blushing: he was the one who was twenty-six and Jay forty.

Jay touched Robbie's knee and said, "Not that I don't think about it."

Robbie stared at Jay's hand on his leg.

Jay withdrew his hand. "But I'm not going there again," he said.

"No," Robbie said. "No, you shouldn't."

"I'd like to know about him," Jay said, "and whatever is going on. It's okay, Robbie, you can tell me. I'm not going to like you less."

AND SO THIS WAS HOW on the first day of winter, Robbie finally invited Jay up to the house while Carlo was out (although Robbie was never sure when Carlo would return). Robbie let Jay give himself his own tour. They ended up in the bedroom, Jay standing at the window, Robbie sitting at the foot of the bed.

"It's quiet up here," Jay said.

"I like quiet," Robbie said.

"Open. Safe."

"Safe?"

"What a view," Jay said. He was staring at the back patio. "Is that the tree?"

Robbie joined Jay at the window. It had begun to rain and the Reservoir was disappearing in the mist. He looked at the more immediate hillside of the property and out at the patio, the stone darkening as it became wet. He stared at Jay, and in the diffused light, the blond scruff along Jay's jaw sparkled. Robbie wanted to touch it to see if it was as soft as it appeared. Jay blinked but didn't say anything. They were standing very close to each other.

Then Robbie looked out again at the patio, and suddenly his pulse quickened.

"You don't look so hot," Jay said. "Are you okay?"

Robbie's dream, his recurring dream of waking and seeing Carlo at the window or seeing Tom at the window—it was no dream at all. It had happened, and not with Tom but with Carlo. Robbie had woken up at one point during the night Tom killed himself and seen Carlo standing at the window, gazing out, and Robbie had tried to stay awake but fell back asleep. This was what happened, he was sure of it.

"Thanks for showing me your house," Jay said.

Robbie did not want to think about what he might have been piecing together, and he said, "I need to get out of here. I haven't eaten much. Should we go to the diner?"

They went to the diner down on Glendale and then parted ways, and as soon as Robbie was home again and alone at the end of the afternoon, he had to know: he could pretend all he wanted

nothing had happened, but something had happened. He opened
Carlo's night table drawer: pills, bracelet, foreign currency, pocket
diary, et cetera—nothing. He went through Carlo's dresser draw-
ers. Carlo's trouser pockets. He unzipped tennis racket covers. He
had no idea what he was looking for. He patted down Carlo's
coats. He opened and shut all the kitchen cabinets. He checked
the garage this time around, tool bins, the drill case. Their luggage. He pulled out books from the shelves and found only dust.
Again he stumbled on nothing in the guest room closet. He circled through the whole house and found nothing and ended up
once again checking amid the stacks of extra sheets and pillowcases, the spare comforter in the built-in linen closet in the hallway. One more time he stood on tip-toes and flung open the
upper cabinet. There on the left was the book box with his grandfather's toys, and there on the right was Carlo's art supply kit—
Wait a minute. Hold on.

The two men were alike in so many ways: Their favorite color
was forest green. They preferred colder weather to warm. They
never tired of dark chocolate. They loved clean square lines, glass,
brushed steel. And, with the exception perhaps of Robbie's desk
at the office, they were neat the same way, orderly, things had
their place. Robbie hadn't noticed it before, but for as long as he
could remember, in the upper cabinet, they had stowed the box
of toy soldiers on the right, Carlo's art kit on the left—the reverse
of the way they were now.

A part of him knew he was being ridiculous. And a part of
him wasn't sure—maybe he had it turned around, and even if the
storage box and art kit had been swapped, so what? What was he
looking for anyway?

Robbie went back to the kitchen, into the pantry for the step ladder, and carried the ladder across the house to the hall. He climbed up two steps and saw that like the file boxes in the guest room closet, the book box with the toys remained sealed with packing tape. However, he noticed that Carlo's art kit, a wooden briefcase, mostly dusty, was not dusty everywhere. There were finger marks. Robbie could tell that the kit had been touched recently. He pulled it out. He stepped back down the ladder and set the kit on the floor, undid its twin metal hasps, and pushed back the lid. And he gasped.

For inside the briefcase there were stiff brushes and dull palette knives and silver tubes of oil paint that looked like dented miniature race cars—and lying atop the knives, brushes, and paints was a pencil sketch on a page of graph paper. The sketch was a portrait of Carlo, his face and torso, his naked torso.

Carlo's head was turned to the right, his chin angled down toward his collarbone, his eyes cast down, his right hand resting lazily across the left side of his bare chest, his palm flat across his heart. The charcoal channel of hair that ran down Carlo's chest, the more feathery hair on his forearm, the orion of freckles between his index finger and thumb—the artist was good, he was very good. He'd captured Carlo's whole being in that gesture, modest yet knowing, open yet covering himself up, gazing elsewhere yet present, very aware of, in wordless dialogue with his viewer. His viewer, which was to say the portrait artist.

Robbie stared at the bottom of the page, first at the date, the day a man had hanged himself, and then at the signature in neat small caps, that of the hanged man himself: TOM FIELD.

6

AND SO IT WAS WINTER AGAIN. On the shortest day of the year, first there was rain, then wind, then wind and rain. Carlo had headed out early, not to the office but to the home supply center to pick up the fountain filtration system and pump and other hardware, and then to the stone yard, where he needed to look over his order of slate before heading home again to await its delivery.

All he'd done these last weeks was work on the fountain, refining his design—a four-by-four pool, elevated one foot, would sit at the back edge of the lower terrace, pressed against the brush, leaving room on the terrace for a hammock and two chairs, and the fountain itself would gurgle up in the rear-most corner of the pool, an asymmetric plan—and figuring out all the proper piping and pumping and recycling of water. Also how to run the electrical. Also how to program the control box. All he'd done these last weeks was finish laying in the piping and grading the terrace. He'd built forms for the fountain pool, and with Gabriel's help one afternoon, he'd poured a quick-setting concrete, making sure (according to everything he'd read online) the drainage would work well, and then even the jaded teenager had to grin a toothy grin because at last there was a there there.

So Carlo made it from the stone yard back to the house, up the rain-slick hill roads, to await the delivery of his slate and saw Robbie's car parked on the street and thought maybe Robbie would be home and could help when the stone arrived. However, Robbie wasn't home. Carlo found the step ladder in the hall and the upper cabinet flung open, his art kit on the floor. On the bed: Tom's sketch.

Carlo sat on the bed, frozen. Everything was catching up with him.

It had occurred to him to get rid of the drawing, but it seemed wrong to destroy something Tom had made, another betrayal. He supposed in time he'd throw it out, and Carlo had thought his art kit was safe (sometimes he'd hidden small gifts for Robbie in it). No one could have seen him hide the drawing except Tom (and Carlo was pretty sure he didn't), and obviously Tom did not tell Robbie it was in there.

A trunk honked, the delivery. The rain was coming down hard now, a cold rain at that, and the men from the stone yard were in a foul mood. Carlo was not at his best and so there was a disagreement about where they'd deposit the slate—not around back like Carlo wanted, only on the front driveway by the garage.

Fine, fine. Carlo threw up his hands. And so the men lowered the pallets at the foot of the driveway, and no one was home to help, and the boy was nowhere when he was needed, and so Carlo himself had to load the slate in a wheelbarrow and maneuver the heavy cart around the side of the garage. It was cumbersome but easy enough with the pre-cut pieces that would be positioned around the sides and base of the fountain pool, but the terrace pieces were large and difficult to lift, only fit one at a time in the wheelbarrow. And Carlo kept slipping in the mud, his ankles turning. And the rain came down and came down, and he was soaked and his boots were coated in muck, his jeans, but he managed to get the stone around to the back patio, great. Great, great—he couldn't actually use the wheelbarrow to get the stone down to the lower terrace—no path was clear and the drop was too steep anyway—and he should have waited until he could get Gabriel to help him, and everything was catching up with him, and the only way to avoid being sunk entirely was to keep moving, to carry the slate down the hill by hand.

Which he started to do, but when he picked up one of the smaller rough-edged islands of slate, the wet stone was slippery against his work gloves, and so he had to carry the piece with his bare hands. And he managed to get a good grip on the flat, heavy piece of slate, even though it was difficult to hold, and he headed down the hill with it along a foot-wide path through the tea bushes and sage and other brush, slipping as he went, losing his footing, sliding on his ass. He got up and headed down and slipped again, but he made it down the hill, and if he was crying, he wouldn't have been able to tell because his face was so wet from the rain. And then he climbed back up to the patio and grabbed another piece and went back down the hill, slipping three times, sliding part of the way on his side. And again, up the hill and down with the slate. And again. And again.

He managed to make a dozen trips up and down the back slope before he sat down in the mud and rain at the bottom of the hill and could carry no more. Everything had caught up with him.

He had walked into the kitchen that night and found Tom at the sink. "What are you doing up?" Carlo had asked, and he said, "You don't have to do the dishes." And Tom had answered, "I was raised a certain way." Tom said: "Nobody else owes me anything." Tom asked: "If not you, then who?"

Autumn was gone and the winter would be a long winter, and Carlo let the rain surround him. He wondered, Must atonement be theater, must there be an audience? And if a man said he was full of remorse but no one heard him say it, did it matter? In the end, with no one to listen, with everyone gone, how would he redeem himself?

HE DIDN'T LEAVE THE HOUSE all the next day because Robbie hadn't taken a car, and so how far off could he be? Carlo had heard it said that if you pictured a lost cat appearing at your back door, summoned thus, the cat would return. Apparently this didn't work for lost lovers.

When the phone rang, he almost picked it up without looking at the caller ID, but he did glance at the number and listened to the message as it was recorded. Detective Michaels requested that either Carlo or Robbie call her back as soon as possible. And Happy Holidays. What an unhappy holiday it would be, Carlo thought, and if the detective needed him, she knew where he lived and worked (and hadn't hesitated to stop by in the past). He didn't return the call. Arrest me, he thought, run me in for resisting a phone call.

No one arrested him, however, and no one came by the house. Carlo's hands were ripped up from carrying the stone down the back slope, but he bandaged them and spent the day finishing the chore, leaving himself with a terrible backache that evening.

The next day was the twenty-fourth and he couldn't stand to be in the house alone, so he got in his car and drove slowly down the street and then even more slowly down the hill toward the lake. Once before he'd happened on Robbie, and he thought it possible again. Carlo circled the lake, hoping to find his lost lover lost in thought, but no such luck. He turned up into the hills on the west side of the Reservoir, continuing the search, pointless though he knew it was. The rains had left the roads slippery and narrowed by fallen branches and palm fronds.

Along an especially tight curve, a military car-truck ahead of Carlo slowed and then came to an abrupt halt. Carlo slammed his foot against the brake. His car skidded and nearly hit a parked station wagon. His fender did tap something like a trash can or mailbox, and he got out of his car to see if there was any damage.

The driver's-side door of the car-truck swung open. The television producer climbed down to the street.

"You," he said. "I thought that was you."

"We could have had an accident," Carlo said.

The producer looked in every way creased: the seat of his trousers, the flaps of his shirt, his forehead. On the back of his hand, a club stamp had not yet been washed off. What hair he had was presently in motion.

"I go away to rest up for pilot season and come back and my useless assistants tell me you've done nothing you promised—

no plans, no permits, no nothing, and you don't answer your phone, don't return email—what the fuck?"

One green vein had popped up along the producer's neck, and Carlo thought a way out of this morass might be if his client had a stroke.

"Nobody in this town," the producer said, red at his temples, red in the neck. "Not with me, they don't."

"I don't think this is the best time or place to talk about your house," Carlo said. "So if you wouldn't mind moving your car—"

"Oh, I mind," the producer said.

"Please."

"*Please*," the producer echoed.

"Please move your car. I'm wedged against the curb there. I can't back it out, but I might be able to drive forward—"

"I'm not moving my car. And let me tell you something," the producer said, "I'm about to own you."

"Excuse me?" Carlo asked, and he was experiencing then the very same urge he did when he confronted Lonny in the liquor store. He wanted to grab the producer by his wrinkled shirt and throw him up against his truck. He wanted to watch the man fall to the pavement only to pick him up again and throw him again against the truck.

"I am about to own you, see," the producer said, "because I will sue you, and I will win, and I will own your office, I will own your house, I will own your car there—Hey, where do you think you're going?"

Carlo had slipped back into his driver's seat. He reached over to the glove compartment and opened it. All he had to do was let the dim noon sun catch the gun in his hand, and then the producer would back down. Of course that might not work, and Carlo might need to fire a round into the treetops. That might get the producer to move his car …

How tired he was, how deeply tired Carlo was of being sane.

"I'm talking to you," the producer said, and waddled toward Carlo's car.

Carlo blinked at the gun.

"We're having a conversation here," the producer said.

"I quit," Carlo said.

"You *what?*"

"I quit," Carlo said again, shutting the glove compartment.

"No you don't, no way," the producer said, and he threw his chubby fists in the air and began ranting about how no one in his career ever walked off one of his sets, ever. If someone was going to do the walking off, it was the producer, and before he turned around and lurched back toward his car, mounted it, and tore off, he said, "No, I quit, I quit—*I* quit."

Carlo grinned for about half a minute. The only money coming in for the foreseeable future would have been from building the producer's house, and now that was gone. What had he done?

HE HADN'T CELEBRATED CHRISTMAS GROWING UP, and even with Robbie, the holiday had never meant so much to him, but all alone, he ached for their merest traditions: sleeping in, the recitation of an instruction manual for a new machine they'd purchased as their gift from them to them, or hanging the new work of art if it was a year of art. Maybe a movie. He was in quite a grumpy mood—not even a phone call from Robbie to say he was alright, or to allow Carlo the chance to explain (to begin to explain) about Tom's drawing, and the rest. Did he deserve to be abandoned like this? No. Possibly. Yes, yes he probably did.

Gabriel came by mid-afternoon. There was little Carlo could do on the fountain because the lower terrace remained muddy, so he was merely sitting atop the wobbly stack of gray slabs when the boy appeared, bearing a gift, only one gift as if he knew already that Robbie was gone. Carlo felt terrible, he had nothing in return. A small box contained a bright-striped scarf.

"It was for my father," Gabriel said.

"Why didn't you give it to him?" Carlo asked. "I can't take his present."

"He left on a trip with his girlfriend this morning, so I wouldn't worry about it."

Gabriel ran his fingertips over one of the cut stones. He seemed so skinny, his arms too long, too thin.

"I hate eggnog," he said. "I really do."

"Me, too," Carlo said.

"I hate it more than you do, I'm pretty sure."

"I doubt it."

"My aunt's is way worse than store-bought."

Carlo managed a chuckle. He was staring at the lake.

"Anyway," he said.

"Anyway," Gabriel said.

"You haven't by any chance seen Robbie around the neighborhood, have you?" Carlo asked.

Gabriel's shoulders dropped. He looked suddenly pained.

"Like, you know, with the blond dude you mentioned?"

Gabriel didn't say anything.

"Never mind," Carlo said. "I didn't think you would have."

The two of them looked out at the Reservoir, like firewatchers, as if something were about to happen.

"Robbie is one stupid fucker," Gabriel said, "isn't he?"

Carlo didn't know what to say. Or he knew what to say, that Robbie didn't deserve the boy's wrath, however Carlo enjoyed having someone on his side. The gift, the misguided sentiment—he became teary, unexpectedly moved.

They went inside and Carlo made sandwiches. Now was the time to tell the kid the truth about what happened with Tom. Now was the time to tell *someone.* He considered getting in the car, the boy riding shotgun, to see if he couldn't find Robbie.

"He's one stupid fucker," Gabriel said again.

"Okay, okay," Carlo said, and hushed him this time.

IT WAS, HOWEVER, highly unlikely Carlo would find Robbie by patrolling the streets, especially since Robbie had not left Jay's apartment in three days. After he found the drawing, he'd walked down the hill and since they'd been together only a short while before, Jay had appeared surprised to see Robbie, who stepped into the apartment but didn't take off his scarf or coat. He was shivering.

"Look at you," Jay said, "your lips are blue," and took Robbie's hands and rubbed them.

"I'm thinking dark things," Robbie said.

"What? Thinking what?"

They stood there a moment, and then Robbie tugged one hand free and with it grasped the back of Jay's neck, his fingers sliding up through Jay's hair, pulling Jay close, their faces close, mouths close.

"Isn't this a bad idea?" Jay had whispered and closed his eyes, and maybe it was a bad idea, Robbie had thought, but then welcome to a world where a kid got a rush dreaming he was a human kite aloft outside a burning tower, a world where the man you'd trusted half your life might in some shadowy way be responsible for another man's death. Robbie had waited until Jay opened his eyes again, and then he kissed him.

Most of their time the following days had been spent in bed. Jay went off to work his shifts at the bookstore and came home with groceries. Christmas Eve was all about sex. The next morning, they slept in, or rather Jay slept and Robbie watched him turn onto his side and pull a pillow over his head. He was not used to spending the night with a man who, impossibly, was an even deeper sleeper than Robbie himself. He was not used to spending the night with a man who wasn't Carlo. Robbie pushed back a stretch of blanket, exposing the bowl of Jay's hip. Robbie didn't know the exact hour because there had apparently been a blackout and the alarm clock was flashing midnight. It was, literally, a lost time.

From the moment they'd added sex to their friendship, their regular conversation had noticeably dwindled, which was fine because Jay made sex so sexy. To look at his long-fingered hands and thin wrists, one wouldn't expect strength, yet there was something supremely confident about his touch, reassuring, rejuvenating. There was one moment during the love-making for which Robbie found himself yearning, and not a dual climax, everyone going everywhere, hardly that. It was the point, say, in the middle of the story after Robbie had stood up to pull off Jay's jeans, his underwear, and then stepped out of his own jeans and underwear, when he lowered himself back across Jay's body, when they found themselves suddenly and entirely naked together, the moment when their hips were snug and Jay's arms came around Robbie once more, when their cheeks brushed, always Robbie's left to Jay's left, with Robbie's nose ending up near Jay's ear—when Robbie pulled back a bit and lifted himself up so he was looking at Jay—it was when they were holding each other with their bodies warm the same way, and how they fit then, as if they'd been coming together like this for years, it was at that moment that time passing became imperceptible. Who they were beyond this apartment, everything from any previous life, fell away.

While Jay was out, Robbie fantasized about what the future with him would look like: One day soon, Robbie would retrieve a few things from the house (he'd worn the same jeans all week, but borrowed Jay's T-shirts and freeballed it and didn't need to worry about socks, since he wasn't going out at all), and then he and Jay would light out toward some new Western city and rent an apartment with high ceilings and an enamel stove, and each would find work, and they would learn the new city together, its farmers' markets and revival cinemas. They would share shirts and make omelets for supper. After a time, they would pack up their few belongings and move on to another city, and one day perhaps they'd settle somewhere for good. They would not need friends in the world or family, it would be only the two of them. Their exile from everyone (*everyone*) who once knew them would be total.

Whenever Jay was home, however, Robbie didn't conjure this or any other vision. They rolled around, and Robbie made noise in a way he'd stopped doing with Carlo. Perhaps this was what Robbie needed, to make noise with someone new, but it became difficult to know if it was what Jay needed, as well. In the beginning, sure, but thereafter, post-sex, Jay started gazing at the wall or out the windows, anywhere but at Robbie lying next to him.

"Merry Christmas," Jay said, awake now. "What time is it?"

Robbie had to find his watch in his discarded jeans, which meant getting out of bed and stepping over to the couch. It was going on noon.

"Ah," Jay groaned. "I should be on the road."

He scrambled out of bed, stepped into the shallow bathroom, took a record-fast shower, and, wrapped loosely (enticingly) in his towel, began gathering laundry in a pillowcase to do at his parents' house. Robbie made toast and prepared cereal for Jay.

"I can't believe you're abandoning me," he said, watching Jay dress.

"Are you going to do what we talked about?" Jay asked.

The night before he'd insisted that Robbie had to go home and see Carlo today. It *was* Christmas.

"I told you," Robbie said.

"You should go home to him," Jay said.

Robbie tried to be light: "You always take his side."

Jay stopped what he was doing and sat on the edge of the bed. "You weren't supposed to find the drawing," he said.

Robbie rolled his eyes. "So you keep saying," he said.

It made no sense, and it made perfect sense: Tom was not a stranger. Carlo knew him, but Robbie had given up trying to figure out what had gone on between them, who Tom was to Carlo. And then for Tom's part, well, Tom was Tom. He might have been playing an angle, making a pass at Robbie on the tennis court that first afternoon: revenge. Coming over for dinner even though Carlo couldn't have wanted that: spite. Tom committing the ultimate act of self-annihilation—why, because he meant to injure Carlo? And did Carlo deserve this retribution? What if he did? What if he had brought about the entire sequence of misfortunes that autumn, grave and ruinous? What if all fell to him?

"I can't go home. I told you," Robbie said. "I half woke up that night and saw Carlo standing at the window."

"And so?"

"I have dark thoughts," Robbie said.

"So *you* keep saying. But I think you know what happened," Jay said.

"I don't."

"You do."

"I saw Carlo at the bedroom window," Robbie said, "and he had to have been looking out at the patio, and then—I don't know."

"What do you *think* happened next?"

"I'm telling you, I can't say."

"You can say," Jay insisted, "but you *won't* say."

He finished getting dressed. He sat on the couch to tie his sneakers and Robbie sat next to him, gently gripping his arm.

"Don't be mad," Robbie said.

"I'm not mad," Jay said.

"Do I have to leave?" Robbie asked.

"You should go home. For today. Then come back."

"I can't."

Jay sighed. "I'll see you later on," he said and left.

Robbie removed a jar of green tea from the refrigerator (he'd found some bags in the back of a cabinet and been drinking it steadily). He sipped the tea straight from the jar and stepped over to the piano and swung his feet around the bench. He studied the sheet music. He had been reteaching himself to play, although his technique was slow coming back. An hour a day, he told himself, an hour every day, although he suspected it wasn't a regimen he'd stick to. Also he wanted to try to recover his French and planned on picking up a Paris newspaper if he ever made it over to the international newsstand, if he ever left the apartment. Once upon a time, in another lifetime, he'd been able to think in French. This was when he was an exchange student. It had been a long while since he'd thought about the disorientation he'd suffered when he first traveled abroad by himself, those early alienating nights. He knew no one, no one yet knew him, and he wanted to go home but couldn't—too high the cost of return, too far, too soon, too great the sense of defeat to give up and make his way back. He was almost forty but he felt like he was sixteen again and in Europe and unable to go home. Nothing had changed. But he reassured himself with the additional memory that eventually he got over his homesickness the way one did, and he had a grand time in France—didn't he?

THE NEXT DAY Carlo drove around the neighborhood, and what did he look like, a long lost relative who couldn't locate an address? He saw family members carrying foil-covered platters into warmly lit houses, and he saw kids in the street playing with brand new plastic things. He didn't spot Robbie and on some level knew he wouldn't, but he headed west at five mile an hour, which was tricky to maintain and not either irritate other drivers buzzing around the lake or arouse suspicion among all the walkers and joggers braving the wind to orbit the Reservoir. It was easier to skim the hill streets and the foothill streets, the flat streets with their evenly spaced bungalows. He made it as far as the middle school on Fountain and parked in front of a small church that it had never occurred to him to enter. Pale gray stucco, tall black doors, cold, imposing, uninviting, and yet … One of the doors was ajar. He stepped inside and waited for his eyes to adjust.

The church was smaller than he imagined it would be, white walls, neat pews, cork soundproofing panels, a low dais, at the center of which was a modestly decorated Christmas tree. He took a seat in the back row, folded his hands across his lap, closed his eyes. He tried (failed) to unclutter his mind. What a mess he'd made of things. What should he do? He wasn't praying, but for the first time in days, a tension in his shoulders eased up, in his neck. He thought if he could remain still long enough, his old clarity would return, a pragmatism. He relaxed, but the spell then was broken quickly when a woman entered the hall from a side door and rolled in an industrial vacuum cleaner, its cord like a lasso in her hand. She plugged it in and began cleaning the carpeted dais. It didn't seem right to Carlo that a church should need to be vacuumed. Some mystery was diminished.

When he got home, Gabriel was down on the lower terrace. He was attempting to position the cut stones around the fountain pool. The rain would return soon.

"Are you growing a beard?" the boy asked.

"I misled you," Carlo said. And then: "I misled everyone."

The boy set the slate slab down on the ground and cocked his head.

"Two hours after we all went to sleep that night, I found Tom doing the dishes in the kitchen," Carlo said, and once upon a time, his own story had seemed complex to him, impossible to narrate and convey the shifting moods of each moment built out from the previous moment, when in truth, his story was as simple as could be. He told Gabriel the truth and then the two of them stood there, Gabriel impassive as Carlo bowed his head, as if awaiting a verdict.

However, Gabriel only blinked a few times and then began to climb back up the slope toward the house, his feet slipping in the mud.

"Gabriel."

The boy kept going.

"Say something," Carlo said.

The boy turned around. "Like what?" he asked. "Like basically you've been lying to me?"

Carlo had allowed him to believe one thing, not another, and so yes, that was a lie.

"Like what? Like how I thought your boyfriend was the scummy one, but actually you're both scummy?"

Carlo wasn't sure he saw a connection, but he accepted that a web of dishonesty existed for the kid. Oh, Gabriel, you're only a boy, he wanted to say, how could you understand, but that was the point: he'd failed a child and the child understood perfectly well what had gone on.

"Well, you know what?" Gabriel asked.

Carlo shook his head: No, what?

But Gabriel didn't say anything more. He swung around and continued up the hill and was gone, and Carlo didn't hear a sound anywhere, no cars, no people, nothing in the sky, nothing carried in the wind. He was alone. He was finally all alone.

AND THEN DECEMBER WAS GONE, and it was the end of another year, another bright Saturday, but in no way a peaceful day. A cold gale trampled the tall trees all around Silver Lake and lifted shingles off rooftops and swept wave after wave across the Reservoir. It was a wind that showed no sign of letting up, not until it had moved everything movable, street signs, birds in flight, even, it seemed to Robbie, the afternoon sun: one of Jay's windows did not close all the way, and enough air periodically rushed over the sill to peel back the curtain, throwing a narrow blade of light into a frantic dance.

The end of another year, Robbie thought, unlike any other because this would be the first in twenty he didn't spend with Carlo. New Year's Eve, their habit was to stay in and fix a leg of lamb with roasted new potatoes and sautéed cabbage, nothing special, but this in and of itself, the dinner, staying in, was a sustaining ritual. Midnight, the two of them alone in their house, safe in their own history. What was Carlo doing now? Was he sleeping in, maybe with the benefit of a narcotic? Had he left the pill bottle out on the night stand in case something went chemically awry? Had he moved yet to the center of the bed?

Robbie turned his attention back to the atlas open in his lap.

He was trying not to think about Carlo but thinking about Carlo just the same. Jay meanwhile was puttering. He rearranged the shirts hanging in his closet. He refiled books Robbie had withdrawn from his shelves. He washed out the mason jars Robbie had been using for green tea. When Jay sat at the edge of the couch next to Robbie and began putting on socks and shoes, Robbie asked him where he was going.

"I made plans," Jay answered.

"Plans, what plans?"

"I have friends, you know," Jay said.

"Okay. I'll come with you."

Jay stopped tying his shoe.

"You don't want me to come with you," Robbie said and fell back against a cushion that was all give. He wanted to take Jay's hand, to massage his long fingers, but the moment wasn't right for that. Something was coming to an end.

"You want me to leave," Robbie said.

"I never wanted to be a cuckold," Jay said.

"Technically Carlo is the cuckold."

"Whatever."

The wind tearing through the ballpark across the street was rattling something, loose fencing or trash cans or light posts.

"Sunset hikes in the hills," Jay said, "and midweek sleep-overs and deciding one Sunday breakfast that keeping two apartments is silly. Getting a place together, decorating it with no money. I want to fall in love the old-fashioned way," Jay said. "You understand. You did that once."

"Once," Robbie said. "It was different."

He placed his hand on Jay's knee and Jay set his hand atop Robbie's.

Robbie asked, "Why did you let me stay here all this time and have, like, a huge amount of sex with me?"

It was a relief to see Jay grin. "I'm twenty-six?" he said, he asked.

"Don't make me go home," Robbie said.

"I'm not making you do anything. You brought up leaving."

"I'm not going home," Robbie said.

"Fine."

"Ever."

"You weren't supposed to find the drawing."

"Here we go again."

"Well, you weren't."

"That doesn't change anything," Robbie said. "Maybe *I* am the cuckold."

"Would that be enough to make you break up?"

Robbie's answer was no, but he didn't respond.

"Do you think that's what happened that night? With you asleep in the other room?" Jay asked.

"I don't know," Robbie said.

"But you do know."

"Jay."

"You do know what happened. You have a theory."

"I do?"

Jay nodded.

"Okay," Robbie said, and he was angry now, "fine." He was angry he was being pushed. He said, "I'll tell you what I think."

After all, what he thought happened that September night was really very simple: From the bedroom, Carlo watched Tom out on the patio. He watched Tom tie a noose. He watched him stand on the chair and then stand on the fence to tie the rope. He watched him stand on the chair again and slip the noose over his

neck—and Tom in turn saw Carlo standing at the window, Tom
knew Carlo was watching him. Tom took his time. He was waiting to be stopped, but Carlo didn't stop him, and what could
Tom do, as if answering a dare, but take one step closer to death?
He drew the knot tight and waited and nothing. He stood up on
his toes and waited and nothing. He let his hands fall to his sides
and waited and nothing. And Carlo watched Tom kick away the
chair. He watched the rope pull against Tom's neck. He watched
him asphyxiate. He watched Tom's body lose its being, he
watched his body go slack. He watched the urine run down Tom's
pant leg and he watched the drool run from Tom's mouth. Carlo
watched Tom leave this world, and then Carlo took a sleeping
pill and got in bed next to Robbie and joined him in sleep. That
was what happened.

"You don't think that," Jay said.

"What if I do?"

"But you don't," Jay said, "you don't, you don't. Do you really
think your boyfriend would do something that heinous? This man
you've been with for twenty years—you don't think he's capable of
what you're saying."

In truth, Robbie didn't know what he thought but felt justi-
fied in his own behavior if he could believe the worst about Carlo.
Although Robbie had to wonder what it said about him that these
grim pictures came so fluently. At that moment, he did not like
himself very much.

"Tom had dying on his mind," Jay said. "We've talked about
it. He didn't want to be stopped. He would not have gone
through with any of it, if he thought he was being watched."

"You can't say that for sure."

"Maybe I can," Jay said. "You gave me a detail."

"I did? What detail?"

"And you know your boyfriend didn't watch Tom die. It's not fair to say that."

"Fair to whom—why are you on his side? And what detail?"

Jay finished tying his shoes.

"When will you be back?" Robbie asked.

"I'm not sure."

"You want me to leave."

Jay was looking at the floor, out the window, everywhere but at Robbie.

"Where will I go?" Robbie asked.

Jay put on a fleece-collared denim jacket.

"What detail?" Robbie asked.

Jay kissed him on the cheek, wished him a happy New Year, and left.

MEANWHILE, Carlo at the house was recognizing he could not live the way he'd been living. In the main room there were newspapers and magazines everywhere, the couch cushions all askew, blankets and pillows brought in from the bedroom since he didn't want to sleep in the bed alone, empty wine bottles, empty water bottles, coffee mugs, goblets, socks, shoes, sweaters everywhere. A couple of cereal bowls, an open bag of cookies, an orange peel. He couldn't account for what he'd done these last days but in some vague way, perhaps only calendrically inspired, he was filled with resolve and therefore spent the first part of the day cleaning up.

He needed to keep moving because whenever he stopped, he suffered memories: Like the time he'd been sitting high up on the library steps and Robbie happen to walk by on the quad below, not noticing Carlo, and there was something about Robbie's stride, short yet fast, determined yet springy, something about the way he left his parka unzipped even though it was cold out and the way he wore his bookbag high on his back, the way he appeared to be singing to no one but himself that drew Carlo to Robbie. That stride, that confidence—maybe Carlo had observed it recently, but it had been missing for such a long time, it seemed. What if Robbie were happier now wherever he was, on his own, then shouldn't Carlo let him go? Wouldn't that be an act of love, even if Carlo himself were destroyed? His life would be nothing, he would have nothing.

He did not need to be in a good mood about being alone, but sooner or later he was going to have to accept his station. He decided to drive down to the grocery store and pick up ingredients and busy himself in the kitchen cooking; not the traditional leg of lamb, but roasting a chicken might occupy him. But then the idea of cooking for only himself was depressing. He had gone through all the soup and canned goods in the pantry, and all the wine. He put off going to the grocery store until the late afternoon and then finally ventured out.

The streets were layered in leaves and twigs, and palm fronds strewn across the boulevard looked avian and skeletal, as if large birds had been thrown from flight and smashed dead by the wind. Carlo had electricity at his house, but down the hill it was out: the traffic lights were operating on backup power, pulsing red. On the way to the grocery store, he ended up at a café and stood in line, ordered to-go and paid for his latte like a normal person, albeit an extremely scruffy one, and the caffeine in his system when he'd eaten little both gave him a jolt and the shakes.

In the car again, he held the steering wheel with both hands. He was jittery, and therefore not sure at first whether what he saw while waiting for the light to change at Hyperion and Griffith Park was what he thought he saw: a long black sedan, *the* long black sedan with a band of young guys in it, heading toward the high school.

Carlo was in the right lane, and watched the car stream past, and he didn't have a clear view because another car came in close behind the black car. He made the turn and followed the black car, too.

The other car peeled off at St. George, but the black sedan turned left and, maintaining some distance, Carlo turned left as well. The car turned right again in front of the brick school, up Tracy, as did Carlo, and he didn't know what he was thinking, what he thought he'd do, but here they were, yes, his young assailants with their wild black hair and wild eyes, yes, the one with his drooping chin and drooping moustache, the other maybe a brother or cousin, but minus the moustache. Don't look, they barked, but he'd looked, now he was looking again. They had to slow down at the bend in Tracy, and then they made a left on Monon, a dead end.

It all began with them. If they hadn't ambushed him and humiliated him, he would not have met Tom at the police station, and then not gone to see Tom a month later and had sex with him, and then Tom would not have surfaced at the office that otherwise benign autumn afternoon. He would not have played tennis with Robbie and won over Robbie and then come home with him and had too much to drink and become so dark and disconsolate—Carlo never would have met up with Tom in the kitchen after Robbie was to sleep and then, then Carlo would never have failed Tom Field. Tom never would have killed himself on a cold morning and Carlo's life with Robbie would never have been cleaved into a before and an after. After all this, then, here they were again, the carjackers, and as he followed them down Monon, once a river and now a narrow street of unassuming houses, followed them all the way to the thicket of brush beneath the white concrete pillars and trusses and arches of the Shakespeare Bridge overhead, he knew he had to achieve some kind of vengeance and in revenge, closure.

The black sedan stopped at the dead end and pulled into the single space parallel to the bridge overhead. The doors flung open and the three young men hopped out, immediately lighting cigarettes. They didn't appear to notice Carlo's car as he drifted closer. They were leaning against the side of the sedan, facing the brush, their backs to him. They looked tense in the shoulder, all of them wearing black leather jackets, expectant, as if they were ready to meet someone, ready for a transaction, most likely up to no good.

Carlo put his car in park, and only because he'd stopped in the middle of the street, effectively blocking any other car from approaching the black sedan, or for that matter, preventing the black sedan attempting a getaway, did first one and then the others turn and look at him. Carlo stared the tallest one in the eye. He had a moustache and a full beard now, too.

Why don't you try me again, Carlo thought, and fixed his gaze on the young man. Try me.

But the man looked away, up at the bridge, at nothing.

Carlo wondered what Tom would do, and he knew damn well what Tom would do. Carlo opened the glove compartment and removed the gun, its grip heavier than its barrel, but secure in his hand. He held the gun in his lap and stared and waited.

The tallest man glanced back again and could see Carlo still staring at him. He shrugged, What?

Carlo didn't blink.

What? the man seemed to be asking, and his pals watched him as he came round the sedan and began moving toward Carlo's car. What do you want?

And Carlo sat up in his seat, his gun concealed, his finger wrapped around the trigger, ready now, ready. Alone in the world, he had nothing to lose.

ROBBIE LEFT JAY'S but didn't know where to go and ended up walking around the Reservoir. There was no dusk to speak of, night had fallen. He wandered up to Neutra Place and peered at the glass houses, the lights coming on, wondering why the life in-side, the careful arrangement of things, seemed alien to him when for better or worse it looked no different than his own house and life, at least once upon a time. His hands in his pockets were fists. He was angry at Jay for kicking him out, angry at Carlo, angry at happy people cooking happy New Year's Eve dinners.

He shuffled along toward Glendale and down Glendale to the diner, where he saw a group of cops eating burgers and fries. Robbie slipped into the rest room and took out his cell phone. He didn't know what he would say, but he'd decided to set the record straight. He wanted Carlo to have to admit his role in Tom's de-mise—he wanted Carlo at last to pay. Robbie dialed the number on the card Detective Michaels had given him almost three months earlier.

"Hi there," the detective said, cheery. Was she at a party already? There was music in the background. "Thanks for returning my call finally," she said.

This naturally confused Robbie.

"You got my message?" Detective Michaels asked.

Robbie explained he'd not been home in more than a week.

The detective must have moved to her office or a private room wherever she was because the background music was gone. "I see," she said. "It was a courtesy call to let you know our finding."

Robbie waited.

"To be frank," the detective said, "I think there may be more to the story about what happened that night."

And she paused and Robbie held his breath. Yes, more. What?

"But I can't justify keeping this case open when in the end, we'd still end up finding that Mr. Field committed suicide," the detective said.

Robbie slumped against the tiled wall, he sat down on the floor.

"But you were calling me?" Detective Michaels asked.

He was picturing Tom lying dead on the patio, remembering that brief moment when he thought Tom might be pulling a crude prank. A suicide: What kind of lonely.

"Did you have something you wanted to tell me?" Detective Michaels asked.

Robbie was picturing Tom that morning, and suddenly he understood what detail Jay possibly was referring to.

"Mr. Voight?"

"Happy New Year, Detective," Robbie said.

IT WAS A LONG WALK HOME up the hill and down the hill again, down their street, and Robbie was so beat that when he finally arrived at the house, he couldn't make sense of what he witnessed:

First, Carlo pulling into the driveway and throwing open the car door and jumping out, Carlo was holding in his right hand what appeared to be—no, what was—a silver pistol.

And second, the lower part of the old pepper tree was illuminated, and for a moment, Robbie thought Carlo had strung up Christmas lights, until he realized the broad boughs were outlined in flame, and that the wind was drawing the blaze up so that the tree was fast becoming no longer a solid thing but a negative of itself, ghostly white in the dark.

Then there was a cry, a man crying, but not Carlo—Carlo was not the one screaming.

Robbie couldn't take his eyes off of the gun in Carlo's hand, which he wanted to connect somehow to the tree on fire. And Carlo had a blankness about him, a hollow gaze like he'd seen something, or done something awful, and this gun—it looked like a natural extension of his arm, his finger comfortably wrapped around the trigger, like Carlo wasn't even aware he was holding a weapon. If it was possible in a glance no longer to know someone, then Robbie no longer knew who Carlo Stein was.

Robbie heard the cry again, both men did, and it looked like a lower limb was crashing down in flames. But it wasn't a branch, it was a person emerging from behind the tree, throwing something square and flaming away from him. It was a person standing, and falling, and standing again, flailing his arms. It was a man on fire who was screaming, who was in agony, lit up as bright as the tree. A tree on fire, a man on fire.

The man shouted, "Help!"

He shouted, "Help, help!" and the man on fire was not a man at all: it was Gabriel.

CONFUSION THAT LAST NIGHT OF THE YEAR, who should do what. Robbie yelled, "The hose, the hose,"—because this was what he thought should happen, first shower the boy with water, and then the pepper tree because the pepper tree was close enough to the eave that the fire could set the house ablaze, too.

Carlo called out to Gabriel, "Don't mov,e"—by which he actually meant stop trying to stand up—"don't move, roll. Roll on the ground, roll on the ground." He smelled gasoline, noxious burning gasoline.

The wind whipped up beneath the tree and blew the flames up over the house.

And then Carlo seemed to wake up to the fact he was holding a gun and flung it behind him onto the front seat of the car and ran toward the front door, and Robbie thought that Carlo was heading to other corner of the yard to turn on the faucet and dash back with the garden hose—Robbie therefore ran toward the house, as well, the two men both heading inside.

"No, no, get him to roll on the ground," Carlo shouted at Robbie.

Robbie turned back toward Gabriel, who was motionless.

"Roll!" Robbie screamed.

The boy was engulfed and Robbie wanted to jump on the kid to smother the flames, but he didn't know if he could because it seemed that Gabriel was now surrounded by a bed of fire, the lawn on fire, too. There was fuel spilled everywhere and about the only thing that wasn't on fire was the chucked gas can itself lying on the sidewalk.

Carlo appeared with a blanket pulled from the bed. He threw the blanket over the boy and jumped on the kid, and the kid was beneath him and he felt, he heard the squelched flames, in contrast to the tree, which flared up with new wind.

Robbie ran over to the hose and turned the faucet and began to aim the spray gun at the tree, but the gun was rusty and loose, and the water was coming out in a trickle.

Carlo yelled at him again, "Call 911! Call 911!"

Robbie ran inside to the kitchen phone and was dialing it as he dashed back out, as if bringing the phone closer to the injured boy would somehow make the ambulance come faster. Of course, it was New Year's Eve and while not late in the evening, late enough that it was a busy time at emergency services and the pick-up seemed slow.

Carlo peeled back only enough of the blanket to reveal Gabriel's blackened face and Gabriel was unconscious but Carlo said, "It's okay, sweetie. Everything will be fine, sweetie." And for some reason, again, "Don't move, sweetie, don't move."

He thought nothing would be fine, and neither did Robbie, speaking with the dispatch: "Fifteen, he's fifteen. There's a fire—yes, send the fire truck—and I think it was started with gasoline. I think he set a tree on fire, and he set himself on fire, too."

Carlo was cradling the boy in the blanket and everything smelled noxious and the tree was losing limbs and the house was in danger and no ambulance could yet be heard—and the boy was shivering, unconscious but shivering.

"Get him wet," Carlo barked at Robbie.

Robbie dragged the hose as close as he could, and of course there had to be a kink in the hose, of all the worst possible moments.

And Carlo shouted, "Get us both as wet as you can."

Which Robbie tried to do.

"Call 911 again," Carlo said.

Which Robbie also did. "I called before," he said. "You need to come faster. We're losing him."

"You're fine, you're fine, sweetie," Carlo said—his voice sounded like it was coming from outside him, it wasn't him speaking.

"He set himself on fire," Robbie said. "By accident."

Or was it an accident? Each man separately had the same thought: Was this an act of self-immolation? Was this another suicide at their house?

"Robbie," Carlo yelled because he couldn't think what else to cry out.

"Hurry," Robbie said even as he'd been advised an ambulance was on its way.

"Robbie," Carlo said again.

Robbie held the phone between his chin and collarbone, the

hose still running in the other hand, and he knelt down next to Carlo with the boy—Gabriel no longer moving. It was pitch black but by the light of the burning tree, Robbie could see Carlo, who was frightened, the two men both frightened.

"I hear them coming," Robbie said, a lie.

Carlo was shaking his head, as pale as the morning they'd found Tom.

Gabriel's body looked like it was weighted beneath invisible bricks—who possibly could breathe against such weight?—and he was going to die in Carlo's arms, at fifteen, burned all over, his lungs scorched, too.

Robbie ran out into the street, and he could hear a siren but it was still so distant and not getting any louder.

Carlo could feel the boy with each breath settling toward the earth, weighted, sinking, too late. A siren in the distance, louder, approaching. But it was too late.

ONCE AGAIN a death at their house. The ambulance was there, and also a ladder truck had come and put out the pepper tree on fire.

After the ambulance drove off, and then the fire truck, the two men remained far apart, at opposite ends of the house. They did not console each other. They were not going to see each other through a new ordeal. Each was in his way already certain he never wanted to be touched again by the other.

The police once more. Another investigation. All the neighbors in the street that night.

Gabriel's aunt was hopelessly distraught, considering herself in part to blame for not keeping track of the boy. But she couldn't comprehend what sort of perverse pageant had led up to this disaster—something untoward, she suspected. She considered the two men corrupt in some way she couldn't specify and said so. They didn't argue with her. All this death. Atonement was pointless, regret pointless—it brought back whom exactly?

Carlo moved in with a friend and closed down the office. He was afraid to go out even in the neighborhood because of what happened by the bridge, which he told no one about, but for which there could be retribution, and it was only a matter of time, wasn't it, before it caught up with him. He took a job at the friend's gallery and looked for a place to live. He drank too much and knew it. At night he didn't get very far reading the novels into which he'd try to escape. He could not escape.

Robbie slept on Jay's couch for a week. He found a studio in Hollywood and also a place at a large architectural firm. It was supposed to be temporary, but he didn't want to borrow money from Carlo, so he stayed on at the job. He dated around, nothing came of it.

They sold the house.

Each man had his separate youth before college, and each now had his life apart: The twenty years they spent together were twenty cold stones, indistinguishable among all the other flat rocks in the drought-dry bed of a bitter arroyo. It was easiest for one and then the other to pretend all the years in Silver Lake never existed, and so that was what they did. The End.

7

No, NOT THE END, NOT THAT. Although such an ending, or some variation thereof, would always haunt the two men, the possibility the night could have turned tragic, the grief then that would have cloaked them. Loss in one's life the way loss had entered their lives made one forever aware that for every plot, there was always a ghost plot, the same story told another way.

What happened was this: As Carlo sat in his car and gripped the gun in his lap, and as the tallest man rounded the sedan and began moving toward Carlo's car, Carlo looked up at the Shakespeare Bridge spanning the gully. Whenever he drove on Franklin across the eighty-year-old bridge, he never cared so much for the quaint gothic spires, but beneath the bridge, its concrete engineering revealed, he was filled with simple awe. On the one hand, the many pillars and trusses seemed excessive compared to contemporary structural standards, yet the twin high-curving, barely ornamented arches were oddly delicate and inspiring. It would be going too far to say that given the heat of the moment, he was recalling what it was so long ago that made him want to become a builder, and yet in that instant, something was reawakened in him, a fondness for futurism, an erstwhile excitement about his own future. Process had always fascinated him as much as what process yielded, and all he ever wanted was to be in on, to participate in the secret history of how things were made. It was clear to him he had quite a bit to lose by brandishing a lethal weapon in the name of revenge. A blink, no more, and he understood what a foolish man he'd allowed himself to become.

Also, looking back now at the black sedan, he could see, too, that it was *not* the ambush car (this car was newer and rounder in the hood), and that the man coming toward Carlo was *not* his assailant. None of the men here beneath the bridge had anything to do with that night.

The tallest guy was holding his cigarette between his thumb and forefinger like a dart, holding it in the air as if he were going to flick it at Carlo's windshield. He was almost standing next to Carlo's car, when Carlo shifted into reverse and pushed back from the dead end a good ten yards before backing into the nearest driveway, screeching into a turn, and zooming up Monon toward Tracy. He turned back on Tracy and crossed St. George at the light, and it wasn't until he was halfway down the block that he realized he still had the gun out—it had slipped down the seat to the floor of the car. He skidded into the parking lot outside the closed art store, looked around, got out with the gun in hand, walked over to the dumpster, threw back the lid, pushed around the trash until he noticed a bag only partly cinched, shoved the gun inside it, reburied the trash bag, ran back to his car, and sped off down Hyperion. He was quite sure what he'd just done was illegal, but he also thought it unlikely anyone would find the gun before it was crushed by a sanitation truck.

And so when he pulled into his driveway, Carlo was not holding the gun. He arrived home several minutes before Robbie, but already the pepper tree was on fire: a few white flames ran up the trunk and along a lower branch. Gabriel must have noticed that he'd spilled the gasoline because a length of lawn was on fire, too. And then Gabriel flung the can away from him to avoid catching on fire himself, but not fast enough and the flames ran up his jacket sleeve and down along his side, down his pants, so that he fell, and stood, and fell again. This was when Robbie showed up, when Gabriel was already dancing about, on fire.

What happened was this: The two men reacted fast. One man ran for the hose while yelling at Gabriel, telling him he needed to drop to the ground, stay on the ground, and roll over and roll over and put out the fire that way. The other man thought to grab the rug from the entry, and he headed straight for Gabriel with it. He enveloped the boy with the rug and used his own body to smother the flames. At that point the man with the hose had reached the boy, and the man with the rug pulled it back and off the boy, and the man with the hose was able to hold his thumb over the end of the hose to create a good spray and douse the boy thoroughly so there was nothing burning. Then he aimed the hose at the tree trunk and the source of the fire. He washed the lower branches with water, as well as whatever bit of the lawn was in flames. Everything and everyone was soaked and the fire was out.

The boy lay on the ground and was crying, groaning, in shock, shivering—he had been burned—and one man returned to his side and told the boy everything would be fine, not to worry, there, there, sweetie, it was okay. In the darkness it was hard to see how badly he'd been hurt. They wanted to get him medical attention as quickly as possible, and because it was New Year's Eve, because they lived in the hills and the narrow streets were packed with parked cars, they thought it would be best to drive the boy to the hospital themselves, if he could stand, which he could, and if he was breathing well, which he was, despite the fact he was sobbing.

One man retrieved a heavy coat from the house to drape over the boy's shoulders. They walked him out to the car in the driveway and one man got in the backseat with the boy and held him and continued to tell him he'd be fine, certain he would be, even as the boy himself was trembling, and the other man drove. He drove to the hospital not along the route he preferred but the one the other man always said was faster, which maybe it was, maybe it wasn't. He drove fast and ran a red, and they got lucky with the traffic and made it to the emergency ward and walked the boy in.

It was only then, with the car parked, in the waiting room, sitting together in the corner, that one of the men started shaking, considering only now how things could have gone down. Also he was still wet and had to laugh about that—thanks for soaking me, too.

Carlo was the one shivering, and Robbie took his hands.

Robbie said, "He'll be fine. The nurse said the burns don't look too bad."

To which Carlo responded, "I know."

"We'll all be fine," Robbie said.

They sat in silence, Carlo staring at the floor, Robbie looking at Carlo.

"What?" Robbie asked.

"I'd met Tom before," Carlo said.

Robbie blinked. He said, "I figured."

Then Carlo revealed the circumstances, all the details, and hearing the whole sad story, Robbie slouched a bit in the plastic waiting room chair. Carlo told him about what happened when he returned the windbreaker, and ever so slightly, Robbie flinched.

"I need to tell you the rest," Carlo said.

"What if I don't want to hear the rest?" Robbie asked.

TWO HOURS AFTER THEY PUT TOM TO BED in the guest room and went to sleep that night, Carlo was awakened by a noise he hadn't heard in years, car tires spinning against packed ice and snow on a winter hill. Obviously not that, but he couldn't identify the grinding sound. Robbie didn't stir. Carlo waited, the noise did not recur, but he was going to need help if he wanted to fall back asleep, and he opened his night table drawer and removed a bottle of sleeping pills. A water bottle on the floor had one sip left. As he was about to set the pill on his tongue, he heard the gnashing of gears again, greater in distress but less prolonged. He dropped the pill back in the bottle, pulled on the pants he'd been wearing earlier, and quietly shut the bedroom door behind him.

Tom was in the kitchen, at the sink, doing the dishes, and when he saw Carlo he turned and said, "Sorry, sorry."

Carlo held his forefinger to his lips: Not so loud.

"Sorry," Tom whispered.

Then he held up an aggrieved piece of flatware, which explained the noise: a fork had been mangled in the disposal.

"I hope it wasn't a family heirloom," Tom said.

"Not really," Carlo said. "What are you doing up? You don't have to do the dishes."

"I was raised a certain way," Tom said.

Like Carlo, Tom was only wearing his jeans. He didn't appear remotely intoxicated, or tired, whereas Carlo had a headache, the early onset of a hangover.

He took the dish towel from Tom and proceeded to dry the already clean plates in the drainer. To make less noise, he didn't put the dishes away but instead stacked them on the counter with minimal clatter.

"I owe you a fork," Tom said.

"You don't," Carlo said.

"Oh, but I insist."

"Just don't run the disposal again. We don't want to wake Robbie, too."

Tom scrubbed the burned skillet in which he'd braised the chicken. The baking pan he'd used for the rolls, the fry pan for the spinach. And meanwhile, a yawning Carlo dried whatever he was handed. They were standing close to each other, which was at first awkward in their mutual shirtlessness, and they talked for the sake of talking, not about anything significant, the seasons here versus the seasons back East, and so on.

But then there was a let-up in the chatter, and Tom said, "Well, here we both are. Finally."

"Here we are," Carlo said.

"You do know how lucky you are," Tom said. "The house, the career, the boyfriend—you do know."

His voice had become louder, and as if he could lower the volume with his own softer tone, Carlo whispered when he said, "I've been very fortunate."

"What?"

"I've been very fortunate."

"And yet you believe all there is is the ground beneath your feet," Tom said. "Nothing more than that? That's it?"

"I wouldn't characterize it that way," Carlo said.

"You're afraid to answer the question."

So Carlo answered the question. He said, "Fine. Yes. The ground beneath my feet. That's it."

"And when we die?"

"When we die, we die," Carlo said.

"That's not a very pretty thought," Tom said.

He was flicking free the espresso grounds from the coffee filter, shaking his head, less in disgust it appeared than defeat.

"Tom, you can believe in what you want to believe in," Carlo said. "We don't have to agree."

"I wish we did," Tom said.

"But why? You have Robbie, more or less. Why do you need me, too?"

Tom stared at Carlo and Carlo couldn't read him. He dried the wine glasses and then the dishes were all done. He suggested they return to bed.

"No, no, not yet," Tom said, tapping his first two fingers against Carlo's bare sternum. Tap, tap, tap.

Carlo stared at Tom's hand as if he expected it to do something else.

"I'm tired, Tom," he said.

"Not yet. Do you have any paper?"

"Paper, why?"

"Do you?"

Carlo opened a drawer and removed a letter-sized graph paper pad and pencil. He leaned against the kitchen counter, one palm flat against the granite. With his right hand, he was scratching his left clavicle.

"Stay like that," Tom said.

"Like how?" Carlo asked. "Like this?"

Tom, with the pad balanced in the crook of his arm, began to move his drawing hand fast across the page. Glancing up at Carlo, down at the pad, up, down. Thinking that if he let Tom draw him, then they could go to bed, Carlo maintained the pose. They didn't talk. Tom was serious, and the way he scrutinized Carlo, the way Tom touched his tongue to his lip and cocked his head, Carlo felt pinned by the artist's stare, a specimen, trapped. Carlo shifted his weight.

"Don't move," Tom barked.

No longer warmed by washed dishes, Carlo got goosebumps and his nipples hardened. He couldn't deny it, this was erotic. Tom worked at the drawing a while and when he was done, he signed it and ripped the page from the pad.

In the drawing, Carlo was looking away, yet his naked chest appeared thrust forward, as if something unseen yoked him and held him back. He appeared thin along the jaw, haggard. Here now, explicit, was what Carlo never saw when he stared in the mirror and faced off his same old self day in, day out: A man turning forty. A man once certain but no longer certain what he wanted in life. A man whose mind was a hundred places at once, never settled, never at peace. His first reaction to Tom's handiwork was surprise, but surprise gave way to discomfort. He did not want Tom Field to know him this well.

Tom, on the other hand, seemed especially pleased with his effort and said, "I think I would have done well in fifteenth-century Florence."

"You do have quick fingers," Carlo said.

That night they met at the police station, in the men's room, when Carlo was changing out of the clothes he'd soiled into borrowed prison overalls—that night Carlo suffered the same uneasiness around Tom because Tom saw Carlo for who he was: frightened, diminished, small. Was this why he'd gone to Valley and fucked Tom, to regain control, to prove himself strong? And was Carlo now stronger? No: he remained a hapless, hopeless victim, stupid, stupid.

They were standing close again, looking at the drawing.

"I did buy a gun," Carlo whispered.

"You what?"

"I said I bought a gun. The day I came to your apartment, I went to a gun store."

Tom squinted at him. "You didn't tell me that. And by the way you were talking earlier tonight—"

"I never picked it up. I didn't want it in the house."

"You bought a gun and didn't pick it up. Who does that? I don't believe you."

"Why wouldn't you believe me?" Carlo asked.

"You told Robbie you had an accident?"

"I didn't want him to worry. What would he do with his worry? Nothing but worry more."

"Is that the real reason?" Tom asked, and then he said, "And you make all these claims you're monogamous—"

"It was only that one time," Carlo snapped.

"Right. If you say so."

"I don't expect you to understand," Carlo said. "It's not like you've been in any kind of real relationship."

Tom stared at his bare feet.

"Or not that you mentioned," Carlo said. "Sorry."

They stood in the kitchen, Tom continuing to look at his feet, Carlo wishing he could take back his callous comment.

Tom said, "That night at the station. In the men's room."

"I need to go to bed," Carlo said. "When I don't sleep, I get depressed."

"You'd pooped in your pants," Tom said.

Now Carlo was the one staring at the floor.

"And correct me if I'm wrong," Tom said, "but I don't think you are someone who generally poops in his pants."

"That's great, thanks. That's enough."

"So to avoid future pants-pooping situations," Tom said, "maybe you should go and get that gun. Maybe you'd want some way of blowing away anyone who—"

"Don't you get it? I don't want anything to do with that night," Carlo said, and this sounded inane, he knew, because that night (like this night) would always have something to do with him. "And I regret, I deeply regret that we fooled around, okay?" He held up Tom's drawing and said, "This is lovely, thanks—"

"No, no, no," Tom said—he grabbed and released Carlo's elbow. "Not yet. Don't go, not yet."

"When I don't sleep—"

"After I finished my cigarette," Tom said, "I was free to go, but I stuck around the station and talked to you, and not because you're so adorable in overalls, but because you were frightened, you poor lost puppy. I stayed and I talked to you," Tom said, "about all your modern houses and all the European cities you know your way around and your handsome boyfriend—your whole life we talked about."

This was true enough, Carlo thought.

"I did that for you. I talked to you so you could go home in peace. I talked to you so you could go back to your life. Nobody asked me to," Tom said. "I did that for *you.*"

He began pacing back and forth the length of the kitchen.

"What do you think it means," Tom asked, "that you forgot about me?"

"I didn't forget about you," Carlo said. "I told you. I didn't recognize you at first because you weren't blond anymore."

"But then you came to my place, and trust me, it's not like I thought you wanted to get involved or even have a fling. But you needed something, didn't you? Which I gave you, I think."

"Tom."

"What?"

What Tom was saying was true, but Carlo couldn't think straight and wanted to get away, very far away from him.

"You said you lived in Silver Lake," Tom said, "and that you had your office on Silver Lake Boulevard. You never told me your last name, but it wasn't hard to find the place. Although my car really did break down."

Carlo absorbed what Tom was telling him.

"We both need sleep," Carlo said.

"I stayed with you. You were upset. I talked you down."

"And I thank you for that, but—"

"*You* came to *me*."

"I don't deny—"

"Talk to me now."

"I don't do well without sleep," Carlo said.

"Nobody else owes me anything," Tom said. "If not you, then who?"

Carlo scratched his head. He rubbed his eyes. He'd had enough.

"Look, Tom, you seem sober. If you want to leave."

"Leave?"

Carlo examined his portrait again, and he said, "I think you should go now. Yes. I think it would be a good idea if you left."

And Tom asked, "That's it?"

"That's what?"

"That's all you have?" Tom asked. "That's it?"

Carlo left him in the kitchen. He tip-toed back across the main room toward the bedroom, but he was still holding the drawing. He didn't want to risk Tom seeing him discard it because as much as he wanted Tom to disappear, he didn't want to hurt his feelings—and he also didn't want Robbie to find it in the morning. He didn't want to explain what had gone on just now, didn't want to get into it, maybe not ever. He opened the built-in linen closet in the hall, opened the door all the way. He lifted one foot onto the lowest shelf, grabbed hold of a middle shelf, and pulled himself up to reach the top shelf. He grasped his wooden art kit with his free hand and caught it with his other hand as he stepped back down, landing on the floor with a thud. He paused for a moment and listened for any stirring in the bedroom—none. He set the case and the drawing on the floor and lifted himself up again, held himself in place, and shoved the book box with Robbie's grandfather's toy soldiers to the left, thinking he'd stash the drawing behind it, but the box fit too snugly on the shelf. Back on the floor, he glanced over his shoulder—did he see Tom peering out of the kitchen, watching? No. Carlo knelt, undid the tarnished clasps of the wooden art kit and placed Tom's drawing atop the paint tubes and impasto and apothecary-like bottles of medium, the brushes and palette knifes. Then he closed the case and pulled himself up once more and returned the art kit to the top shelf.

In bed, Robbie was still sound asleep. Carlo washed down a sleeping pill with the remaining sip of water in the bottle on the floor. And then he lay on his back waiting for the pill to take effect. He could hear Tom moving around the house, first in the guest room, then in the main room, then back in the guest room. He wished the pill would deliver him elsewhere, but even after some time had passed, he wasn't drowsy and lay awake tracking Tom's continued movements, aware that he had neither gone to sleep nor departed.

A good hour after leaving Tom in the kitchen, Carlo finally heard what he thought might be Tom going out the front door, and he thought he heard a car door open and shut, or a trunk, but then Tom walking through the house again. Carlo heard something heavy rolling, the sliding door to the patio being pulled back. Then noise from the patio, a metal chair dragged across the stone. Then silence.

Carlo waited a few moments before he got out of bed—Robbie shifted onto his side—and crept across the room to the window. Light from the house spilled onto the terrace, although it wasn't easy to see what was going on, except that Tom appeared to be pacing again like he had in the kitchen. Short steps, fast steps. There was an object lying on the table, but Carlo couldn't make out what it was. Tom kept stepping back and forth across the slate and stopping beneath the tree and gazing up, and then he would resume pacing.

At one point when he stopped moving, Tom stared back at the house, at the bedroom window, and Carlo leaned back—he didn't think Tom spotted him. He knew he should go out and talk to Tom, who glanced up at the tree again and began pacing again.

Nobody should be alone in the world. This was what Carlo's father said to him when Carlo came out. Years later he realized his father wasn't speaking so much about teenage Carlo as he was about himself, explaining his own life.

Tom stood beneath the tree.

Carlo was frozen at the window, his hands suddenly heavy, his legs weighted, too.

Like a standoff: Tom on the patio, Carlo in the bedroom, neither moving.

Until finally Tom sat down at the edge of the chair, his elbows on his knees, his head in his hands.

Carlo let his shoulders drop. His head heavy now.

Go outside, he told himself. Go.

But he did not go out to Tom, and instead Carlo got back in bed. Instead Carlo lay down next to Robbie. And he had the sense that what had been chasing him all spring and all summer, and what would follow him across the fall and winter was the fear, the cold conviction that against his father's wishes, it was only a matter of time before he, before Carlo ended up all alone. And with this thought that night, that morning, at last he fell asleep.

"I DIDN'T TAKE CARE OF HIM," Carlo said.

While he'd been telling Robbie what happened, several men who looked like brothers had come in the waiting room, which was not crowded, but for some reason they didn't sit down and stood in a row in front of the wall-mounted television in the corner, watching the latest news on a slow news night.

"I should have stayed with him, I didn't, he died," Carlo said.

Robbie didn't speak for a long while. Carlo expected him to say he was the worst person, Carlo was, and Robbie didn't see a way to continue in a life with him.

"You should have, yes," Robbie finally said. "And maybe you could have stopped him that night, but not necessarily the next night or the night after that."

"You said you thought he didn't mean to—"

"When I told you that Tom's death was an accident," Robbie interrupted, "I was wrong."

"We don't know," Carlo said.

"We don't, and then we do," Robbie said. "There's a detail, there was something I never understood. When we found Tom, he wasn't wearing shoes. He ended up with splinters in his feet—remember? And why no shoes, because he was in a hurry?"

"No?"

"No, I think he didn't put on his shoes because he didn't want to make too much noise when he walked around the house or even out on the patio. He didn't want to wake us. He was deliberate. He wanted to end his life."

"I don't know. Don't you think that's too small a detail to attach so much to?" Carlo asked.

"I don't think so."

"I think Tom wanted to come close to death without experiencing death," Carlo said. "He set up the rope. It was a test. And at the last second, he got too close. He fell off the chair, he died."

"You're saying at the very final instant, it was a mistake."

"I'm saying," Carlo said, "that I have to believe at some point, too late, it was an accident."

"I used to think that, but now I don't. Anyway, we can't know," Robbie said.

"We can't know," Carlo echoed, "so we have to decide for ourselves what he was thinking."

"You believe he wanted to get close."

"I guess that's what I need to believe," Carlo said. "So, yes."

"I wish I could agree," Robbie said.

If this was what Carlo needed to think, it was because he couldn't understand no longer wanting to experience the early winter dusk falling all around him. He could not imagine no longer wanting to see through as many seasons as possible.

"If he'd lived another day," Carlo said, "who knows? Maybe that next day, things would have turned around for him."

"Possibly," Robbie said. "We can't know," he said again.

"I guess not," Carlo said, and they sat a while and didn't speak. Then Carlo said, "Tom Field." He said, "Tom Field, Om Ield."

Robbie smiled, but a tear formed, as well.

"Tom Field. Om Ield," Robbie repeated. "Meld," he said.

The two men were staring at each other in silence: How old they were in that moment, how old.

A FEW DAYS LATER, they went over to Gabriel's aunt's apartment. The boy had told his aunt he did not want to see them, but Gabriel's aunt, grateful the men caught the boy when they did, perhaps fearing charges could be brought against her nephew (though bringing charges never once occurred to either man), said Gabriel didn't have a say in the matter. Gabriel's aunt said she knew the two men had been good to her nephew over the years, and she hoped they would forgive the boy for whatever he'd done. No, no, the two men told Gabriel's aunt, it was the boy who needed to forgive them for however they'd tangled him up in the tragedy at their house that fall.

Then the two men talked to Gabriel alone. They tried not to be overtly amused by a teenager's bedroom, the posters, the batik fabric across the top of the dresser. The candles next to the computer. Was that possibly an old teddy bear amid the bevy of pillows?

Gabriel sat up in bed. He pulled a flannel sleeve down over the bandage running the length of his arm. He had burns along his right side; they would heal. He was told to expect minor scarring at his hip. The side of his face had been burned, too, and was presently oily with salve, but he would recover. In the hospital, they'd had to shave his already shaved head as well as his right eyebrow. He did look a little strange, but he seemed to be his same old self once they started talking—or no, maybe he was not his same old self, not so sweet, not so innocent. The boy's voice had flattened out and he sounded weary and bitter when he conveyed what he knew about all the vandalism at the house.

He did not know for certain who had tagged the trash cans and thrown the garbage all over the front yard, but it was the kind of random prank that the crew of kids who hung out with Lonny (yes, Lonny) sometimes pulled when they were drinking. But was this a mocking response to Tom's death and what might have been rumored as the unsavory way Tom died? Probably not, but they would never know. And as for the two plum trees and whether they succumbed to the wind or were snapped against an angry boot, Gabriel didn't have an opinion. He didn't think it was the kind of thing Lonny would do, but then Gabriel could certify that Lonny was responsible for the effigy. Lonny had taken one of Gabriel's old shirts and a tetherball he found in Gabriel's backyard and then strung it up during the night—in retaliation, Lonny claimed, for Carlo having roughed him up at the liquor store.

"That kid could have made a mess of you," Robbie said to Carlo.

"It *was* pretty pathetic on my part," Carlo said. "But, Gabriel, do you know this for sure about Lonny and the effigy?"

"I was with him when he did it," Gabriel said.

The boy hadn't tried to stop his friend, not in front of some of the other kids also lurking around, plus Lonny was not someone you wanted to get in the way of when he was both vengeful and stoned.

"And also …" Gabriel started to say.

"And also what?" Robbie asked.

The boy seemed reluctant to go on. He was scowling at Carlo. He said, "I didn't owe Lonny money like I said I did. I was scamming you."

"Oh," Carlo said.

"And Lonny wasn't with me when I set the tree on fire. You lied. I didn't care if your whole house burned down. I still don't."

Carlo shivered. The boy was becoming one more stranger to them. He had to believe it was not too late to repair the splintered trust, and yet he'd be fooling himself if he didn't admit he was worried. If a sweet kid could grow up and light up a pepper tree, and if a man could hang himself while the two men slept, then logic meant nothing, reason nothing. In time the boy might become that man. They needed to do everything they could to prevent that from happening, but could they?

Gabriel leaned back and stared at the bedroom ceiling, scarred by half-scraped-off celestial decals. He appeared to soften a bit. He said, "I don't know. Maybe I was changing my mind. I thought about putting out the fire, but I'd spilled gas on the lawn and on my arm, and then I caught on fire—"

"Luck," Robbie said. "Luck I decided to come home when I did. Luck Carlo was there, too. We've been lucky, we've all been lucky. Except for Tom, that is. Except for poor Tom."

Carlo looked at him and he was thinking in some ways, yes, much of the life they'd led together before that autumn had been charmed, but there was also a part of him, he had to admit, reluctant to assign away what had happened to chance. He wasn't yet but wanted to be at peace with the knowledge some things could never be understood.

BACK TO NEW YEAR'S EVE. Once the nurses at the hospital said Gabriel was asleep and once the boy's aunt arrived from a party, the two men went home. In bed, they held each other the old way. They wanted to take a trip somewhere but had run out of money and therefore would need to fall in love again without the benefit of a room with a view in a canal city. They talked about the office, its revival or maybe each of them moving on into separate jobs beyond their partnership. They talked about needing to do things alone, taking courses, lessons in something, they weren't sure what. They talked, but not everything was said about affairs or why secrets were held for so long, though in time everything would need to be said. They had changed in ways they could not yet qualify, and they were going to live now with a kind of uncertainty about their future. Each in his way knew the possibility existed, perhaps even the likelihood that they may not always be together. No matter what happened, however, they needed to remain close, because what an uncommon history theirs was, and how rare to know each other the way they did. To be known in the world and to be seen, everyone lived for that—nobody alone, or never alone for so very long.

And so it was the first day of a new year, and when the sun was up, Robbie stood at the bedroom window and was taken by the color the lake, a self-possessed lapis lazuli. Also he thought he spotted something oblong going into the water off the concrete shore at the opposite end of the Reservoir, something fluttering then sinking.

"What is it?" Carlo asked when he joined Robbie at the window.

"I don't know," Robbie said, although he had a suspicion.

The two men dressed and went out front to look at the pepper tree. The trunk was black but they were able to rub off a layer of soot. Some limbs needed to come down before they came down on their own, and so they got their ladder and their saw, and when they were done trimming, the old tree didn't look so terrible. They were enjoying the yard work and so they moved around to the back of the house and pulled out some dead brush and weeds, and they went down to the fountain and talked about what it would look like and Robbie was enthusiastic, willing to help finish it. And then back up on the patio, Robbie was sweeping while Carlo was looking back at the glass house, which seemed to him for the first time not modern at all, but instead simply old. They lived in an old house and who really knew how well it was built? It had survived some wind these last weeks and decades of other natural battering, but it was possible one day it could come down.

Carlo expressed his newfound concern to Robbie, who said, "Oh, you're a silly man. It's lasted this long, hasn't it? Earthquakes and storms and now fire—well almost. That house is not going anywhere. Who's a silly man?"

"I am," Carlo said.

"What are you?"

"A silly man—Hey, look."

"What?"

"There," Carlo said and pointed at the Reservoir.

There was something again on the water in the distance. It looked like a raft of some kind, a raft with two people on it. Carlo went back inside to fetch their binoculars but by the time he returned, binoculars were unnecessary.

It was a raft and it had pushed closer toward the center of the lake, and the men could see plainly that the raft was in fact a small boat with a stubby mast. Two people stood up in the boat and worked at a white crescent of fabric, trying to loosen a sail, or maybe the sail had been released from its rigging but wouldn't unfurl. There wasn't enough wind up, although earlier it had been gusty, and Carlo wanted to shout to whoever it was down there to be patient for the wind to return. The two people in the boat kept struggling with the sail, one at the helm, one at the mast. They couldn't catch any breeze. Perhaps some lakes were not meant to be sailed.

It was cold out and the day would be short again and yet the two men didn't go inside. They sat next to each other on the back steps, their legs not quite touching. They sat there a long while.

Robbie was thinking that while he was skilled at his profession, he'd gone through life, his forty years, not knowing how to do so many things: He couldn't really sew or cook. He couldn't change a tire. He couldn't build a chair. He couldn't actually build a house himself. He couldn't use a compass or pitch a tent. He couldn't swim a mile. He couldn't rescue a snake-bitten child, he wouldn't know what to do. Oh, of course he could *do* all of these things—he would figure out what he needed or learn on the spot or train. But he didn't want to be who he had been in the sense he didn't want to be so dependent. He had changed but wanted to change more.

Meanwhile, too many images stayed with Carlo, his mother at the end, her mind gone, not recognizing him, or maybe recognizing him, he never knew. Tom hanged. The boy on fire. It was all too much, and Carlo felt weak but he let himself be weak.

He let his hands get cold, he let his teeth chatter. He stared up through the leafless bough of the Liquidambar at the noonday sky, and there was something strange yet wondrous about the way the top branches moved with a wind the listless lower branches showed no knowledge of, a vatic murmur above that went unheeded down below.

Robbie reached his arm around Carlo and tried to warm him up and wasn't able, and he nodded toward the house to say let's go inside, and it would have been at this point, as they stood at the same time, that the two men looked out at the Reservoir and noticed the boat in the center of the lake achieving its geometry, the white triangle of a full sail coasting from southeast to northwest across the water, gliding, banking, righting itself, curving around and tilting the opposite way, coming back now at the two men as if drawn along by their inhaled breath.

"How long do you think they've been planning this?" Carlo asked.

"I bet you they've talked about getting out there since -the day they moved in," Robbie said.

"I wonder how they got the boat over the fence."

"Very carefully. And in pieces, the hull, the sail."

"You think?"

"Si, signor."

"Nobody has come along and stopped them," Carlo said.

"The police have better things to do," Robbie said.

"Look. They're headed back the other way."

"They'll go around and around the rest of the day, providing no one stops them and the wind stays up."

"It will have to die down," Carlo said.

"You never know," Robbie said. "Anyway, they've got the wind for now."

The two men watched the boat circle the lake, one man cold and the other exhausted, but they could not yet go inside. The boat on the lake was like a comet in the night, a date zero from which a calendar began, a new story they would likely be telling anyone who would listen for years to come.

Author photo by Art Gray

PETER GADOL is the author of five previous novels, including *The Long Rain* and *Light at Dusk.* He lives in Los Angeles and teaches in the Graduate Writing Program at Otis College of Art and Design.

THE ART OF F. SCOTT FITZGERALD

By SERGIO PEROSA